The Cat Caliban Mysteries by D. B. Borton . . .

One for the Money

After thirty-eight years of marriage, Cat's starting a new life—buying her own apartment house and working for her P.I. license. She'll be using her investigative skills sooner than she thinks . . . when she finds her upstairs apartment comes furnished—with a corpse!

Two Points for Murder

When a high school basketball hero is gunned down, Cat knows there's more to the murder than meets the eye—and she's determined to blow the whistle on the killer. . . .

Three Is a Crowd

Cat missed the protest movement of the '60s . . . she was too busy with a husband, house, and kids. But now she's learning more about those wild years—investigating the death of a protester at a peace rally. . . .

Four Elements of Murder

Cat looks into the death of an environmental activist—and finds herself in a mess of murder and deceit . . .

MORE MYSTERIES FROM THE BERKLEY PUBLISHING GROUP . . .

CAT CALIBAN MYSTERIES: She was married for thirty-eight years. Raised three kids. Compared to that, tracking down killers is easy . . .

by D. B. Borton

ONE FOR THE MONEY
TWO POINTS FOR MURDER
THREE IS A CROWD
FOUR ELEMENTS OF MURDER
FIVE ALARM FIRE

ELENA JARVIS MYSTERIES: There are some pretty bizarre crimes deep in the heart of Texas—and a pretty gutsy police detective who rounds up the unusual suspects . . .

by Nancy Herndon

ACID BATH
WIDOWS' WATCH

FREDDIE O'NEAL, P.I., MYSTERIES: You can bet that this appealing Reno private investigator will get her man . . . "A winner."—Linda Grant

by Catherine Dain

LAY IT ON THE LINE
SING A SONG OF DEATH
WALK A CROOKED MILE
LAMENT FOR A DEAD COWBOY
BET AGAINST THE HOUSE
THE LUCK OF THE DRAW

BENNI HARPER MYSTERIES: Meet Benni Harper—a quilter and folk-art expert with an eye for murderous designs . . .

by Earlene Fowler

FOOL'S PUZZLE
IRISH CHAIN
KANSAS TROUBLES

HANNAH BARLOW MYSTERIES: For ex-cop and law student Hannah Barlow, justice isn't just a word in a textbook. Sometimes, it's a matter of life and death . . .

by Carroll Lachnit

MURDER IN BRIEF
A BLESSED DEATH

FIVE ALARM FIRE

D. B. BORTON

BERKLEY PRIME CRIME, NEW YORK

FIVE ALARM FIRE

A Berkley Prime Crime Book / published by arrangement with the author

PRINTING HISTORY
Berkley Prime Crime edition / June 1996

For information address: The Berkley Publishing Group, 200 Madison Avenue, New York, NY 10016.

The Putnam Berkley World Wide Web site address is http://www.berkley.com

ISBN: 0-425-15338-X

Berkley Prime Crime Books are published by The Berkley Publishing Group, 200 Madison Avenue, New York, NY 10016.

PRINTED IN THE UNITED STATES OF AMERICA

10 9 8 7 6 5 4 3 2 1

To Carol Blum,
who shared her family, her city, and
her enthusiasm for its herstory,
and who served as my comrade-in-arms
during several Northside Halloweens

Acknowledgments

My gratitude goes first to Gail Russell and her Wednesday night pottery class, culinary club, and plant swap at the real Arts Castle (Delaware County Cultural Arts Center) in Delaware, Ohio. Special thanks to Laura, Amy, Andrea, Lisa, Tim, Pam, and Rich, along with apologies for any jokes I stole. Arts Castle donors are advised that as far as I know, no dead bodies have ever been found there, just happy living artists—give or take a few malcontents whose pots have just exploded in the kiln.

Pat Carter's video project on Rookwood Pottery for the University of Cincinnati Center for Woman's Studies was a source of inspiration and information, as was Anita Ellis's *Rookwood Pottery.* Greg Blum shared his expertise and his library. Trace Regan took my medical questions seriously and answered them graciously.

Special thanks to Frances Bartram, who served as my first reader, and to my editor, Laura Anne Gilman.

One

Me and Kinky were parked behind a couple of five-ways down at Skyline Chili in Clifton. Five-ways were to Cincinnati what cheese steaks were to Philadelphia: its distinctive culinary contribution to the world. Kinky was poking his fork down through the layers of cheese, onions, beans, chili, and spaghetti, scowling.

"Don't think of it as being in the same food group as Texas chili, Kinky," I told him. "It's East European."

Kinky glanced up, then looked around, as if searching for evidence that this joint was an enclave of ethnic haute cuisine. Tell me another one, his eyes said.

We were interrupted by a waiter in a white jacket, hurrying to our booth with a white telephone.

"Telephone for Mr. Friedman," the waiter said.

Now this should have tipped me off that something was amiss. Skyline Chili—or "Skilini's," as the local wags pronounce it—does not run telephones, white or otherwise, or jacketed waiters for that matter. It was one in a chili parlor chain which featured downscale dining, even in the heart of one of Cincinnati's more upscale neighborhoods. Both the telephone and the white jacket were splashed with tomato sauce, but still.

Kinky told me that the cat was calling to say that his building was burning down.

"How can she tell?" I asked. It was a reasonable question; Kinky was always complaining about the heat in his New York City loft.

But, all of a sudden, I could feel it. A wave of heat washed over me and left me soaking wet. Goddam, I'd heard of reaching out and touching somebody, but this was ridiculous! I dropped my fork.

And woke up.

I was sitting up in bed, scanning the darkness in confusion.

Goddam, it wasn't Kinky's place that was on fire—it was mine!

I fumbled for the light and switched it on.

Sadie and Sophie, who were sacked out on the foot of the bed, raised their heads and gazed at me in sleepy feline confusion. Not a whisker twitched. I sniffed the air.

Hell, it wasn't my place that was on fire—it was me!

I threw off the wet sheets and raced to the bathroom, nearly tripping over Sidney, who had heard the commotion and come running to investigate. By the time I got the water on, the heat was receding. Behind it came a chill like a Canadian cold front. I stood in the shower, my dripping nightgown clinging to me tight as a corpse's fist. I sneezed, and felt a tiny explosion of wet heat between my thighs.

Sidney was watching me curiously. I think it was gradually dawning on him that I was not up for a game of Kitty Tease.

Menopause. I love it.

Mind you, I'd waited for it long enough. For some time now, I'd found it downright embarrassing to be caught carrying tampons around. Fifty-nine and a half years was a long time to wait. I'd felt like a goddam gynecological miracle. Even so, the Change, when it came, kind of crept up on me. I'd thought my PMS had been lasting longer than usual for a while, and my periods were coming fast and heavy. But I didn't really keep track. I mean, what was the point? If I turned up pregnant—well, let's just say that since I seemed an unlikely candidate for participation in the Second Coming, we'd have to consider the *Rosemary's Baby* scenario.

When I finally realized what was happening, my sixtieth birthday party paled by comparison to the celebrating I did.

Until I found out that there were things you could carry around that were even more embarrassing than tampons.

Not that I thought anybody should be embarrassed, if I listened to my rational self. This was 1985, for crissake, and we seniors were fast becoming everybody's favorite voting bloc and marketing target. Hell, judging from our President's domestic policy, senile dementia was all the rage. I'd even thought about writing President Reagan and proposing that he do his bit for gray pride and appear on an Attends commercial. Then I remembered that I wasn't speaking to Ronnie, for all sorts of reasons I won't go into.

So anyway, there I stood, dripping wet, wishing a genie would show up and grant me three wishes. I'd use up one getting my estrogen back. That gave me two left to wish menopause on my worst enemies, and Ronald Reagan was high on the list. Maybe, out of deference to my upstairs neighbor Moses, I'd zap Marvin Warner while I was at it. Moses still had a good chunk of his life savings frozen at Home State S&L while the Feds tried to sort out the mess. The whole ordeal had considerably soured his disposition.

Meanwhile, speaking of sour dispositions and freezing, I was now cold, wet, cranky—and wide awake. I went back to the Kinky Friedman mystery I'd been reading before I went to bed.

You know how people are always saying that everything looks better in the morning? Well, if you believe that, I have some waterfront acreage in southern Louisiana to sell you. People also say that you get moody during menopause. Sleep deprivation will make anybody moody.

I'm an expert on what people say because I'd been getting an earful from my tenants at the old Catatonia Arms. My favorite lines are the ones delivered as if I weren't present in the room, or as if senility were one of the side effects of estrogen withdrawal.

"Boy! She sure is crabby today!" Al the attorney, who is normally the soul of tact, would say to Mel, her roomie.

"Crabbier than yesterday?" Mel, who is not, would say.

"She's going through a rough time, poor dear!" Kevin would say, and pat my hand as if he knew just how I was feeling. Kevin often mistook his bartending license for a counseling license, and confused his customers' experiences with his own. "Aren't you, Mrs. C.?"

"I remember when my wife went through the Change," Moses put in gloomily, shaking his head. "Seem like she took something for it, though. Perked her right up."

"That's probably what killed her," Mel said, proving what I said earlier about tact.

Al gave her a reproachful look, but agreed with her.

"Women are a lot more careful now about what they take, Moses," she said. "There's a lot of evidence that links estrogen therapy with uterine cancer."

"Well, that's not what she died of," Moses grumbled.

"On the other hand, Mrs. C., it's supposed to reduce the risk of heart disease," Kevin offered.

"Since when did you learn so much about menopause?" Mel challenged.

"I thought that was common knowledge," Kevin said. "I read *Newsweek.*"

"Anyway, the important thing is for Cat to take charge of her own health," Al said.

I opened my mouth to start taking charge, but I wasn't fast enough.

"I'm just saying, if there's some kind of pill she could take, she ought to look into it, that's all," Moses said.

"They're even saying now that men go through some kind of menopause, too," Kevin put in.

"Well, don't look at me!" Moses said defensively, because everybody was. "Ain't nothing wrong with me 'cept my arthritis."

"When's the last time you saw your gynecologist, Cat?" Mel asked.

I jumped up from where I was sitting, feeling twinges of protest from my own joints.

"Hey, time out! Sympathy I will take any time. Advice I will take only when I ask for it—and P.S., don't hold your breath. In the meantime, if you don't want moody, don't talk about me like a goddam surgical team standing over me in the operating room!"

Leon, a young friend and sometime sidekick of mine, chose that moment to stick his head in the door.

"Hey, you guys! Hey, M-miz Cat!"

"Watch out, Leon," Mel advised him. "She's testy."

Leon frowned at her. "What that mean?" I knew that the concept wasn't beyond him, which people sometimes automatically assume because of his mild retardation. *Testy* just wasn't part of the vocabulary of teenspeak.

"Crabby," Al told him. "Cranky."

"Oh," Leon said, enlightenment spreading across his forehead. He shrugged and turned to me, the only one in the room with the politeness to address me directly when he was talking about me.

"You always that w-way, M-miz Cat."

Two

I was taking charge of my own health: that's what I said, and I should have stuck to my guns. But no.

Two days later Kevin comes around with this brochure advertising classes at the Northside Cultural Arts Center. I'd seen the place: it was a refurbished Victorian mansion on Chase east of Hamilton Avenue, a house whose Gothic pretensions had given it the popular nickname, the Arts Castle. Kevin had decided that I needed an outlet for my menopausal aggression, and for some reason he thought that pounding clay was the answer.

So that's how I landed in Jan Truitt's Beginning Ceramics class, Saturday mornings at ten, along with most of the human residents of the Catatonia Arms. Kevin went along because he's always looking for new experiences. Al went along because she wanted to be able to converse more intelligently with Mel, who was a potter by trade. Moses claimed that he was going along for support, but I suspected he had some notion of producing a complete set of dinnerware for his daughter by Christmas. I thought this was an entirely unrealistic fantasy, but if I'd told him so, he would have accused me of being cranky again. I invited my friend Mabel to join us out of deference to her passion for the arts, but it conflicted with her Barbie crochet class. Personally, I thought Barbie's tastes ran more to leather, suede, and space-age plastics, but it had been a while since I'd hung out with her.

In addition to my team, there were four others. Brenda Coats was a middle-aged black woman, short and comfortably plump, like me, but with delicate features and the most interesting almond-shaped violet eyes; her hair either hung in loose, medium-length waves, or was braided and pulled back into a bun. She had a colorful wardrobe of loose-fitting pants and tunics, and an armful of noisy brass bracelets that she removed whenever they started to get in her way. Ram Chatterjee was a dark-skinned, awkward, self-conscious fifteen-year-old with the kind of dark eyes and long lashes that would one day, to his great surprise, get him elected homecoming king. Gerstley Custer, who looked like an accountant and seemed not to have a nickname, was actually an art history professor at the University of Cincinnati; it was impossible to guess his age, and most of the time you didn't think to try because he was so bland and unprepossessing you forgot he was there. His foil was Mimi Finkelstein-Fernandez, who wore her long frizzy black hair in a Raggedy Ann and favored bright clothing color-coordinated with her two-inch fingernails. Her speech proclaimed her New York origins, but I didn't know enough about the neighborhoods or boroughs to pinpoint where she was from. When the instructor told her that the fingernails would have to go, she detached them nonchalantly and slipped them into her purse. She smelled like she had a relative in the perfume importing business. I sneezed a lot in her presence.

Jan Truitt, our instructor, was a friend of Mel's. She wore her long dark hair in a thick braid that she pinned up to keep it out of her way. She was a short, slender woman with more muscles than you would have credited just to look at her. Luckily, she had an even temperament and a sense of humor.

And speaking of temperament, if you are menopausal, premenstrual, pissed off, or just crabby by nature, let me give you a word of advice from your friend, Cat Caliban: working with clay will do nothing to improve your disposition.

From Day One I was at the bottom of the class, with Moses breathing down my neck to edge me out. We started with pinchpots. For the uninitiated among you, these are named for the handbuilding process used, and not, as some of us might imagine, because they make you want to pinch yourself to make sure you haven't stumbled into a nightmare where all your sins get punished by being forced to spend eternity doing what you are least competent at. At the end of two hours I had a small pot that looked like a miniature Hunchback of Notre Dame. This did nothing to take my mind off menopause.

"Can pots get osteoporosis?" I asked in a low voice, nudging Moses.

"Mine's got a tumor," he said morosely.

We glanced furtively around.

Al was studying her pot in alarm. I don't know what she was worried about; it was a little lumpy, but unlike Moses' and mine, it looked like something somebody intended to make.

Gerstley Custer had a neat little vase and was blithely running a fork up the side to score the clay. Moses and I exchanged a look: he'd moved on to surface decoration. No fair.

Brenda Coats was crimping the edges of a flat dish. Mimi Finkelstein-Fernandez was putting ridges into something that was recognizably a seashell, even though she'd been chattering nonstop ever since the clay had been doled out. Kevin's bowl had a smooth surface, a nice, graceful line, and a rolled lip. And Ram Chatterjee, who had worked in total silence, held a beautiful little pot that looked more sculpted than pinched. When asked, he confessed that he'd "fooled around a little" with clay at school.

"I thought you said this class was for beginners," Moses groused in my ear.

Jan had something complimentary to say about every pot. It must have been a stretch where Moses and I were concerned, but she pronounced our pots "interesting" in a way that dismissed round, smooth, uniform pots as dull.

"I don't want to be interesting," Moses confessed to me.

I sighed. "I know what you mean."

Across the table Kevin sparkled at us. "Isn't this fun?"

From pinchpots we graduated, more or less, to coil pots. At this point Moses and I had a collection of small, misshapen pots that listed to the side like a mob of drunken sailors. I could see the dinnerware set fading from his mind's eye. With coil building you were supposed to make a uniform roll of clay by rolling it between your hands or on the worktable, then coiling it around and on top of itself into the shape you wanted, then smoothing out the ridges. My coils looked like a python that had swallowed the contents of Noah's ark.

For inspiration, Jan showed us a film of a Native American potter from New Mexico who used this method to build pots half as tall as she was.

"Maybe she started when she was two," Moses observed. This was our latest theory, Moses's and mine: that we were too old to learn pottery. We'd decided it was like language learning—the older you get, the less natural aptitude you had. Or maybe between the arthritis and the hardened arteries, you didn't have the flexibility that you had once had.

Look at Ram. Here he was, turning out coil pots as easily as he had produced pinchpots. And not one of them interesting, we noticed. Just well-proportioned, sleek, and graceful. Case closed.

After the coil building came the slab building. At first this technique looked promising to me. You rolled out a slab of clay on a slab roller that looked like a piece of antique laundry equipment. You did this by turning a large wheel like a steering wheel, which rolled the roller over the clay and produced, with little effort or expertise on your part, a smooth, flat sheet of clay with a uniform thickness. This slab could then be cut in various shapes, like rolled cookies, and the shapes joined together with watered-down clay, called slip. So far so good.

But do you remember that box-folding part on the aptitude

tests your kids used to take in school, the one where they gave a diagram of a flattened-out shape and asked you what it would look like if they folded it up? That's the kind of aptitude you need for slab building, and I didn't have it. Never had, never will. I couldn't, for the life of me, figure out how the sides of something would fit together and how they would look afterward. So I made boxes, with all the sides square. Even "interesting" stuck in Jan's throat when she contemplated the results. Al was the only one who liked my boxes—but then, hers didn't look all that different.

Moses, meanwhile, with all of his carpentry experience, was in his element. He took to bringing a T square and a protractor to class.

"If I'd known you had to know math for this class, I'd never have signed up," I grumbled.

"Math, geometry, chemistry, and physics are all useful to potters," Jan cheerfully affirmed.

"How 'bout astrology?" I muttered under my breath. "That's the one I should've used before I signed up."

In the meantime, we had all gotten to know each other better, though some better than most. Mutual suffering will do that to you.

I thought at first that Mimi was going to be hard to take, especially early on a Saturday morning. But she kind of grew on you after a while. For one thing, she was a fountain of sympathy as well as a storehouse of aphorisms—from both sides of her family. "Well, as my *bubbe* used to tell me," she'd say, surveying the damage, or, "My *abuelita* always said . . . " When you showed her a disaster, she'd slap her hands to both cheeks, and exclaim, "*Chica! Qué pasó? Pobrecita!*" And when she created one herself, she'd pull at her hair with clay-covered hands, and wail, "*Oy vay!*"

Like I said, her foil was Gerstley Custer, and it was only through Mimi's persistence that we learned that he was a U.C. art professor and specialist in pre-Columbian pottery, and had worked with museums and on digs all over Latin America. I thought he looked kind of sickly for someone who worked in the sun a lot, but maybe those *National Geographic* specials use trick photography and makeup to make everybody look better. When pressed, he sometimes served as Mimi's translator to the rest of us, but to call him her interpreter would be pushing it.

Brenda Coats, the boutique owner, could be crusty. That didn't bother me, though; I knew all about crust. I noticed, too, that she tried to keep quiet when she was in a bad mood. Other times, she could be funny and generous and kind. She kind of took Ram under her wing, and he responded by opening up more. He was universally liked, a painfully self-conscious kid who could laugh at his own self-consciousness.

Luckily, everybody had a sense of humor—even me, on my better days.

By now you might think I was getting discouraged after five weeks of demonstrating my incompetence. You might even suspect that I was actually moodier than when I started. And you'd be right. But I wasn't really sorry I'd taken the class. Not yet.

Three

Call me an optimist, but I admit I harbored secret convictions that I would do better once we started throwing pots on the wheel. No matter how many times Mel warned us that wheel throwing was by far the most difficult technique, I thought that once I had a piece of electrical equipment to help out, the whole business would go much more smoothly. I thought this even though my relationship with all the domestic machinery I owned could best be described as an uneasy truce regularly disrupted by hostilities.

First, we had to learn to wedge the clay so that it would be the proper uniform consistency for throwing. Jan taught us a spiral wedge and cautioned us against confusing wedging with kneading. This was not an issue for me, but Kevin, who was on a first-name basis with the Pillsbury Doughboy, took more time than usual to master the technique.

Then Jan demonstrated how to throw a cylinder. Then we tried it. Suffice it to say that if you have never thrown pots before, you have a real treat in store for you.

The first challenge is to center the clay on the wheel head. You begin by throwing a ball of clay down hard on the center of a circular bat mounted to the wheel head. The better your aim, the less work you have to do to get the clay centered. On my first try I missed the bat altogether. As Mel pointed out when she questioned this story, the wheel head and bat are the size of a large pizza, so people don't normally miss.

The next ten tries were nearer the mark only because the clay hit the bat. Not one came remotely close to a bull's-eye. What's more, every time the clay hit the bat, Moses, who was sitting at the next wheel over, got splattered. He'd retaliated, and by now we looked like we'd been in a mudfight. I was worn out, and my pitching arm ached. I glanced around for Jan, and seeing that she was busy with Mimi, I surreptitiously shoved the clay over to the center, scraped off the telltale trail with my thumb, and slapped it a few times to make it stick.

I started up the wheel with the foot pedal, and the goddam clay flew off and hit me in the stomach. The next few times around, it waited until I started pushing on it to come loose. The evil lump hit the wall with a loud splat, stuck there a moment, and then slid to the floor.

Jan advised me to get some more clay and a dry bat.

That's when I discovered the next drawback of pottery as a recreational activity for seniors.

"Moses?"

"Hmmm?"

"I can't straighten up."

"Hmmm?" He frowned at me. He was concentrating on moving a pile of clay to the center of his bat, about four inches.

"No kidding. My back hurts like hell. You try it."

He shot me a look of annoyance over his bifocals, and pushed off from his low stool.

"Ow!" he yelped.

"See what I mean?" I was upright by now, and flexing my shoulders to see if the damage was permanent.

He ratcheted himself up to a vertical position.

"Mel didn't say nothin' 'bout no back injuries!" he complained.

"She's twenty-five years younger than we are," I pointed out. "She probably doesn't feel anything."

"Yeah, or maybe we just workin' too hard."

"Well, I wouldn't mind that if I had something at the end to show for it besides a chiropractor's bill."

"Maybe you should go see my mom," Ram piped up on the other side of me. "She does therapeutic massage."

For a minute there, I confess I began to suspect that this kid was a plant, going from class to class, exploiting the elderly in their moment of greatest need.

Moses sighed. "You better take down her phone number, Cat."

"Maybe we should just drop the course," I said. "It would probably be cheaper."

"One, we already paid for it," Moses objected. "Two, we only got four weeks left. Besides, you wouldn't want folks to think you were a quitter, would you?"

"I wouldn't mind," I said. But he'd already sat down at the wheel again, his jaw set with determination, so I started over with a dry bat.

If you've never tried to throw a pot before, and if you've seen a professional potter do it, you might believe that once the clay is centered on the wheel, the rest is easy. The thing is, wheel throwing engages three of your limbs simultaneously, and each of them is doing something different. The first time you try it, you will conclude that control, much less careful coordination, of all these activities is impossible. Coaching doesn't help much at this stage. If the instructor tells you to slow the wheel down, all of your limbs suspend their activities at once, and the whole process comes to a screeching halt, putting a bulge like a goiter into the piece on the wheel. Then the instructor will tell you not to make any sudden moves like that, and suggest that you hold a small sponge in your right hand. What for? you think. The chance that you might use something in your palm when you are concentrating so hard on your fingertips is nil.

What you're supposed to be doing at this stage is pulling the clay up by applying even pressure as it passes between your fingertips. If the pressure isn't even, or if the clay wasn't centered to begin with, you will have what is known among pottery pros as a "thin spot," and your piece will either tear, so that you find yourself holding the top of it suspended in midair, or fold in the middle like the Dakota Badlands, or collapse. I speak from experience.

All of which goes to explain why I was the last person in the world who should have been delegated to check the kiln on the night of October twenty-fifth.

For some reason, everybody thought it would be good experience for me, boost my self-confidence. The real reason probably had something to do with the fact that it was a Friday night, and everybody else seemed to have better things to do than baby-sit a kiln. I considered presenting an affidavit from my children affirming that I should not be allowed near an oven of any kind, or from my washer repairman that I should not be entrusted with electrical equipment. But no.

All I had to do, they said, was check to see that the kiln was off, and turn three switches. Jan wrote down the instructions, and I practiced a few times, just to make sure. How hard could it be?

So I drove over to the Castle, about three minutes from my house, on Friday night at about ten o'clock. To tell you the truth, despite my self-defense lessons from Mel, it was a little creepy to let myself into the darkened building. I went in the back way from the small parking lot, flipped on the lights, and marched briskly down the hall to the ceramics studio, passing the office and rest room on my left and the kitchen, a.k.a. the "culinary arts studio," on my right. If there were any ghosts in there baking rhubarb pies, I didn't want to know about it.

On the left past the rest rooms was a small cubbyhole with a photocopying machine, a soft drink machine, and a pay phone. Next to it on the wall facing me was the door to the large room partitioned lengthwise down the middle to create the ceramics studio, on the far side, and the jewelry and stained glass studio on the near side. I hit the lights for both sides of the room, and walked through the jewelry studio into the ceramics studio, my instructions clutched in my hot little fist.

There it was—my nemesis. The kiln was cylindrical, like an old-fashioned washtub, but it was about my height and bigger around than I could reach.

"Listen up, machine," I said to it. "I'm not the regular kiln checker, I'm just a substitute, and this is my first time, so I don't want any funny business."

I stooped over it to check the switch. Sure enough the gizmo had fallen. That meant the little clay matchstick-like cone inside the kiln had melted when it was supposed to, when the temperature had reached cone 05, and triggered the release which made the gizmo fall and shut the kiln off. Relief flooded my body.

My job was to turn the three switches on the front of the control panel from "high" to "off." This was an extra safety precaution to ensure that the kiln shut down. But someone had already done my job.

Shit, I thought. Somebody else had horned in. You might think I was relieved, but I wasn't. I'd spent days psyching myself up for this responsibility. My feelings were hurt. I thought somebody had decided they couldn't trust me to get it right.

I felt tears welling up in my throat, and resolutely swallowed them down. Damn those hormones, anyway.

I licked my finger, like you do when testing a hot iron, and felt the top of the kiln. It was cold.

That was odd. I'd been given to believe that it would still be pretty hot, and been cautioned against opening the thing.

I frowned at it, puzzled.

Then my gaze shifted and fell on the large counter adjacent to the kiln. At the far end were several pieces from the bisque firing we'd unloaded last Saturday, including one of my own stellar contributions—a bulging piece somewhere between a flowerpot and a bowl, heavy enough to sink the *Lusitania*. But at the near end, next to the kiln, stood maybe ten tall pieces of unfired greenware in various states, from whole to chipped or cracked to shattered.

Little ants popped out of the roots of my hair and raced for the back of my neck. Why hadn't these pieces been fired? It was possible that they had been left out of the kiln because they didn't fit, especially since they were all on the tall side. But how had they been cracked? And, more important, would anybody believe me if I said that I found them like that? I could see it all now: I would be blamed for something that wasn't even my fault.

I looked around for an explanation—a window left open to admit gale-force winds, a crazed squirrel who had been trapped in the building when it closed, a pent-up poltergeist. Nothing.

I gingerly touched the kiln again. Still cold.

Frowning, I bent over and pulled on one of the ceramic pegs that covered the peepholes into the interior—what we pottery pros call "pulling the peeps" (and no, I do not make this stuff up). I put one eye to the hole and peeped. And gasped. Once again I saw nothing, but this time it was a nothing that replaced the fired pots that should have covered the shelf.

Throwing caution to the winds, I opened the kiln, prepared to fall back when the heat hit me. There was no heat.

I nervously reviewed my instructions, both the ones I had in writing and the ones I remembered. Had I volunteered to load the kiln and turn it on, and forgotten? Surely not. I'd been forgetting a lot lately, but surely nobody would have let me do anything that required any skill, aptitude, or experience.

Reassured, I peeked over the side. The top shelves were littered with ashes and fragments, but no pots.

"Aww," I said sadly, taking a pinch of ashes between my fingers and wondering whose pots had been reduced to rubble. And again, whether I'd be held responsible. I wasn't attached to my own pots, God knows, but some people were attached to theirs.

I picked up a fragment and studied it. The ants changed course and scampered back up the other way.

The clay we used was a brown stoneware clay. When bisqued, it turned a tan color, with darker spots, and became very hard. What I was holding wasn't tan at all. It was sort of an off-white, with a pattern of tiny horizontal cracks across its surface. A piece of it chipped off as I fingered it.

It was the color of bone.

Four

"Moses, I got a problem here at the Castle. I think you'd better come right away."

In the background I could hear the masculine banter of a poker game in progress.

"Now, Cat, you can do it without me. Just follow your instructions."

"I can't. I'm having a problem."

"Now, Cat, you know what the book says. It's all hormonal. If your heart's racing, just sit awhile."

Kevin had bought me a book with a small section on menopause and given us a dramatic reading of selected contents, including the part about panic attacks. This now qualified Moses as an armchair gynecologist.

"Moses, trust me on this: it's not my goddam hormones. Now just get your buns over here and we'll see if your heart races."

I hung up on him.

Maybe I should have called the police, but I wasn't one hundred percent sure about what I was seeing. I figured calling a retired cop was the next best thing. Plus, it was less embarrassing if I was wrong.

Moses arrived clutching his thirty-eight.

"Good thinking," I said. "You can put some of these pots out of their misery while you're at it."

I led him to the kiln and watched his face while he studied its contents.

"Now, tell me that isn't what I think it is—that somebody slipped some porcelain ringers into our kiln."

Porcelain clay was white; I knew that much from reading Jan's handouts.

"No, that's exactly what you think it is," he said gravely. "That's bone. And that there"—he pointed at a small lump—"that's a tooth. And that big one—there's your porcelain. That's a set of dentures."

"A big raccoon with false teeth?" I suggested hopefully.

He shook his head. "Too much of it. Have to be a whole raccoon family."

"Maybe that's what it is."

"Could be." He didn't sound too confident of that possibility. "Crime lab should be able to tell. You touch anything in here?" He himself hadn't touched anything, not even the side of the kiln.

"Just the kiln. And I picked up a pinch of ash to get a better look. That little piece right there is the one I handled."

He nodded and glanced around. "I'd better call in."

"Aw, c'mon, Moses." He stopped in the doorway and turned. "You know I'm a detective in training. Give me a few minutes here to practice my investigative skills. What difference will it make? They'd have a hard time taking the body's temperature. Besides, you could give me some pointers."

"I was never a homicide investigator, Cat, or a scene-of-the-crime man."

Moses Fogg, like most black cops of his generation, had spent his career in one of two places: patrolling a beat or working Juvie. As a matter of fact, that was one reason we were trying to persuade him that he'd enjoy coming out of retirement to get his private investigator's license—the very license that stood between me and a rewarding career as a private eye. I had everything but the experience, as defined by a state that didn't recognize more than thirty years of unlicensed domestic detection as experience. I could remedy this situation if Moses got a license and let me work as his operative. But it was a tough sell. Moses claimed to be enjoying his retirement. Plus, he said that following husbands and wives around and taking pictures of their extramarital escapades wasn't his idea of a good time.

Now, however, he turned back and looked around the studio, which I took as a sign of interest.

"Who turned the kiln on, and when?" he asked.

"Yvonne, the secretary, was supposed to have turned it on this morning," I said. "But she couldn't have."

"Why not?"

"It's not hot enough. A normal firing takes about twelve hours—that's what Jan told me. Even if she started when she got in at nine, it should still be warm now." I pointed to the clock: it was eight-fifty. "And, anyway, it was already turned off when I got here. I mean, the dials were switched off."

Moses stuck out his bottom lip and fingered his mustache. "Could somebody have turned it off early? Before it went the whole twelve hours, I mean."

Obviously, Moses hadn't been giving one hundred percent of his attention to Jan's discussion of kiln firing.

"Not if Yvonne did her part right," I told him. "We know it reached the right temperature, because the cone melted. Look—you can see it in that little doohickey there, between the prongs. When the cone melts, it shuts off automatically."

He leaned over and studied the cone.

"What do you mean, 'if she did her part right'?"

"Well, you don't just turn the kiln on to high right away, even though that's where it will end up." My voice sounded strange to me; suddenly I was an expert on kiln firing. I started to enjoy it. "You turn it on low for an hour, then on medium for an hour, then on high. I don't know too much about it," I confessed in a sudden burst of modesty, "but I guess if you weren't worried about pots cracking, you could accelerate the process by turning it up to high right away. That would cut two hours off. I'd think that the kiln would still be warm, though. I just don't know."

He nodded. "We'll have to ask Jan. And Yvonne, of course. Was she supposed to load the kiln, too?"

"Uh-uh. Jan was going to do that when she came in last night for that lecture on African pottery. But she didn't want to hang around for the two hours it would take to turn the kiln on." I pointed to the damaged greenware on the counter. "That stuff must have been on the top shelf when somebody decided to use it to fire—uh, whatever."

"Let's see." Using his handkerchief, he picked up one of his own slab-built vases, which was now missing a section from one corner, and lowered it into the kiln. "Yeah, it fits, all right. Damn! That was one of my favorite pieces!" He replaced it carefully.

"So what we've got is this: John Doe has a dead body."

"Or Jane Doe."

"Right. They stash the body in the kiln and probably turn it on. It's possible that they just intended to hide the body, and that it was Yvonne who came along and turned the kiln on. But that's not likely for two reasons. One, Yvonne has presumably turned the kiln on lots of times before, and isn't likely to make a mistake. Two, the kiln is too cold—or at least, we think it is."

"So if they stashed the body *and* turned the kiln on, that means they wanted to hide the identity of the victim," Moses speculated.

"If it was a victim," I cautioned. "We should probably leave open for the moment the question of how the corpse got to be a corpse. And maybe they didn't want to hide its identity so much as hide the fact that there was any body in the first place."

"You mean, they were counting on us not knowing the difference between bone ash and pot fragments? That's a big gamble. And besides, they smashed our pots taking them out to get the body in there. They must've known we'd notice that."

"You have a point," I conceded. "They weren't exactly careful. But they were probably in a hurry. Anyway, a lot depends on how much they know about kilns and firing temperatures."

"And cremation," Moses added darkly.

"Right. What did they think we'd see when we opened the kiln? Ashes? A skeleton? A pot roast?"

"If they ever had a relative cremated, they might have thought the ashes would look like that," Moses said.

"What do you mean?" I asked. My husband, Fred, had not been the religious type, but he'd wanted to be buried in a coffin, just to keep his options open. Me, I'd always favored cremation myself, having seen too many vampire movies to want to spend eternity hanging around a cemetery.

"When somebody's cremated, the funeral home takes their ashes and pulverizes 'em so they're more uniform. That way, the relatives don't have to look at pieces of bone that look like pieces of bone."

"So the perpetrator we're after either knows a lot about pottery and cremation—"

"Or not much about either."

"Well, that's a big help," I told him. "I'm glad we did this exercise. I feel better already."

"Yeah, Cat, but no matter how smart they are, they already made their first big mistake."

"What's that?"

"They didn't count on a trained detective being the one who would open the kiln."

Five

"I hope it's nobody we know," Moses said as we sat in the kitchen watching a parade of detectives, photographers, scene-of-the-crime technicians, and other miscellaneous investigators file past, and waiting to be questioned.

"Yeah," I said, "like somebody from our class. I mean, I envy their talent, some of 'em, but I don't want to see them dead." Strangely enough, this sentiment even extended to Mimi Finkelstein-Fernandez. My mood in her effusive presence had mellowed from irritability to appreciation—as long as I stood upwind of her perfume. She kept us laughing at something besides our failed pots.

"'Course, if we were really leaving our options open, we'd consider the possibility that the bones were old bones that somebody wanted to get rid of," Moses said. "They might be any kind of bones."

"Sure, that's how I'd handle it, if I were cleaning out a closet and discovered a skeleton tucked away in the corner. I'd run right down to my local arts center to see if by any chance they had a crematorium in the back."

"Some artists use bones in their work, don't they?" he asked. "Seem like I read somewhere about a sculptor who uses 'em some kind of way."

"Yeah. After all, Jan's always trying to get us to study the natural world and use natural objects to put texture into our surfaces. Maybe somebody brought 'em in for show-and-tell."

"That don't explain why somebody smashed our pots, though."

"Maybe Lottie did it," I suggested.

Lottie Gambrel was the woman who worked part-time as

building janitor. Jan had a running battle with her because, according to Jan, her standards were too high for an arts center. If she saw dirt, she went after it, no matter how many artworks she had to move to get to it. As a result, Lottie had numerous breakages to her credit, especially in the pottery studio. Once clay was bisqued, it was pretty durable, but before that, when it was still greenware, it was extremely brittle—hard to trim but easy to break. Studio etiquette frowned on the handling of another potter's greenware.

Lottie was a reasonable suspect for the smashed pottery, although she'd never done that much damage before. I was pondering this possibility when Frieda Katz, director of the center, arrived.

Frieda wore her thick, straight black hair in a short wedge cut, kind of like those ancient Egyptians you see pictures of. She wore fashionable glasses with large square red frames, and she usually exuded a determined if rather frenetic enthusiasm. She lit a cigarette nervously and collapsed into a chair.

The center was her life. A tireless fundraiser, she was said to be brilliant at attracting money. She'd also been given high marks for her ability to manage an often temperamental and even fractious board of directors. I didn't really know her, but she'd stopped by the pottery class often enough to make it clear that she didn't keep bankers' hours.

"This is terrible!" she exclaimed. "Which of you found the—uh, remains?"

I raised my hand. "That was me."

She turned troubled dark eyes on me. "And was the building locked when you arrived?"

"If you don't mind," a voice in the doorway interrupted politely, "I'd like to ask the questions. In private. Ms. Katz, we can use the office across the hall? Thanks. Ms. Caliban, I think I'd like to talk to you first."

For a pleasant change, the investigation apparently was not

being handled by my old nemesis, Sergeant Fricke. The man in the doorway was a plain-clothed, distinguished-looking black man in his mid-fifties, I'd say, clean-shaven, with accents of white in his hair. He introduced himself as Lieutenant Arpad.

He took me through a blow-by-blow account of the evening's events.

"Are you the person who normally checks the kiln?" he asked.

I started. He'd pronounced it "kill," like a lot of people do. But Jan pronounced it the way it was spelled, and everybody in the class had followed her lead, so it took me a minute to realize what he was asking. Normally, we didn't have a kill to check.

"I don't know if there is a normal person," I said.

"That's why they picked you, huh?"

I grinned. I liked this guy. Fricke had the sense of humor of a newt.

"I've never done it before," I told him. "My classmates said they thought it would be good experience, but between me and you, I think I got the job because I didn't have anything better to do tonight."

"Same here," he said.

Eventually we worked our way around to kiln firing, and I explained the process and the timing of it. I even got to trot down the hall to the studio and show him the wilted cone in its little metal enclosure.

Like Moses, he asked me what I'd touched, and arranged to take my fingerprints for comparison. He asked about the pots on the counter adjacent to the kiln, and I explained.

"So you think these pots were actually in the kiln, on the top shelf? I guess we'll find out when we talk to whoever loaded the kiln."

I explained about greenware being fragile, and even threw in our speculations about Lottie. I didn't want to get her in trouble, but I figured if this was a homicide, the police would need to clarify who did what.

As he lingered over the greenware, I pointed out Moses' vase.

"Foggy made that? No kidding. Hmm." He smiled. "We don't watch out, he'll grow a goatee and move to Mt. Adams." Mt. Adams was an artsy little hilltop neighborhood near the Art Museum and the Art Academy.

"I don't think so," I reassured him. "You haven't seen his other stuff."

As if in retaliation, he strolled over to the bisqueware and, reaching into the middle with a gloved hand, selected my pot. He almost dropped it before he added a second hand to support it.

"Didn't realize how heavy it was," he said apologetically, as if he didn't notice my red face. And no, it wasn't a hot flash.

He held the pot out so that I could see it. "You recognize this one, Ms. Caliban?"

"It's mine," I croaked, ducking my head. "I made it."

"You did?" He looked impressed. "You must be pretty strong." He said this as if it were a compliment. Maybe he intended it that way. People who don't know pottery don't always know that it's not supposed to double as ballast.

He turned it around carefully so that I could see the other side.

"Did it look like that the last time you saw it?"

I felt sick. My pot had a few new cracks in it, radiating out from what looked to be a point of impact. A dark stain showed against the speckled tan of the clay, and stuck to the surface at the center of its concussion were several strands of curly black hair.

Six

I'd figured class would be canceled next morning, what with the pottery studio sealed as a crime scene and all. But Arpad had apparently decided that he needed to talk to all of us anyway, so he'd take advantage of our regularly scheduled meeting time on Saturday morning.

I am not exactly at my best at ten A.M. Since I'd given up caffeine for menopause, I'd been crankier than usual. Worse yet, this morning I was functioning on five hours of sleep, courtesy of another one of those middle-of-the-night hot flashes. Which is to say that I wasn't in the best condition to observe my fellow students as they reacted to the news about the kiln-turned-crematorium. Those who hadn't already heard about it on radio or television learned what had happened from the army of reporters swarming all over the Castle's front yard.

Gerstley and Mimi appeared suitably shocked and distressed. After expressing these emotions—or rather, after Mimi expressed these emotions for both of them—they went on to inquire after a large hand-built bowl and a slab vase, respectively.

"I doubt it," I told them.

"But the vase wasn't very tall," Mimi persisted hopefully. "It wouldn't have been on the top shelf. God forbid I should show disrespect for the dead, but a vase is a vase. I had a spot all picked out for it in my mother's apartment, which—with any luck at all—she would never have to know that a dead person got roasted on top of it."

Ram was positively gleeful. "This is so cool!" was his comment. "Do we get fingerprinted?"

Brenda Coats looked so disturbed that I was reminded that

she was a board member. Maybe she was worried about lawsuits? Could a board member be sued for negligence if somebody got murdered on the premises? Or was she just concerned about getting fingerprint ink on her pants? I was willing to bet it was harder to wash out than clay.

I'd heard Frieda Katz's voice coming from the office when I'd passed it earlier. Jan arrived next, and Frieda joined us in the hall outside the studio. Neither one appeared to have gotten any more sleep than I had.

But Arpad took the prize in that department, with circles under his eyes as big as doughnuts. Moses had told me that Arpad's nickname was "Rap," an ironic one for such a clean-cut, distinguished-looking guy, and I was studying him to see if I could get used to it.

Arpad explained that he wanted to take us into the studio to see whether anybody spotted anything unusual or out of place.

"The fingerprint technicians are finished for now, but I'd still like you to be careful not to touch anything," he said. "Just walk around and look. If you see something, holler. If it needs to be picked up, we'll pick it up with gloves."

We shuffled in like a tour group. All eyes were drawn to the kiln. Then they shifted to the collection of shattered greenware on the counter. Fingerprint dust covered everything—the kiln, the pots, the counter. Gasps and moans followed.

"If it weren't for the ashes in the kiln, I'd assume Lottie had done that," Jan admitted.

"Except Lottie wouldn't leave the mess behind for you to find," Frieda pointed out.

"You're right. She wouldn't deny that she did it, but she would clean it up. And I don't want to be around when she sees that fingerprint dust."

"I don't think Lottie's been in here lately," I said. "Look."

I pointed to a spot on the wall over one of the wheels, where we could see two curved brown lines. Jan had a habit of drawing on the off-white wall with a clay-covered finger when she wanted to illustrate something she was explaining. She'd draw the line of the pot you'd thrown, for instance, and then the line of the pot you should have thrown. At least, that was how it went for me. Usually, she was in the process of explaining why my pot had collapsed as soon as I'd got it pulled up.

"You're right, Cat," Jan said. "I drew that Wednesday night. In the advanced class," she added for Arpad's benefit. "If Lottie had been in here since then, she would have washed it off."

We continued to behave as if we were on a guided tour in a non-English-speaking country. Even Mimi had been stricken silent, and Gerstley had turned into a black hole. I kept stepping on his feet. We shifted to the far end of the counter and the adjacent double sink.

Ram scrutinized the sink. He looked disappointed. "Didn't you find any bloodstains?" he asked.

"I can't tell you that," Arpad said. He was wearing those disposable plastic gloves they all wear at crime scenes.

"Wait! What's that?" Ram pointed excitedly to a minute brownish-red splash on a far corner of the sink.

"Looks like red glaze to me."

"Oh, God! That's right!" Mimi said. "I guess we should look at the glazes, too."

"Why?" Kevin asked. "You think somebody glazed the victim before they fired him?"

"No, really!" she said. "I saw this movie once where this serial killer who worked in a candy factory kept hiding the heads of his victims in vats of chocolate and candy coating."

We all stared at her.

"Listen," she told us, raising a cautionary hand, "you don't even want to know what they put on TV in the middle of the night in New York. You know why there's so many weirdos in the city? They all stay up and watch these sick flicks and it does something to their brains. I'm not kidding!"

The mixed glazes stood in large plastic buckets piled on top of one another and pushed under the counter. We all dutifully squatted down to study them.

Kevin pointed to the slip bucket, an open bucket that stood nearest the sink. It contained scraps of hardened clay that were slaking in water so that the clay could be recycled and reused.

"You'd better check that," he said. "Anything could be down there."

"Yeah," Ram enthused. "Maybe the murder weapon is there."

I wasn't about to confess that the murder weapon had already been found, and those in the know kept silent, whether out of deference to me or to Arpad, I wasn't sure.

"That's a good idea," Arpad said. "We'll check it out."

A "good idea"? Had this guy gone through the same training program as my old enemy, the surly Sergeant Fricke? He was downright polite. Maybe Fricke had been sick the day they covered community relations.

I tried to stand up, and couldn't. Kevin hoisted me up by the elbow, then gave Moses a similar hand up.

"You'd better check that clay, then, too," Jan said, and pointed to the heavy rectangular tray where the slaked clay was spread out to dry for reuse.

"Okay," he said amiably. He was actually taking notes.

We shuffled to the right, and contemplated the tall set of shelves where trimmed greenware waited to be fired.

"I guess you'd better look inside all these tall, narrow pots," Jan pointed out thoughtfully. "I guess somebody could have hidden something inside them."

"Yeah, like from a jewel heist or something," Kevin said. Ram's enthusiasm was catching, and Kevin was hardly immune.

"Not a jewel heist these days, Kevin," Ram said. "It's probably drugs."

"Got it," Arpad said, writing.

"Oh, look!" Al exclaimed, pointing. "One of the thingummyjiggers is gone from my wheel!"

"Oh, wow!" Ram said, and raced to inspect it.

Mounted to the average wheelhead are two small bolts, which fit inside two holes in the bats used for throwing and secure the bat in place. One of these bolts was missing.

"I don't see what significance it could have," Gerstley mused, and then looked almost embarrassed that he'd been caught venturing an opinion. "I mean, most murderers don't commit murder by forcing the victim to swallow something they'll choke on."

"Yeah," Mimi said, "and I have vitamin pills that are bigger than one of those bolts."

She had vitamin pills? I thought. Wait'll you're my age, cookie. Especially if you're surrounded by health nuts who think hot flashes can be cured by the right combination of herbs, extracts, and other naturally occurring chemicals with names that sound like geriatric trailer parks.

Personally, though, I shared their skepticism about the missing bolt. After seven weeks of pottery class, I was pretty accustomed to seeing things turn up missing. Me, I was willing to bet a Peewee Potter had dropped the damn bolt down the drain just to see what would happen.

We examined, in their turn: the two long worktables, all the stools (with a note to Arpad to check the undersides), the overflow shelves, the window ledges, the slab roller, the assigned shelves for our work in progress, the wedging table. Arpad continued to take notes, though I doubted we were telling him anything he hadn't already thought of—and probably done. In fact, nothing very exciting occurred until we reached the assigned shelves for the advanced class.

Since the advanced class wasn't on the same schedule we

were, they'd already completed several glaze firings—the second firing for a finished piece—and several glazed and finished pieces stood on these shelves.

"What's that?" Jan asked, bending over and pointing. "Pull that out."

"Which one?" Arpad asked, bending over a little stiffly, I was gratified to notice. "This one?"

He straightened up and held out a vase that didn't look like anything I'd ever seen around the studio.

I wish I could tell you who gasped, but I was focusing on the vase. All I can tell you is that several people did, and I might even have been one of them. In retrospect, I guess some of those gasps were more knowledgeable than others, but at the time they sounded pretty much alike to me.

The vase we were looking at seemed to be about eight or nine inches tall. It was in one of those classic forms, full with a narrowed neck, exquisitely shaped. But what was most remarkable was the decoration. The background was a dark brown, and swimming across its surface was a school of brilliant red goldfish. Their scales and the surrounding water shimmered with gold.

"Oh, my God!" Kevin said in a hushed voice, reaching out almost involuntarily, and then pulling back. "It's a Goldstone—a Rookwood Goldstone."

Arpad turned it over. Impressed into the bottom was an odd mark, like an oval turned sideways, bisected by a column and surrounded by thirteen little upside-down commas that looked like flames.

Seven

"I don't know much about Rookwood," Kevin said modestly over lunch later.

Don't believe it. Kevin was our own Alex Trebek, only he didn't carry around those *Jeopardy!* cheat cards that Alex did.

"But I have friends who collect it," he added.

"Not me," Mel said. We'd picked her up on our way to lunch so that she wouldn't die of curiosity before we got home. "My friends can't afford it."

"Hold up," Al said. "I know Rookwood Pottery is supposed to be famous and all, and I know when you move into a Cincinnati apartment that has a tiled fireplace, all your friends ask if it's Rookwood. But I don't know any more about it than that. What makes Rookwood such a big deal?"

"Okay," Kevin said, clearly pleased to be asked. "Rookwood Pottery was founded in the late nineteenth century by Maria Longworth Nichols, then Maria Longworth, daughter of one of Cincinnati's leading citizens."

"Go on," Al prompted.

"Rookwood recruited from the Art Academy—or whatever it was called—and trained its own artisans, as well. Nichols was a big fan of Japanese pottery, so a lot of Rookwood shows that influence—hence the goldfish, for example. What Rookwood was most known for was its glazes and its magnificent slip painting—animals, flowers, landscapes, and portraits."

"You mean, like that blue slip we got at the studio?" Moses asked.

"Yeah, so that will give you some idea how much training and skill it required to paint with slip. Our blue slip will look a lot bluer when it's fired than it looks now."

"It hardly looks blue at all now," I observed.

"Right. So imagine painting with a whole palette of slips that don't look anything like they will look when the pot is fired."

"Don't worry, Cat," Moses told me. "We won't have to do that till we get to the advanced class."

"I doubt you'll do it then," Mel said, to my relief.

"Yeah, even the experts were impressed, and Rookwood began to win all kinds of international prizes early in its history. And it got a lot of public exposure at the Chicago World's Fair in the early 1890s. It sent decorators abroad to study, and imported one of its most famous decorators from Japan."

"Too bad you don't know more about this stuff, Kevin," Mel said through her veggie burger.

"Listen, there are people who can look at a piece and tell you who the decorator was," he said. "Or date it from the glaze line. Or tell you whether it was one of the decorator's favorite pieces or not. I don't even know all the different glaze lines. I just know about Goldstone and Tiger Eye because those are the most famous."

"Goldstone is what we saw on that vase this morning, right?" I said. "So what's Tiger Eye?"

But Kevin liked to tell a story his own way. "One day, not too long after the pottery was founded, a glaze firing came out of the kiln with some amazing effects. It looked as if the surface of the pots had been dusted with gold. They'd never seen anything like it before. The trouble was, when they set about trying to reproduce the effect, they couldn't. For years and years they tried to control it, but they never figured out how. It just occurred randomly."

"So that was called Goldstone?" I asked.

"Goldstone or Tiger Eye. The distinction has to do with the concentration of the gold effect."

"What was that symbol on the bottom?" Moses asked.

"Oh, that was the Rookwood logo. Here, I'll draw it for you." He took out a pen, and started drawing on a napkin. "It's a reversed R superimposed on a P, for Rookwood Pottery. The tail of the R here looks like a flame, and then there are other flames all around it." He studied his drawing critically. "I'm probably getting it wrong. I don't know how many flames, but I think it varied."

"So what's the bottom line?" Moses asked. "How much was that vase worth?"

"Offhand, I couldn't say. But you can imagine. Since the pottery couldn't produce the effect at will, there aren't that many pieces of this kind out there."

"Yeah, but give us an idea what we're talking about here, Kevin," I protested. "Several hundred dollars? Several thousand? Enough to kill for?"

"Well, if you put it that way, Mrs. C., sure. To any given collector, it could be priceless. Say you specialized in Goldstone, or say you wanted an example of every Rookwood glaze line ever produced—some people do that, you know—and the only one you didn't have was Goldstone."

"So what you're saying is that price may not be the most important measure of how valuable this thing is?" Moses asked.

"Well, it's certainly one measure. But what I'm also saying is, some collectors are real fanatics. There's nothing they wouldn't do to get their hands on a piece they want for their collection."

"Yeah, but Kevin," Al objected, "if somebody killed for it, why didn't they walk off with it?"

"Good question," I said.

"Well, it wasn't exactly a purloined letter," Kevin pointed out. "I mean, we had to bend over to see it on that lower shelf."

"Somebody hid it, but hid it someplace where they could get to it easily," Moses observed.

"What do you mean?" I asked.

"Well, they couldn't put it in our main supply cabinet, because that was locked. But there's that smaller cabinet on top of the main cabinet—that's never locked."

"Or maybe they couldn't reach it," I put in, the shortest member of the group.

"Ooh, that's good, Mrs. C.! That's very good!" Kevin nodded approvingly. "That would also explain why they didn't put it on a top shelf! That means we're looking for a short murderer!"

"Or a short murderee," I corrected him.

"Oh, that's right." His face fell. "I don't suppose there's any chance we'll be able to tell how tall they were from their ashes," he said to Moses.

Moses was smearing ketchup around on his plate with a french fry I was lusting after. Between my daughter Franny and the Mel and Al duet, I'd been lectured so often on the effects of fat on women my age that I did most of my fat consumption in private these days. But Moses, whose arteries were nothing to write home about, pretended not to notice the looks Mel was giving him.

"I don't know for sure," Moses confessed. "But I'd guess they can give us a height-weight range from the weight of the ashes and maybe the density of the stuff. I know a guy over at U.C. who specializes in that kind of thing. My guess is that Arpad will consult him.

"But getting back to my point. There's a cabinet under the sink where you could hide something, too. It's not locked."

"Which means—?" I said.

"Damned if I know what it means, Cat. If you gave a quick look around, you might not notice one vase surrounded by other ones. But if you were looking for a Goldstone vase, and you knew that's what you were looking for, wouldn't you spot the difference pretty quick?"

"So if the victim was murdered for the vase, the murderer

either was in too big a hurry to do a very thorough search or didn't know what he was looking for," I concluded.

"Or she," Mel amended.

"I don't know, Mel," Kevin said. "You didn't see Cat's vase. It would take a lot of upper-body strength to lift that thing high enough to use as a weapon. *You* could do it, but you work out."

"Maybe the killer just dropped it on the victim," Moses agreed. "Coulda been an accident, even."

"You'd better shut up about my vase if you don't want pinchpots in your Christmas stockings," I grumbled.

They made a visible effort to look serious.

Finally Kevin said, "I don't think you'd better, Cat. What if a stocking fell on one of the cats?"

That broke them up. I glowered at them.

"C'mon, Cat, lighten up," Al said, provoking new gales of laughter from the gallery. "What'd I say?" she asked. Then, "Oh," and she was off, too.

To my utter horror, tears welled up in my eyes and overflowed. Everybody froze, including Moses, who held a french fry suspended in midair. They stared at me.

"Well," I wailed, "it's no fun to put in all that time and effort doing something you can't do, and making things that everybody is going to poke fun at!"

They exchanged guilty looks.

It was getting worse and worse. You know how it goes. Your damn sinuses clog up and your lips puff up and go numb and your voice squeaks and even you can't understand what you're saying.

"Well, gee, Cat, you're just a beginner," Mel said. "Nobody expects you to be an expert overnight."

"Well, so is Kevin a beginner, and he makes great stuff!"

"Actually," Kevin said quietly, handing me a handkerchief, "I took some classes in college."

"Well, Al is a beginner, and she makes bowls that look like

bowls and plates that look like plates. And even Moses is good at slab building. But I'm not good at anything! That's why the murderer picked my pot!"

I'm not sure how much of this they understood, but they got the gist of it.

"Look, Mrs. C.," Kevin said gently, "we talked you into taking this class because we thought you'd enjoy it, and it would help you relax. Aren't you having any fun there?"

"Well, yeah," I admitted tearfully. "I mean, I like the people, and I like Jan, and nobody tries to make me feel bad that I'm so lousy; in fact, everybody mostly tries to make me feel good, and when I finally do something right, I *do* feel good, but it's frustrating, too."

I had just about run down and was back to being nearly intelligible. I blew my nose and felt a familiar response in my lower regions.

"And now I have to go to the bathroom!"

As I left the table, I heard one word of the whispering that followed in my wake: *gynecologist.*

"Don't feel so bad, Cat," Moses consoled me when I got back. "I'm givin' everybody doorstops for Christmas."

"Mine were all vases, till I trimmed right through the bottom of them," Al said. "Now they're all flowerpots."

"I say we just forget about trying to pull all that clay up," Kevin offered. "It never stays where we put it anyway. I say we just make pizza stones, and be done with it."

"Pizza stones!" Al exclaimed. "That's a great idea, Kevin."

"It's harder than you think to keep flat pieces flat," Mel cautioned, eyes and eyebrows elevated to the sky. Maybe that's where the patron god of pottery hung out, thinking up entertaining new ways to make pots fall apart.

"Could we get back to the weightier problem at hand?" I said, just to show I hadn't lost my sense of humor. "There was other stuff on the bottom of that Rookwood vase, Kevin. What was all that?"

"Yeah—there was a number of some kind," Al recalled.

"You'll have to ask an expert," Kevin said. "But the number was stamped into the wet clay, so I'd guess it's a shape number. You see, Rookwood used the same shapes over and over again, and they were catalogued in a notebook I've heard people refer to as a 'shape book.'"

"You mean they were molded instead of thrown?" I asked, glimpsing new possibilities for my own career as a potter.

"Rookwood did use mold casting as well as throwing to facilitate mass production. If I remember right, a piece might be thrown, and then a mold cast from that. But they always used some wheel-throwing as well, and it seems to me that most of the famous pieces—the vases, I mean, not the tiles—are thrown."

"And what about the letters cut into the bottom? Are those the initials of the thrower, or the decorator, or did one person do both?"

"No, I think throwers threw and decorators decorated, but I could be wrong. As far as I know, the initials usually belong to the decorator. It's the decorator's reputation that makes a piece valuable."

"There was a paper label, too—something about Paris," I said.

Kevin nodded. "It was a label from a Paris exposition. Rookwood often sent pieces to major shows and expositions abroad, so I'd guess that one went to Paris."

"Does that make it more valuable?"

"I don't know for sure, but I do know they usually sent only their best pieces. I'd guess a French showing would be pretty important, so they probably sent la crème de la crème. I don't know whether the label itself adds value, though. It might."

"And then there was some kind of faint stamp that had been applied to the surface in purple ink. I couldn't make it out very well. It looked sort of like a triangle."

"You got me there, Cat. I just don't know."

"How'd you get to know so much, Kevin?" Al asked.

Me, I'd given up asking how Kevin knew about anything. I'd decided that a world-class education was one of the perks of tending bar for a living.

But Kevin looked sheepish and Mel grinned.

"He had an old boyfriend who was a collector," Mel revealed.

"Darryl wasn't old," Kevin protested.

"You still on speaking terms with him?" I asked. "We might have a few questions for him."

" 'We'?" Moses threw me a look. "Cat, I don't remember the part where Rap asked you for advice."

"Are you kidding?" Kevin rose to my defense. "He asked everybody for advice. But I'm not speaking to Darryl!"

"Please?" I pleaded. "I'll wash the pawprints off your car."

"Cat, Rookwood experts are a dime a dozen in Cincinnati. You could ask the owner of a gallery who specializes in Rookwood. For that matter, you could go right to the top and talk to Dan Pratt at the Art Museum."

"Yeah, don't be a party pooper, Moses," Mel told him. "Cat's in training so she won't disgrace you when you finally cave in and get your license."

"Now, aren't we all glad we rented from Cat?" Al said, beaming. She was trying to recover some of my goodwill after ridiculing my pots. "I mean, I've never been a murder suspect before."

"Yeah, well, I hate to burst your bubble," Moses said. "But ain't none of y'all a serious suspect in this case."

"What do you mean?" Al asked indignantly. "We all got fingerprinted, didn't we? That looked pretty serious to me."

"What do you know that we don't?" Kevin added, narrowing his eyes at Moses.

"I know that Yvonne didn't turn on the kiln yesterday morning 'cause it was already warm. She did turn the temperature control switches off, though, 'cause that switch on the side was already down. If she's telling the truth, that means somebody turned it on the night before."

"You mean, somebody who had a key, or somebody who broke in?" Kevin asked. "You mean, somebody met somebody there in the middle of the night?"

"The kiln was warm, Moses," I asked slowly, "or hot?"

He grinned at me. "Just what I said. Warm."

"And the cone had already melted and triggered the shutoff. So even if somebody turned it right to high, it must have been on most of the night."

"Right. So the person who turned it on was probably in the building Thursday evening."

"Attending the lecture on African pottery," Kevin speculated.

"Attending the lecture on African pottery," Moses confirmed.

"Which gives us how many suspects?" I asked.

"Thirty-three," Moses said, "beginning with our teacher."

Eight

Moses' leading suspect agreed to see me on Tuesday. She lived in a rambling farmhouse tucked in among the nurseries on Gray Road, behind Spring Grove Cemetery. The working pottery and showroom for Spring Grove Pottery were located in a converted barn in back of the house. Jan gave me a tour, increasing my sense of the complexity of the whole enterprise. Pottery is not for dilettantes, take it from me. If you don't know what you're doing, not only can you destroy a week's work in an instant, you can burn the place down or poison yourself. And I'm not even mentioning dust allergies and arthritis and carpal tunnel syndrome. Cross-stitching is a hobby; pottery is a way of life.

"I have to get back to work by two," Jan warned me. She'd pulled her long hair back in a ponytail, the end of which looked as if it had been dipped in white slip. "I'm in the middle of a huge dinnerware order."

I was tempted to ask if Moses had ordered it, but I bit my tongue.

Jan moved a pile of *Ceramics Monthlys*, and we sat down in a pair of dusty director's chairs. I caught movement out of the corner of my eye. A large orange tomcat was arching and stretching on a nearby drying shelf crowded with greenware. He blinked at us sleepily, then began his slow progress along the shelf, stepping delicately, swaying sinuously, as he negotiated a path around the drying pots. At the end of the shelf he crouched, then leaped to the adjoining counter three feet below. A cloud of dust rose when he hit the counter, and the shelf unit swayed just a fraction of an inch. He sneezed, knocking the cobwebs off his whiskers.

"We tried to break him of that when he was younger," Jan

said, half-apologetically, the way you do when a guest spots one of your cats in the kitchen sink or on top of the stove. "But it didn't take. And anyway, he's very careful. He's never damaged anything."

I nodded. Cat training ranked right up there with writing my congressman as a doomed undertaking.

"Did you make a list?"

I had asked Jan to write up a list of everybody she could think of besides herself who had attended the Thursday night lecture on African pottery.

"I did, but I don't see what good it will do you," she said, handing over a sheet of legal paper. "I didn't know everybody there, and I've probably forgotten half the people I did know. I'd like to help, but you know how it is. Frieda probably recognized more people, because that's part of her job as director. But even Frieda won't have known everybody who was there, and won't remember. You'd either have to go around interviewing a lot of people, or else put an ad in the paper, to come up with a complete list. And even then, anybody could have walked into the building during the lecture and walked out again without ever being seen."

"Yeah, I know," I admitted. "I'm just fishing right now. Can you think of anybody you remember seeing before the lecture, but not after?" She gave me a look of exasperation. "Okay, I withdraw the question."

I suddenly felt this overwhelming desire to dazzle her with my detection skills. I'd had this feeling a lot lately, and Moses had confessed one night that he'd felt the same way. As our ceramics disasters mounted, we wanted to demonstrate that there was something—anything—that we could do and do well. Unfortunately, I couldn't think of anything dazzling to say. So I went back to the list, flawed as it was.

"When did you arrive that night?"

"I got there about six forty-five. The lecture started at seven-thirty, and I had the kiln to load."

"Anybody there when you arrived?"

"Frieda was in the office, I know. That's all I remember, but there could've been other people around. I went straight to the studio to load the kiln."

"Did you see anything unusual or out of place in the studio?"

"The police asked me that, Cat. I didn't see anything. I sure didn't see a pile of broken greenware on the counter next to the kiln. I would've had a heart attack! That was all stuff I put into the kiln, on the top shelf. And I was very careful. You tell Moses there was nothing wrong with his vase when I loaded it."

"Oh, he knows that," I assured her.

The orange cat, now advancing across the cement floor, sniffed at my toes and looked as if he might sneeze again. I watched him warily, hoping he wouldn't decide my ankles needed marking.

"By the way," Jan said, "we salvaged some pots from the firing. The police let me unload it while they watched. Of course, they've confiscated all the pieces for testing, but we'll probably get them back by the end of the week. I'm afraid that carved piece of yours didn't make it. Those heavy pieces often don't dry out completely, which makes them really vulnerable if the temperature inside the kiln rises too quickly. But your little plates survived," she said brightly.

"Those were bowls," I mumbled. "Cat bowls."

"Oh. Then I guess they fell some more. But they came through the bisque."

Luckily, the cats weren't all that critical about presentation, just the food itself. As if to console me, the orange cat suddenly landed in my lap. It felt as if somebody had dropped one of my own pots there.

"So, on Thursday night, you finished loading the kiln," I said. "What then?"

She shrugged. "I closed it up, then double checked to see that everything was off."

She probably did, too. I didn't know if all potters were as careful as Jan was, but she impressed me as the kind of person who would go crazy at my house, where the motto embroidered on my sofa cushion was "Hang Loose." For example, I had smoke detectors to compensate for my absentmindedness, but I hadn't checked their batteries since they'd been installed. I thought maybe Moses had, but I kept forgetting to ask him.

"Did you turn the lights off in the studio?"

"Yes, I'm sure I did." Jan didn't like to waste anything.

"What time was that?"

"A little after seven. I went into the office and talked to Frieda and Alex—he was the one giving the lecture—and then I went with Alex to make sure the equipment was set up right for his slides."

"And was it?"

"Yes, but the projector bulb had burned out. Brenda Coats was there by then, and she volunteered to hunt up another, and came back with one about five minutes later. The room was filling up. I sat down near the front, and then Frieda came in and introduced Alex, and he talked."

"Did anything unusual happen during the talk?"

She shook her head. "Jim Hyde came in late—nothing unusual about that. He's campaigning for city council, so of course he asked a question, probably written by one of his aides, so we'd appreciate his appreciation of the arts. Mimi—she was there—she was unusually quiet, but Gerstley was as quiet as he always is. Gil Forrester asked stupid questions—again, nothing unusual about that. Several people had pots they wanted Alex to appraise—there's always some of that. I guess the only other thing unusual was that Brenda didn't ask any questions. She's pretty keen on African pottery, but I don't think she gets along with Alex too well. And then the lecture part was over, and the reception started out in the foyer."

"Did you notice whether the light in the pottery studio was on or off?"

"I didn't notice, so it must have been off."

I nodded. She would have noticed if it had been on.

"So, the lecture was over. Anything unusual happen at the reception?"

"No. Again, Gil made himself obnoxious, but that's normal. Alex was surrounded by people who had pots at home they were sure were worth a fortune. Brenda and Frieda seemed pretty cool toward each other, but that's not unusual, either."

"Anybody strike you as nervous?"

She pondered that a minute. "Not exceptionally so. I mean, Frieda seemed nervous to me, but you wouldn't notice unless you knew her. She's always nervous at these events, and probably more so if they involve somebody like Alex, and even more if Brenda is around."

"Who was the last person out of the building? Do you know?"

"Frieda said she was. The reception was over around nine, and she locked up at nine-fifteen. Yvonne opened up in the morning."

"Did Frieda check the pottery studio?"

"She says she didn't, and I don't have any reason to doubt her. As long as the lights were off, she wouldn't go in there."

"Did you talk to Yvonne about what she did next morning?"

"Yes. She says the switch was already down when she went in around nine-thirty. So she turned the controls to 'off.' She was surprised, she said, but she just figured I'd come in earlier than I'd intended the night before, and turned on the kiln."

"Did she notice anything else?"

"She saw the smashed greenware, but—you know Yvonne." I didn't, actually, but once you've spent some time in a small operation like this one, you hear enough stories so that you feel like you know everybody. "She figured I knew about it. She just thought, oh, too bad."

I nodded. The studios were the instructors' domains, some more so than others—especially when an instructor had been with the center as long as Jan had. Jan and her advanced students had built shelves, installed a wedging table, and decorated the studio to suit her with inspirational pictures of pots. The staff didn't feel all that comfortable intruding.

I had the sense that I was forgetting something, but I had that sense a lot lately. Have I mentioned that before?

"Tell me something about the people on this list," I said.

She gave me an exasperated look. "What do you want me to tell you? Of the ones I know well, none of them seem like murderers to me; of the others, I don't know them well enough to know."

"Well, let's start with Frieda. As the last person out on Thursday night, she becomes the prime suspect."

"But you know Frieda."

"I've interacted with Frieda on several occasions when she wandered in during class, but since those tend to be high-stress occasions for me, I'm not in a very good position to judge her character. I mean, if you asked her to describe me based on what she's seen, she'd say I was aesthetically handicapped at the very least, and possibly suffering from an undiagnosed muscle disorder."

She glanced at me in surprise, as if the part about the stress had never occurred to her.

"Well, Frieda is very good at her job, very devoted to the center. She runs a tight ship, but she makes people feel good about going there."

"How devoted?"

"If you're asking me if she'd kill to protect it, I'd say

probably not, but how would I know? Anyway, I don't think the murder makes very good publicity for the center, and Frieda wants the whole thing cleared up as soon as possible for that reason. I think, too, that she's hoping it will turn out not to have anything to do with the center.

"I want to see it cleared up, too," she continued. "That's why I'm sitting here now when I'm eight cups and saucers away from finishing an order that's two weeks overdue. It's partly that I don't want the bad publicity for the center; I'm a board member, after all. But it's also that the Castle pottery studio is like my home away from home. It's like somebody came into my living room and killed somebody and burned the body in my fireplace. I hope the police solve it. But if they don't, I hope you and Moses will. After all, you've spent time there now. You're family."

To my surprise, my throat closed up. Hell, maybe I was more attached to the place than I thought. But it was also kind of heartening to realize that Jan recognized my competence at something. She didn't judge my intelligence by the way I threw pots.

"Okay, tell me something about Alex, the lecturer."

"Arthur Alexander Parker the Third." She pulled thoughtfully on her ponytail and discovered the white tip with apparent surprise. She frowned, licked her thumb and forefinger, and began washing it off.

"Alex owns the Parker Gallery on Fourth Street. His specialty is pottery, but mostly Chinese and African, not American. I'm sure he's sold some Rookwood, though. Alex is tremendously knowledgeable, and he makes a very engaging lecturer."

"You mentioned that he made Frieda uneasy?"

"Well, his reputation isn't entirely clean. He's been known to offer flawed pieces at auction without disclosing their flaws. You know—a chip or crack that isn't visible from a distance, or something you can't see unless you actually handle the pot. He'll take advantage of an inexperienced buyer who doesn't know how to read catalog copy, or—at least, according to rumor—he'll tell a customer one thing, and when they find out it isn't true, he says they misunderstood him, and they haven't got anything in writing to use against him. That's why experienced collectors only buy from him when they can handle the piece—either in the gallery or in an auction preview. He's charming, though, and he has his own circle of admirers."

"But Brenda Coats isn't one of them."

"No. But the thing you have to understand about Brenda is that she's passionate about African culture, including African pottery. Alex's primary expertise is in Chinese ceramics, but he's been getting more interested in African in the past several years. Brenda thinks he's exploiting a trend. Plus, she knows about his reputation and she doesn't like the idea of him selling African pottery to inexperienced buyers. She thinks he's ripping them off." She shrugged. "He probably is."

"A lot of people seem to be exploiting that trend," I observed.

"Sure they are. And most of them have taken less trouble than Alex to become expert on African art and culture."

"But Brenda's a board member. Did she approve the lecture?"

"Well, she resisted at first; she doesn't like to give him a forum. It's good publicity for him, after all. Some of those people probably will end up paying him to appraise their pots, or they'll go to his gallery now that they know who he is. But she agreed in the end. She knows how knowledgeable he is—even she can learn a thing or two from Alex."

"What's your read on Brenda in general? You must deal with her a lot on the board."

"I like Brenda, but she can be prickly. Everything is a race issue with her, and who knows, maybe she's right. But we get along pretty well. We disagree on some things, but she doesn't hold a grudge—at least, not with me. That's probably because we're often on the same side, too."

"What does she do for a living? I forget."

"She owns a boutique in Walnut Hills. That's where she gets all those gorgeous clothes. I said to her after the first class, 'Brenda, don't you have some old clothes to wear so you won't get your good clothes dirty?' She said, 'These *are* my old clothes.'"

Me, I usually wore an old pair of jeans and one of Fred's undershirts.

I looked at the list again.

"There were two other board members present at the lecture—Ralph Nagel and Jim Hyde."

"Ralph's family owns Nagel Funeral Home in College Hill—that's probably the biggest black-owned funeral home in the city. I think Ralph is in charge now. He's always been a big financial contributor. All his daughters have taken classes at the Castle, and Ralph and his wife have, too. I think they're taking ballroom dancing right now."

Uh-oh. A funeral home owner. Somebody who knew all about cremation. On the other hand, why borrow the Castle kiln when you have your own crematorium at home? Even if you were pressed for time, seems like you could pitch a body out the window into the bushes and come collect it later for a more leisurely disposal.

"I can't imagine Ralph doing anything that would bring the center bad publicity," Jan added. "Heck, he paid to have the Culinary Arts Studio remodeled so he and Ava could take Chinese cooking."

"Is there anybody he doesn't get along with?"

She shook her head. "He gets along with everybody, pretty much."

"And what about Jim Hyde, the other board member who was there?"

"Well, you probably know about him. He's one of your city council members, and he's campaigning for reelection. I made that snide remark earlier about his staff writing up a question, but actually, Jim's probably the biggest supporter of the arts that we have on the council. He's a Democrat, and a moderate—Vietnam vet, naval hero, you know. Personally, I get along with him okay, and we vote together a lot. What can I say? Like a lot of ambitious politicians, he's kind of self-important—loves to hear the sound of his voice, carries a beeper so his staff can reach him night and day—you know, as if the President might call him up for advice on the Geneva summit. He comes across as a bit too hale-and-hearty for my taste. But he's better than some. Although it's hard to like a politician in October of an election year."

I knew what she meant. I had voted for Hyde twice because I liked his voting record better than some. He was more conservative, or maybe more cautious, than I wanted him to be, but our candidate choices were nothing to cheer about. And he'd taken a few stands I really supported—on historical preservation, for example. He'd even come out in support of proportional representation, to the surprise of liberals and conservatives both. The cynic in me said he had an eye to swinging the black vote in future campaigns for the state legislature or Congress, but the fact remained that even some of his liberal counterparts were intimidated by proportional representation.

"Does he get along with everybody on the board?"

"Well, he tries not to make enemies, let's put it that way. But he and Brenda don't get along, as you might imagine. They're two strong personalities. And I think there's some tension around the race thing—you know, he thinks the black community ought to be grateful to him for speaking out on proportional representation, and she's holding against him all the things he didn't vote for that he should've."

"Besides Brenda, there were two other members of our class there—Gerstley and Mimi," I observed.

"Now, Mimi surprised me. She doesn't strike me as the intellectual type. But she was there, all right, and she and Gerstley sat together."

"Is Gerstley interested in African pottery?" I asked.

"His specialty as an art historian is pre-Columbian," Jan said. "But those of us who are fanatics will hear anybody speak about anything having to do with pottery."

"He doesn't strike me as the fanatical type," I mused.

"Still waters run deep." Jan shrugged. "You don't get a Ph.D. in any field without being some kind of a fanatic. Anyway, he's been on digs in Mexico and Central America, I think. He mentioned it in passing one day."

I consulted the list again.

"Malvina Deeds and Constance Petty?"

"They're a hoot!" Jan said. "Retired teachers—you've probably seen them around the Castle. They go to everything because they're interested in everything. Malvina is black, and Constance is white, and they're both in their seventies. They live together in this big two-family house. They might be a couple—nobody knows. All I can say is, I hope I have their energy when I'm that age."

"Anybody else here I should know about? You mentioned this Gil Forrester."

Jan made a face. "He taught pottery at the Castle years ago. I'm prejudiced against him, because I don't think he's very good, and I also think he's lazy. But there's another reason, too. When he taught at the Castle, he appropriated Castle equipment and supplies for his own use. Someone spotted a grinder in his studio one day, and then went back to check and see if ours was in the cabinet. It wasn't. Frieda set him up by marking our equipment and bags of materials, and then as soon as a marked bag showed up in his studio, she fired him. She could've charged him, but she didn't want the publicity."

"So is that why Gil Forrester makes himself obnoxious at center events?"

"No, Gil makes himself obnoxious because he *is* obnoxious."

I suddenly remembered what I'd wanted to ask, so I asked before I forgot it again.

"Jan, who has keys to the building?"

"Well, let's see. Frieda, of course, and Yvonne. Some of the instructors—not all of us, but the ones who have been around for a while and who would have reason to come in after hours to check on artwork. The gift shop volunteers don't have them. Oh, and Lottie had one, of course; she usually cleans after hours."

"That's right, I forgot about Lottie. Has anybody talked to her?"

"No, she hasn't been in, and we haven't been able to get ahold of her. I think somebody went by her house and left a note for her. She usually comes in two afternoons a week; she's very reliable. But it's really odd. I mean, she could have gone out of town, but you'd think she would have told us, unless it was an emergency. She has another job somewhere, but nobody knows where."

She checked her watch, not so surreptitiously, and I began to make noises about going. The orange cat took some persuading, but he finally hopped down and strolled to the door to check for low-flying birds.

I had to pass through the showroom on the way out. By the time I got out the door, I was fifty dollars poorer and two bowls richer.

Nine

I stood outside the Parker Gallery on Fourth Street and checked my reflection in the window. I was wearing khaki pants, a long-sleeved woven cotton shirt, and a light jacket. My short white hair was lying down close to my head, where it was supposed to be. My shoelaces were tied. I didn't see any tags sticking up. Decent. Respectable, even. I took a deep breath and went in.

Art galleries intimidate me. I was not cheered by Jan's reassurance that people who didn't know what they were doing shopped there all the time. I figured most people who walked through the door knew how to keep up their end of a conversation about what they were looking at. They had attended their share of openings and sipped champagne and swapped knowledgeable opinions with other insiders. Their living rooms featured track lighting and they wore expensive, hand-crafted jewelry. They never backed into a Ming dynasty vase or splashed cocktail sauce on a Georgia O'Keeffe. Their cats didn't shed.

Just inside the door, as I surveyed a room full of breakable objects insured for five times the value of the Catatonia Arms, adrenaline flooded my body. The hormone hit my heart like a tidal wave, nearly knocking my heart right out of my chest. It accelerated like a race car on the final lap.

Oh, God, I thought. If I'm going to have a heart attack, let it be at a quilt show. Not here.

I found my way to a chair and sat down.

"May I help you?"

A young man had materialized.

"Not yet."

He studied me with some alarm.

"Should I call for an ambulance?"

"No," I said. I tried deep breathing. It wasn't easy. A golf ball seemed to have wedged in my throat.

"Here." The young man was standing in front of me, holding out a small paper bag. "Breathe into this."

Hell, I'd try anything. So I did.

Gradually my heart slowed. I raised my head.

"Hey, that was great. How did it do that?"

He shrugged. "I don't think the bag has anything to do with your heart. But when my mother has these attacks, she uses the bag to keep from hyperventilating."

I was beginning to think that everybody knew more about menopause than I did.

"Can I get you anything else? Water?"

"Nope. You've done enough—thanks. Actually, I'm looking for Mr. Parker. Is he in?"

"Do you have an appointment?"

I shook my head. "I wanted to talk to him about the recent—incident—at the Arts Castle."

"I'll see if he's available."

Mr. Parker proved to be available, which confirmed my suspicion that people who asked if you had an appointment were instructed to do so just to intimidate you. A middle-aged man emerged from the back of the store. He had curly blond hair going gray and a neatly trimmed mustache and beard. He wore a look of exaggerated concern.

"My dear lady." He clasped his hands in front of him. "Todd tells me you've had a little spell. I hope that you're fully recovered."

"That will probably take another five years—or so they tell me," I said. "Meanwhile, I'm looking into the recent events at the Northside Cultural Arts Center."

"Are you with the police?" His face registered surprise.

"No, I'm just a private citizen with some—uh, experience in investigation."

"Ah!" He beamed at me. "It's so nice to have a hobby, I always say, especially after retirement. Perhaps we should step into my office?"

He made a move to help me up, but I adroitly moved out of his reach and stood on my own. Hobby, indeed.

His small office looked like any other office, give or take a few priceless Chinese vases and some paperweights that appeared to be worth more than the crown jewels. The phone was a white antique, like something out of the bubble bath scene in a silent movie.

I introduced myself, then sat down.

His eyes widened. "Caliban? But then you're the one who found the—er, remains. How perfectly ghastly for you! But then, given your hobby, it must have been rather exhilarating, too. I mean, there you were, all alone in that big Gothic house at night, and then, to find that! Do tell me what it was like. I'm dying to know!"

"It was damned creepy, if you want to know the truth," I told him. "So now I'm trying to find out how those bones got there and why."

"And were they really bones when you saw them? How could you tell?" He leaned forward eagerly.

"Well, they were the wrong color for bisqueware, of course."

"Of course, they would be."

"But the teeth really gave it away."

"The teeth?" He looked shocked. "Oh, my! Well, perhaps the police will identify the deceased fairly soon, then."

"I guess so," I said dubiously. "But first you have to narrow the field. I mean, you can't just run a spot on the six o'clock news that says, 'Do you know these teeth?' "

"No," he agreed. "I quite see your point. Well, needless to say, I am entirely at your disposal—goodness, no pun intended. How can I help?"

I took out my notebook, partly just to impress him.

"You arrived at the Castle on Thursday night when?"

"Let me see—it was just after seven. I wanted to check the slide projector. One can always count on an equipment failure whenever equipment is being used, you know. The Woman's City Club is the worst, though. It's in that church basement where the wiring is so badly designed that whenever someone turns out the lights for slides, unless they know what they're doing, the sound system goes as well."

"And last Thursday night at the Arts Castle," I persisted, "the projector bulb had burnt out."

"Yes, that's right. Mrs. Coats had to go in search of another one."

I scratched an ear with my Bic pen and wondered if that was significant. Probably not, unless Brenda had fought somebody over the last living projector bulb in the Queen City. But I didn't think she'd do it for Alex Parker.

"Do you remember anything unusual that happened, either before, during, or after the lecture that night?" I asked.

"Nothing unusual, no. I honestly wish I could help, but I told the same thing to the police. I didn't notice anything at all—certainly not anyone lurking in the background murdering anybody or stuffing a body into a kiln. I can't even imagine why anyone would want to do that, can you?"

"Maybe so that the victim wouldn't be recognized," I said.

"But whatever for? Believe me, Mrs. Caliban, I've been puzzling this out. And the only thing I could come up with was that this victim was a spouse who had disappeared and finally been declared dead, and then come back after his—or her—mate had collected the insurance and remarried."

"Do you know Kevin O'Neill?" I asked suspiciously. Any theory that ludicrous had "Kevin" stamped all over it.

"I don't think so. Why?"

"Never mind. I think it's far more likely that the victim was cremated by somebody who would be the most likely suspect in their murder."

"Oh, I never thought of that!" His expressive face registered enlightenment. "But you must be right. Your theory is so much more straightforward than my own."

"Of course, neither of those theories explains the Rookwood vase."

"No, that's right!" he exclaimed. "What do you make of that?" He made a tent of his hands and leaned forward.

"Well, we don't know that it was left in the studio Thursday night. All we really know is that it appeared there between Wednesday night at nine-thirty and Friday night, when the room was sealed as a crime scene."

"So you don't think it has anything to do with the body in the kiln? You know, it's quite possible that someone brought it in to show the class," he mused.

"Except that nobody in any of the ceramics classes admits to having seen it before. Did the police show the vase to you?" I asked.

"Oh, yes! Such a lovely thing! You saw it, didn't you? Exquisite. I do hope I'll have the opportunity to handle the sale if the owner is found and wants to sell it. But I suppose that's rather leaping ahead, isn't it?"

"Could you identify the marks on the bottom?"

"Well, the Rookwood mark, of course—everyone knows that one. And the shape number and decorator's initials. That is, I knew that the letters corresponded to the decorator's initials, but I had to look up the signature in one of my Rookwood books. Artus Van Briggle—that was the decorator. Do you know his work, Mrs. Caliban?"

He barely gave me time to shake my head before he continued.

"I don't know Rookwood very well myself, and so I'm not familiar with their decorators. But my books suggest that Van Briggle was one of the important ones."

"And the Paris label?"

"From the Exposition Universelle in 1900. An international

pottery exposition—very important, very prestigious. I believe that Rookwood took one of the prizes. Well, now that you've seen the Goldstone, you can see why—a beautiful design, and that lovely gold sparkle effect."

"What about the purple triangular mark, stamped on the bottom in ink?"

"Oh, I wouldn't know about that." He waved a hand dismissively. "Perhaps some mark the studio used—oh, to mark a piece that was not for sale, for example. They did keep their very best pieces for exhibition. But it could be anything, really."

"Were you able to tell the police how much the piece was worth?"

"Oh, only the vaguest of ballpark figures, Mrs. Caliban. As you can see—" His gesture took in the vases scattered around the small room. "My specialty is Chinese pottery, with a recent interest in African pottery as well. I sell some Rookwood from time to time, but even I would have to consult an expert before I priced it."

"So give me your vague ballpark figure."

"Oh—perhaps as much as five thousand." He said this dismissively, as if to emphasize how little he credited his own estimate.

"I see. And do the pieces you normally handle sell for that much?"

He burst out laughing. "My dear Mrs. Caliban! Some of the pieces I sell date from a hundred years before Christ! I should hope they are worth more than five thousand!"

I was getting pretty damned tired of being laughed at, but restrained myself from seizing the nearest antiquity and pitching it at his head. My pitching arm was still sore from throwing, and if I'd learned anything so far in pottery class, it was that I had lousy aim.

"Of course, to a real Rookwood aficionado," he continued, "that vase would be priceless. He or she might not give a nickel for an antique Chinese vase. Do you see what I mean?"

I nodded. That was what Kevin had said.

"I've heard that you don't get along with Brenda Coats very well." Since I couldn't throw any material objects at him, I'd do the next best thing.

He shrugged. "I hardly see Mrs. Coats enough to get along with her or not get along with her. I don't dislike her, but she seems to resent my interest in African pottery."

"Does she think you're selling it too high?"

"Truly, Mrs. Caliban, I couldn't tell you. I don't run into her very much, and don't speak to her much when I do run into her."

"I hear there's some fake Rookwood around." Pure speculation on my part.

"Yes, I'm sure that's true. It's true of any kind of pottery that is worth money."

"Have you ever seen any?" I tried to look curious instead of accusing.

"From time to time," he acknowledged. "But you're not thinking that the Goldstone is a forgery, are you?"

"Can you tell if it is?"

He looked chagrined. "I'd like to think I could, but given my limited expertise in Rookwood, I probably couldn't give a definitive answer. I will say, however, that the Goldstone and Tiger Eye glazes are extremely difficult to duplicate. Why, even Rookwood couldn't do it. So one would have to be a brilliant forger to produce a successful fake. I'm not prepared to say it couldn't be done, because I've seen some amazing effects in my time. But I'd say it would be close to impossible."

"Do you know any forgers who are that good?"

He laughed. "Not that good, no."

"But you know some," I pressed him. "Any of them specialize in Rookwood?"

His eyes glistened with merriment. "Now, Mrs. Caliban"—

he wagged a finger at me—"you're trying to get me to give away some nasty trade secrets. But as it happens, since I don't specialize in Rookwood myself, I don't know any forgers who do. In fact, my favorite forger, who can produce the most delicate Han bowls imaginable, is behind bars at the moment, wasting his considerable talents making license plates."

I smiled. I couldn't help it. He might have been a rascal, but as Jan said, he could be charming, too. I almost forgot I was pissed off at him.

"Do you know Gerstley Custer, the art history professor?" I asked.

"I've met him," he conceded. "He was there that night—I expect you know that."

I nodded. "Have you ever had any financial dealings with him? Is he a collector?"

"Oh, yes, though not in a big way. I don't imagine art professors' salaries run to major collections. He has some interesting pieces, I believe, which I've seen on display at the Art Museum. No, I've never sold him anything. Pre-Columbian is a field unto itself, and not one in which an amateur like myself can afford to dabble."

I almost asked if amateurs could afford to dabble in African art, but I bit my tongue before it was out. I thanked him for his help and stood up to leave.

"Oh, one more thing. When you left the Castle on Thursday night, did you pass the ceramics studio?"

"Oh, now, let me see. Where would that have been?"

"It's in the back of the building, in the corner on the right-hand wall where the hall turns toward the office and kitchen. If you were parked in the parking lot, you must have passed it."

"Yes, I must have," he said thoughtfully.

"I'm trying to find out if the lights were on," I explained.

"Oh. I really couldn't say. But now, I wonder." He stroked his beard.

"Yes?"

"There's a jewelry studio at the end of that hall. I remember seeing the sign."

"That's right. The pottery studio is in the far half of that room."

"I mention it because when I left the reception at one point to go to the men's room, I noticed that the light in the jewelry studio was on. I don't know why I noticed it, except that perhaps I experienced just the tiniest regret that they were holding a class that coincided with my lecture. Unreasonable, I know, and certainly a bit of vanity on my part, but there it is. Nobody was in the room, though—I could see that. So my ego was salvaged after all."

"You walked into the room and looked?"

"Oh, no—I could see from the doorway that it was empty." He paused, then said thoughtfully, "But, now, you say that beyond the jewelry studio is the pottery studio? I suppose it's on the other side of those tall cabinets. So somebody could most certainly have been in the pottery studio, and I wouldn't have seen them."

"And you don't remember if the light was still on when you left the building?"

"No, I'm so sorry, I don't."

He trailed me to the front door of the gallery and opened it for me.

"You know, Mrs. Caliban, I think detective work is so interesting," he confided. "I've always been fond of detective fiction myself. After all, it's not so very different from my job when I appraise a piece I've never seen before. I do hope you'll call on me if I can help in any way. I'd love to take part in a real investigation! And meanwhile, I'll keep my eyes peeled and my ears to the ground, and if I come up with anything, I'll call you."

He'd given me a valuable piece of information already. Some time between the time Jan went to help Parker set up for the lecture and the time she left the building, somebody had turned on the lights in the pottery studio, and somebody had turned them off. If I could trust Arthur Alexander Parker III's account. And if I could trust Jan's.

Ten

I needed to see Frieda Katz, I decided. But what if she wouldn't see me? What if she was less receptive to my "little hobby" than Parker had been? What if she told me to go away and let the police handle it?

They were *my* bones, damn it. *I* found them. And I tended to take a personal interest in dead bodies that were thrust upon me. Like Jan, I discovered that I resented the intrusion into the pottery studio, where I'd begun to feel comfortable, if not competent. And another thing, I thought: somebody had used *my* goddam pot to do their dirty work! I wasn't sorry to lose the pot, but the killer didn't know that. He—or a muscular she—had a lot of nerve.

Well, if my hormones were going to rage, I might as well get some mileage out of them.

At least I had the sense to take the parkway up to Northside instead of the freeway. Crabby is not a good mood for driving I-75, especially in late October, when the construction crews are rushing to get their final hours in and tend to be on a short fuse themselves. That's when you see those orange barrels laid out in patterns like a cubist painting, and unless you've got an engineer in front of you, you're out of luck.

"Well, I'm in the middle of a grant proposal," Frieda said uncertainly when I found her in her lair. She sat huddled behind a desk piled high with paperwork. "But I guess I could spare a few moments."

She looked like hell—dark rings around her eyes like a reverse raccoon, hair sticking out every which way. She clutched a pack of cigarettes in her fist.

"Is Yvonne around?" I asked. I needed to talk to her, too.

"She went down to Makro. She should be back soon."

I doubted it. Makro was one of those giant members-only discount houses where you could really save money if you were willing to buy enough toilet paper for the Mormon Tabernacle Choir. It was not a store to be taken lightly. You couldn't go without bumping into something that you didn't even know you needed until you saw how cheap it was. You'd go home elated at all the money you saved, until you realized that you'd have to rent a storage locker or hold a yard sale before you could unload the car.

At my suggestion, we took a walk down the hall to look at the large front room—once a parlor—that served as library and meeting room now. The lecture had been held here on Thursday night. Again, I passed the kitchen on the right, and at the corner, the rest room, drink machine alcove, and the doorway to the jewelry and pottery studios. A series of stunning watercolors lined the walls of the hallway. We turned the corner into the hall and foyer where a magnificent staircase led to the upstairs ballroom and studios. To the right was the small room used as a gift shop. To the left, the library.

"Jan is very upset about all this," I told Frieda. "Because of our investigative experience, she's asked Moses and me to look into it." I didn't mention that Moses was on strike.

"Well, I appreciate your concern, Cat, I really do," Frieda said earnestly. "But of course, I have to consider the interests of the center. Lieutenant Arpad strikes me as very competent, and I wouldn't want to do anything to hinder his investigation.

"Ralph Nagel, who chairs our board, has been out of town since before this happened," she continued. "I don't even know if he knows about it yet, and we can't reach him because he and Ava are on one of those fall foliage tours. I really hesitate to act in his absence."

"Oh, I wouldn't want to undermine the police investigation," I assured her. "But Moses and Arpad know each other from Moses' years on the force, so they've been talking a lot." That was half true; I knew that Moses had talked to Arpad at least once, resulting in the information about the narrowed list of suspects. What I didn't say was that Moses didn't necessarily talk to me.

"I guess it's okay, then. What do you want to know? I've already told the police everything."

"Why don't you just give me a rundown of your evening?"

We sat down in a pair of armchairs, and she studied a hand-carved duck decoy on the table between them.

"Okay. I went out to eat at six that night, and came back around six-thirty."

No wonder she looked awful; she was working overtime and eating at fast-food restaurants.

"Jan arrived some time in there—she said something as she passed the office. At around seven o'clock Alex arrived, and then Jan came in to chat. She wrote a note to Yvonne about the kiln."

"She wrote a note?" I echoed.

"Yes, that's why Yvonne was so surprised to find it already on next morning. But she figured Jan either changed her mind and forgot about the note, or else the kids' pottery instructor had come in and turned it on."

"Go on."

"Okay. A little after seven Jan and Alex went to set up the equipment and check it. Brenda came in shortly after that, and she went down to help. Just a little before seven-thirty, I came in here, introduced Alex, and the program began."

"When you walked down the hall from the office, was the light in the pottery studio on or off?"

She frowned. "I think it was off, but I couldn't say for sure. Jan's pretty careful about that, but people come and go all the time. We keep boxes of program brochures in there, and sometimes people are just walking around to see our facilities. And then sometimes the potters come in to check their work, you know—see how it's drying."

I didn't know. I had always assumed that that part of the process came under the heading of an Act of God—either your pot was trimmable when you showed up to trim it, or it had dried leather hard and could only be trimmed with a chisel and chain saw.

"Where were you during the lecture?"

She glanced at me, and then away.

"I mean, where did you sit?" I amended.

"I didn't actually sit," she said, studying the end of her cigarette. "I stood at the back to work the lights."

"Good," I said. "Then you can tell me if anyone left the room during the lecture."

That really made her nervous, which made me nervous.

"I don't know that I would remember all that well," she said tentatively. "I mean, somebody always gets up and goes to the bathroom, don't they?"

"Did they?"

"Well, I'm sure somebody did. Let me think. Two little girls went out, but that was near the end. Marsha Francis went out, but just into the hall; she has a baby, and the baby was fussy, so she walked him up and down. That's all I remember."

"Did *you* leave?"

This turned out to be the question she was dreading. She swallowed nervously, and frowned, as if to concentrate. "Um, I think I ran downstairs to get something."

"Really? What?" I said it casually, but I think she understood what I meant: what was so important that she needed to leave in the middle of the program to retrieve it? And, more to the point, why did she not want to talk about it?

She stubbed out her cigarette. "Theresa Baumgarten had agreed to oversee the gift shop volunteers while Millie Fuchs is in Florida. I had the schedule to give her Thursday night, but I'd forgotten and left it downstairs. I knew if I didn't go get it as soon as I thought about it, I'd forget again." She gave me an embarrassed smile. "I know I give the impression of being extremely well organized, but all the credit goes to Yvonne. She keeps me on track."

It sounded plausible. But why was she so nervous?

"Did you see anybody when you went downstairs?"

She shook her head. "Not a soul. I just zipped down to the office, picked up the schedule, and ran back upstairs."

"Was the light on in the pottery studio when you passed?"

She frowned again. "Sorry, Cat, I really couldn't say for sure. If I noticed, I've forgotten."

"Was anybody standing at the back with you?"

"Well, Brenda for a while. Nobody else."

I sighed and rubbed my forehead. "Have you got any theories about this, Frieda? Any at all?"

"No, honestly. I can't imagine how it happened, or why. It just seems too bizarre! I can't help but think that somebody came in from outside. I don't know—maybe a drug deal that went wrong. The building was open and the lights on, and we're not that far from Hamilton, you know."

Hamilton was the main street that ran through Northside—a major north-south artery that connected Clifton and downtown to the northern suburbs across the viaduct. It was not, as Frieda made it sound, 42nd Street, and downtown Northside was not Times Square.

"Yeah, but as far as I know, Frieda, Queen City drug dealers aren't doing a big side business in Rookwood."

"Then I just don't know."

"Had you ever seen that particular vase before?"

"No, never."

"Do you know anybody connected with the center who collects Rookwood?"

"Nobody who's a major collector. I mean, Rookwood is a Cincinnati tradition, like Hudepohl beer and the Reds. Everybody has a few pieces."

And here I was using old wine bottles and jelly jars.

"Like who?"

"Well, I have some production ware—a pair of rooks and a small vase. Ralph and Ava Nagel have several nice pieces that Ralph displays at the funeral home. I really couldn't say. It's possible that everybody on the board owns a piece or two."

"But you wouldn't categorize any of them as an expert?"

"I don't think so. You can still find production ware—you know, the mass-production pieces—around at reasonable prices. That doesn't mean they can tell one glaze line from another."

"And I gather that nobody's seen Lottie around to ask her what she knows about any of this?"

Her frown deepened. "No, and she's usually so responsible. She doesn't answer her phone, she doesn't seem to be home, nobody knows where she is. Maybe she's off on a fall foliage tour, too, but you'd think she would have told us."

That meant two people out of pocket in the days following the murder, Ralph and Lottie. Was one the murderer and one the victim? If so, which was which? I wondered who else was missing.

But to tell you the truth, I was more worried about Lottie Gambrel than Ralph Nagel. Cleaning people, especially if they are older, black, and female, are notoriously invisible. As a result, they see and hear more than most people realize. That made Lottie a likely witness. Was she in hiding because of something she had seen? Or was she an even likelier victim?

Oh, well, I said to myself as I parked the car behind the Catatonia Arms and ran the gamut of hungry felines planted along the front walk. She's probably got a sister in Paducah who needed an emergency appendectomy.

Eleven

But you know how something nags at you—like when you leave for a two-week vacation to Canada, and you're sure you unplugged the iron before you left, but you won't be able to enjoy the scenery until you've called your neighbor to check? Well, that's what Lottie did to me that evening.

At nine o'clock I couldn't stand it anymore. At nine-ten, dressed in dark clothes and carrying a flashlight, I was standing in front of a big Victorian on Pullan Avenue, about three blocks from the Arts Castle. Like the Castle, it typified Northside's upper-class housing stock in a long-forgotten time before the neighborhood shifted to multifamily houses and apartment buildings like the Catatonia Arms. Lottie lived here? I thought. She probably needed a part-time job just to pay the heating bill.

Somebody lived here. There were lights on, downstairs and up.

I rang the bell. I always prefer legal entry when I can get it. I rang again. And again. Then I pounded on the door. The house looked to be in pretty good shape, but with these old houses, you could never tell if the doorbell worked or not. I tried the door, which was locked. I pounded again. Nothing. Just the sound of the wind picking up, and the clatter of dry leaves.

I walked away from the house and up the street. I crossed the street, ducked behind a hedge, and waited, watching the house. I couldn't see any sign that my clamor at the door had elicited a response from within. Nobody tiptoed out to the front porch and looked around. No telltale curtain movement.

After ten minutes I circled around to the back of the house. The back door was locked, so I crammed the flashlight between my shoulder and cheek as I fumbled in my wallet and surveyed my credit card options. I didn't have many choices left because I kept forgetting to call in and ask for replacements. My new skills in B&E were doing wonders for my debt. With reluctance I extracted my Visa card. What difference did it make? I told myself. Ever since Cousin Delbert had taken it on a shopping spree last summer to buy me enough computer equipment to outfit Naval Intelligence, the Visa folks had refused to finance so much as a candy bar. I don't know what their problem was; they could finance a new world headquarters with the interest they were charging me.

I slipped the card between the jamb and the door, worked my magic, and went in. The room I was standing in was dark, but there was enough light from the room down the hall to show me that I was in the kitchen.

I took a step, and froze.

There was a tapping coming from somewhere inside the house. The sound was rhythmic and steady. I stood still and listened. The sound stopped, then started again. I stood there in the dark until I convinced myself that it was the wind, rattling a loose window.

I crept cautiously toward the light. It had occurred to me that Lottie might be sound asleep, and might also be hard of hearing. The doorbell might be broken, and if she were upstairs she might not hear the muffled pounding of fists on a heavy door. I had never met Lottie, and I had no desire to make her acquaintance now, standing uninvited in her living room.

It had also occurred to me that Lottie might be dead. I sniffed carefully. We detectives have to use all of our senses to gather information. My sense of smell told me that the house was full of something that I was allergic to, and I nearly broke my eardrums stifling a sneeze—with the usual results down below. Damn, I thought, getting older was really cramping my style. I couldn't always count on breaking into a house with a stash of maxipads in the bathroom cabinet!

But what I smelled was dust and mildew—that distinctive old house smell—not death.

To my right was a dining room, and beyond that, the living room, on which two lamps with fringed shades cast a soft light. Both rooms were decorated with furniture that had been around for a while. It was a comfortable, old-fashioned living room, with a clock on the mantel and knicknacks on the glass-covered coffee table. As my eyes grazed the fireplace, I caught myself wondering automatically if the tiles were Rookwood. The faint smell of wood smoke mingled with the other scents in the room.

I turned my attention to a group of framed photographs standing on an end table under one lamp. I sat on the faded, overstuffed floral sofa, planted an elbow on a crocheted doily, and examined the pictures, one by one. This took some time, but I wanted to get a sense of who Lottie was. I'd never seen her—didn't know what she looked like. Unfortunately, the pictures weren't labeled on the back, the way they might be in an album, and I didn't take the frames apart to see if there was writing underneath. They were family pictures of a nice-looking black family, some of them professional portraits, dating back, I'd say, to the late nineteenth century, judging by the Victorian dress.

None of these people looked like murder victims. None of them looked like murderers.

Now, you might think I was putting off going upstairs. You'd be right.

When I finally got up the nerve, I took the stairs slowly, testing each step with a sneakered toe before I put my weight on it. Still, there were a few loud creaks by the time I got to the top—at least, they sounded loud to me. I hoped that they were drowned out by the tapping, which had started up again.

Five doors opened off the hall, and all but one stood ajar.

Here, the scent of lavender was strong, and the smell of wood smoke stronger. Either there was a working fireplace on the second floor, which would have been logical in a house this age, or there was a window open somewhere, and I was smelling something coming from outside. But there was another odor, too—a fuel odor. A kerosene lamp?

Moving quietly, I checked all the rooms briefly, using my flashlight—three bedrooms and a bath. No one was asleep in any of them. I would have to return for a more thorough search later, in case there were any corpses lying around, but for now I needed to check out the third floor, where there was a light on.

I pushed through the door that led to the stairs to the third-floor attic. These stairs were narrower and steeper—a hell of a lot narrower and stepper than I like to deal with at my time of life. My bones were creaking louder than the steps. This time I paused to breathe on every step so I wouldn't be winded when I got to the top and betray my presence with a gasp.

A wasted strategy, as it turned out. I reached the top of the stairs and turned toward the light, which was coming from a room beyond the one I was standing in, when somebody put out *my* lights. I had time to register a faint rustle behind me, and the overpowering smell of smoke mingled with kerosene.

Damn, I thought, as I sank to the floor, if he hit me with one of my own pots, I'll murder him!

Twelve

"M-miz Cat?"

A voice floated to my ears from somewhere far above me.

"What you d-doin', layin' in the b-bushes, Miz Cat? You ain't d-doin' that steak thing a-g-gain, are you?"

I opened my eyes and saw Leon hovering above me like a Sistine angel. Only—it was weird—he had kind of a demonic glow about him.

"No, Leon," I said quietly. "I am not on a stakeout." I refrained from pointing out to him that if I had been, he would have just blown my cover. Training good help takes time, I told myself. Leon had drawbacks as an operative, but he didn't drink. I did, so he came in handy at times.

"I am lying under the bushes because some bastard just clobbered me over the head," I explained patiently, Saint Cat rising to the surface. "Although why he deposited me in the bushes, I really couldn't say," I added, after some thought.

"Oh," Leon said. "Well, d-don't you want to w-watch the fire?"

I looked up at him. Gradually it dawned on me why his face had that funny light on it.

"What fire?" I shrieked, and sat up abruptly.

This was a mistake, as anybody who has suffered a head injury can tell you. I nearly pitched forward on my face.

"Oww! Dammit! Leon, if I pass out again, you go get a bucket of water and throw it on my face—fast."

"Okay," he said tentatively. "You g-gonna y-yell at me 'f I do?"

"I'll yell at you if you don't," I muttered, clambering to my feet with a considerable assist from Leon.

The street was filled with fire engines, police cars, flashing lights, and people. The house two doors up was burning. It was Lottie's house.

"Damn, damn, damn!"

"You g-gettin' testy, M-miz Cat?" Leon pulled out his new vocabulary word with the air of a magician releasing a dove from his pocket handkerchief.

"That the Olmstead h-house," he remarked. "But M-Miz Inez d-don't live there no more. She dead." Leon got around, and he knew the business of the neighborhood better than anyone. In his own way, Leon had as much information as Kevin did, but it was harder to get out of him. My mind wasn't in the best condition to figure out how to do that.

"When did she die?" I asked.

He shrugged. "While back."

"But another lady was living there," I prompted him.

He studied the burning house. "She d-didn't want no paper." The paper route was one of Leon's many enterprises.

"Mrs. Gambrel didn't want the paper?"

He nodded. "That lady. She w-were nice and all, b-but she d-didn't want no paper."

"She worked down at the Castle," I observed, "Mrs. Gambrel did."

He nodded.

"Was Mrs. Gambrel related to the lady that died?"

"Uh-huh. M-miz Inez her c-cousin or her aunt, s-somethin' like that."

"Were you ever in the house, Leon?"

"Uh-huh, lot of t-time."

"Was this when Mrs. Gambrel lived there?"

He shook his head. "Nuh-uh."

"Do you remember if you ever saw a really beautiful vase? Or if Miss Inez ever talked about owning one?"

He considered. "She have them g-glasses with pitchers at the b-bottom, but I d-don't remember no v-vase. This one t-time my m-momma give me some f-flower to t-take over there, and M-miz Inez, she p-put 'em in a p-pickle jar."

Would a woman who owned a Rookwood vase put flowers in a pickle jar? Shit, I didn't even have any evidence of any connection between the vase and Lottie. I was just taking stabs in the dark.

In that case, I thought, I'd better get closer to the light.

Movement introduced me to a few more injuries, but they mostly seemed to be incidental bruises. Whoever had hit me had not taken the opportunity to work me over. That meant he had wanted me out of the way, but temporarily, not permanently. At least, not yet.

Standing with the crowd at the edge of the police barricades, I spotted a familiar figure, leaning against a police car: Lieutenant Arpad. How long had I been out, for crissake? Everybody in Cincinnati knew that Lottie Gambrel's house was burning. Hell, if I looked hard enough, I'd probably spot Dan Rather.

The fire appeared to be concentrated largely at the top of the house, although it was creeping downward. I heard a shout just before the roof went, and the crowd fell back. Falling debris was now igniting the lower stories.

"Lord, I hope there ain't nobody inside!" a woman near me said fervently.

"If it was, they history, man!" gloated a young man, who seemed to be enjoying the spectacle.

"That house is history, young man!" A stern voice behind me put him in his place. "It's a part of your heritage that's burning."

"Ain't none o' *my* heritage," he said sullenly to a friend. But he didn't say it very loudly.

"You right about that, Miz Petty." Someone in the crowd egged her on. "These young people comin' up, they don't appreciate they past. It's been some of this city's history made in that house for sure."

Petty? I turned around to find the crowd coalescing around a petite white woman with blue-tinted white permed hair and glasses. Was this the Constance Petty who had attended Parker's lecture last Thursday night?

"Probably more than we'll ever know now," said another woman sadly. She was a very dark-skinned black woman of medium build with her reddish-black hair cut short and straight. She wore a pair of gold-rimmed glasses on a gold chain around her neck. She was wearing a sweater and shivering—probably at least partly from the cold. Most people appeared to have grabbed what was handiest when they'd heard the sirens, and though the fire was generating a lot of heat, the night air at our backs was cold.

"Poor Malvina," the white woman said, squeezing her arm. "You were always hoping there'd be more papers."

So this was Constance Petty and Malvina Deeds. Retired teachers, Jan had told me, and avid attenders of Castle programming. How had Jan described them? A hoot?

But at that point I heard my name called, and turned to see Lieutenant Arpad waving me over.

"So, what do you think of this?" he asked grimly, gesturing toward the burning house.

"I don't think it could be a coincidence," I said cautiously, wondering if I had any blood on the back of my head. One of the disadvantages of having white hair is that it shows up everything.

"Oh, shoot!" he said. "I don't think so, either. I was looking for somebody to disagree."

We watched in silence as the upper floor caved in.

I think I should make it clear that I had reasons for keeping silent about the evening's escapades that had nothing to do with wanting to solve the case before the Cincinnati PD had done it. Fricke had always brought out the competitive zeal in me, but I wished Arpad well. Trouble was, if I told him about the attack, I'd have to tell him where I was when it happened.

And if I told him that, I'd have to tell him how I got there. The Visa people might be giving me a hard time now, but that was nothing to what they'd say if I sent them a change-of-address form redirecting my bills to the city jail.

Leon chose that moment to speak up.

"M-miz Cat, ain't you g-gonna t-tell him 'bout the b-bastard that c-clobbered you?"

Thirteen

Well, he took it better than Fricke would have, but that's not saying much. Yes, he did recite the penalty for unlawful entry. But he wasn't standing over me in an interrogation room at the time, holding a rubber hose; he was standing over me in an examining room at University Hospital, holding my purse. The hospital had been his idea, and he hadn't given me any choice. I was about to be taken down to X ray.

"You keep saying *he* hit you," Arpad persisted. There are other forms of torture when you have a head injury. "How do you know it was a he?"

"I don't know it was a he," I snapped. "It could have been a transsexual orangutan, for all I know. I didn't see shit. I'm using the masculine pronoun purely as a convenience, and possibly because most violent crimes are committed by men. But if I've offended you by slighting your gender, I'm sorry."

"Smells?" he pursued, ignoring my tone.

"What?!" I shrieked, wincing when I set my own skull to vibrating.

"Any smells? Aftershave instead of perfume, tobacco, anything like that?"

"What I smelled was smoke and kerosene," I huffed, glowering my best glower. "Not coincidentally, since when I came to, I discovered that the house where I'd been standing had turned into a goddam five-alarm fire!"

"Shoes?"

"I was wearing my Adidas. He didn't show me his."

"Was he taller than you? Did you feel him looming?"

"I'm trying to tell you, I didn't feel him anything, for crissake! If I had, I would've ducked."

He sighed. "It's not much to go on."

"Well, excuse me! If I'd known how important it was going to be to you, I would've strapped a video camera to my head."

"I'm taking your clothes to the lab," he said. "If he used anything—uh, breakable—we might find fragments. The arson squad will want them."

"If you find pieces from one of my pots again," I shouted as they wheeled me down the hall, "I don't want to hear it!"

They released me to Moses' custody around midnight, which, from the expression on his face, boded worse for my headache than a night in the Emergency waiting room would have done. A quick check of my purse revealed that Arpad had confiscated my few remaining credit cards. Moses, meanwhile, had chosen to freeze me with a disapproving silence. That was fine with me.

At home I took the painkillers they'd given me and fell into bed.

When I woke up, it was past noon. The painkillers had worn off, and the dull, persistent throb in the back of my head had awakened me. I popped a couple of aspirin in the bathroom and hung a towel over the mirror so I didn't have to see what I looked like. I gazed longingly at my bed, thought of all the things I had to do, and went to make coffee. So much for giving up caffeine.

Then I sat at my kitchen table, my head in my hands, feeling sorry for myself and worrying about Lottie Gambrel, who couldn't come home now even if she tried. Sadie sat across from me, her gloomy countenance reflecting my own misery. Sadie expected disaster, so she was never surprised when it happened. That made her a good cat to have around when you wanted to plumb the depths of your own depression.

I tried desperately to cling to my sick-relative theory about Lottie's disappearance. It was still possible—though not likely, I admitted—that Lottie had left town for a family health crisis.

Moses disabused me of this fantasy later that afternoon, when I was making a desultory pass at the furry sofa with a Dustbuster.

"Cat, come up here!" He shouted from the top of the stairs. "There's somebody I want you to meet."

The tall, stoop-shouldered man in Moses' living room looked a little like a cartoon version of Orville Redenbacher, down to the bow tie. He gave me a broad smile, and pumped my hand.

"This is Buster 'Boney' Brissard," Moses said.

Buster Boney? This guy *was* a cartoon character. His parents must have been hoping for a dog when he was born.

"Dr. Brissard is the forensic anthropologist who just helped the police confirm the identity of the body in the Castle kiln. It was Lottie Gambrel."

Fourteen

I sank into one of Moses' overstuffed chairs. Winnie trotted over and cocked her head at me, then lay down with her chin on my feet. Beagle sympathy.

"Are you sure?" I asked Boney.

"'Fraid so," he said cheerfully.

"I thought you might be interested in how Boney works," Moses said. It was a conciliatory nod toward my career development, and I appreciated it.

Boney brightened, if that was possible, and opened his mouth to speak.

"Jus' the high points, Boney," Moses said, putting a cautionary hand on his shoulder.

"Okay," Boney said, looking just the slightest bit disappointed. "I'll give you my ten-cent lecture.

"The down side of this case was that we had total cremation," he began. "Most fires, you don't get that, so you have more to work with. The up side was that we had all the remains—or at least, we think we did. We can't be absolutely sure that there wasn't something missing, of course, but we have enough to know that the kinds of bones that are usually missing were there—the skull, arms and hands, feet."

I was feeling a little sick. My own skull throbbed in sympathy.

"Unfortunately, we didn't have any bone whole, including the skull. Often you can tell a lot about age, race, and sex if you have a whole bone. From the sutures in the fragments of skull we had, we knew we had an adult. I saw some evidence of arthritic lipping on fragments of the vertebrae, and microscopic examination of another large fragment from the femur showed some wear as well, so I knew we had an older adult but probably not an elderly one—so, say, anywhere from forty-five to sixty-five. Without an intact pelvis or skull, we couldn't be sure about sex. Ditto with race, which shows up in the skull and the long bones. Teeth can sometimes help, but in this case, for example, it wasn't much help except to suggest that the victim wasn't either Inuit or Bushman."

He showed me his own teeth in a wide grin.

"In fact, about all we could contribute from our lab was the age estimate. Oh—and the fact that the body was burned intact—I mean, with flesh on the bones."

"Okay, I'll bite," I quipped. "How do you know that?"

"Well, you saw them, right?" He glanced at Moses to confirm. "See, dry bones show a different pattern of cracking and splitting than green bones do, and green bones warp."

Green bones. Like greenware. I shuddered.

"The police department has its own physical evidence experts, and they worked on the strand of hair found on the pot. Say, I heard that was your pot, Cat!"

I blushed and nodded.

"Tough break," he said, shaking his head, and I don't think he intended the pun. "Anyway, that hair came from the head of a black person. The length meant probably a woman—somebody who used chemical straighteners. Of course, we can't be sure that the hair was once attached to the same body as the bones in the kiln. But the crime lab folks didn't think someone could have been hit that hard with that particular pot and survived. Uh, sorry, Cat."

"That's okay. I'm getting used to ridicule."

"I know what you mean. Try spending your life with skeletons and see what people say. And after all, a lot of what we do in the lab is educated guesswork."

"So tell me about the teeth," I said.

"Oh, right. Well, once the police had a missing person on their hands, and a set of human remains, it wasn't that hard to match them up. The dental expert did that. In fact, you might even say that my work was a complete waste of time, except for the part about burning the body."

"Were you right about the age?"

He smiled. "She was fifty-five, bang in the middle." He took a swig of the beer he'd neglected during his lecture. "It's nice to be right."

I ignored various feline lobbying efforts to get me downstairs for dinner and hung out with Boney and Moses for a while. I swore on a stack of *Reader's Digest*s that I hadn't taken anything stronger than an aspirin all day, so Moses fixed me a gin and tonic. Boney had a trunkful of stories to tell, and the more gin I drank, the funnier they seemed to me. Pretty soon, Boney was drawing bones on the back of Moses' AARP newsletter.

I turned to Boney as I was seeing him out.

"What do you know about osteoporosis?" I asked.

"Don't get it," he said, and winked at me.

Moses had a chicken in the oven, so I fed the cats and went back upstairs to eat dinner and talk over the case. I nearly tripped over the cats on the stairs. They liked what Moses was serving better than what I was serving.

"Uncle Moses," I said, "you've got company."

"All right, all right," he grumbled, wading through cats and dog as he crossed from the oven to the counter. "If y'all want to eat, you mind your manners. Go on, now, and give me some room."

Winnie retreated to the vicinity of her dog bowl and sat down. Sophie and Sadie lined up, joining her vigil. I scooped up Sidney, who leaned much too heavily on his cuteness in situations like this.

Moses set down a bowl of broccoli on the table, and I sighed. Moses and Mel had gone into a freezing frenzy at the end of the gardening season, and the basement freezer was bulging with produce. Me, I'd been too exhausted from hand-to-hand combat with whitefly and Japanese beetles to participate. The thing was, you had to eat whatever was on top because it was too much trouble to find your way down to anything else. That meant that right now, broccoli was in season. I hadn't seen a bean in ages, but I had high hopes for February, when I hoped we'd hit the corn.

I had once thought of gardening as a nice, relaxing activity, but now I couldn't stand the stress. If I ever moved the refrigerator to vaccuum behind it—a scenario, I might add, as likely as the one where Ed McMahon hands me a check for a million dollars in return for my subscription to *Good Housekeeping*—I was sure I'd find a tomato or two skulking back there, possibly sprouting in the cracks in the linoleum. I'd say a zucchini, except the zukes we grew looked like watermelons, and I don't think they'd fit.

"I know how you feel, Cat," Moses said, misinterpreting my sigh. "Who'd want to kill Lottie Gambrel?"

"Did Arpad know about Lottie last night?" I asked suspiciously.

"Naw, they just got the confirmation this morning, while you was sleepin' off your bad habits."

I forked some broccoli onto my plate and reminded myself of its cancer-fighting qualities.

"Yeah. I mean, Jan resented her for being so passionate about cleanliness, but who ever heard of a person being killed for being too clean?"

"You be surprised," Moses said, tucking into his broccoli with apparent relish. "Folks think domestic homicides are all about jealousy or money. I'd be willing to bet a good third of 'em are all about 'bitch told me once too often to pick my clothes up off the floor' or 'he tracked grease on my nice clean carpet.' Or maybe that ain't what they're about, but that's how they happen."

"But domestic homicides take place at home. Lottie wasn't killed at home," I pointed out. "You think her husband showed up at the Castle and put fingerprints on the wall she'd just wiped?"

"It could've happened that way, but I doubt it." He was cutting up his chicken into suspiciously small bites. "No, I reckon we got to find out more about Mrs. Gambrel. Lot of folks aren't what they appear to be." He tossed some chicken to the peanut gallery, which had polished off what he'd already given them in record time.

"Of course, it's always possible that she was killed because of something she saw or something she knew," I suggested.

"That's right," he agreed. "And if it was something she saw or found out by accident, because she was in the wrong place at the wrong time, we may never figure it out."

I liked the way he was using "we" all of a sudden.

"And why burn her house down?" I asked. "I don't get it, unless they find a body in the ashes. Maybe the cremation in the kiln was an experiment. You know, Moses, if it weren't for her house burning down, I might wonder if the killer hadn't mistaken Lottie for somebody else. I mean, she seemed to have been such an innocuous person."

"You got a candidate?"

"Well, there's Brenda," I offered. "She was there that night."

"You goin' on the theory that all colored people look alike?"

"Not at all," I said, refusing to take offense. "I'm just trying to come up with somebody she could have looked like—say, from the back. But I don't even know if they were the same height and build, or wore their hair the same, or any of that."

"I be willing to bet they didn't dress the same, though," he observed.

"No," I agreed. "Probably not, unless Lottie shopped at Brenda's boutique. But she could have been wearing a coat; it was cold enough that night. Maybe even a hat." He threw me a look. "All right, all right, it's a long shot. But Brenda's more cantankerous than Lottie apparently was."

"Cantankerous don't get you killed, Cat," Moses objected. "'Fit did, you and me would've been dead a long time ago."

"And then there's that Rookwood vase," I persisted. "Did Lottie put it there or did someone else? I wonder if any of the experts would recognize it as something they'd seen before. I'd put Kevin on it, because he has the contacts. But you know how busy he is these days."

"Yeah," Moses said through his mashed potatoes. Did I mention the four bushels of potatoes we had stashed in the basement?

"Don't worry, Cat. It'll be over soon."

"What?" The case? Menopause?

"Halloween," he said darkly.

Fifteen

Halloween was the holiday most universally observed and enthusiastically celebrated at the Catatonia Arms. Kevin's religious lapses did not prevent him from collecting his ashes on Ash Wednesday or attending midnight mass on Christmas in a fit of nostalgia. Moses sang bass in the Baptist church choir on Christmas and Easter. Mel and Al sent solstice cards, but they'd also been known to attend Seders presided over by the women students from Hebrew Union. The Fourth of July was a political hot spot, depending on what our country was up to at the time. Columbus Day was always a downer. But Halloween was for everyone.

Now, you might not think of Halloween as a high-stress holiday like Christmas, especially if you're not a single parent with small children. If so, you move in the right circles. You run out the day before and buy a couple of bags of cheap candy, and sit back to await developments. If your kids are old enough, you let them borrow your clothes and your makeup. You plan an early dinner. You turn the porch light on. You toy with the idea of letting the tots choose their own piece of candy out of a large bowl.

In my neighborhood you would get eaten alive. In my neighborhood, Halloween looks like Chapel Hill, North Carolina, the night of a basketball win against Duke. Don't ask me what those folks up in Forest Park and Madeira are doing come the thirty-first of October; all I know is that their kids are in Northside. I'm prepared to believe that somebody is bussing them in from Dayton. Kids are to October what Japanese beetles are to July. No matter how much candy you buy, it won't be enough. And don't think you can get by with apples or pennies. Please. Nor is Northside one of those polite suburban subdivisions where you can discreetly turn out your porch light when your candy is gone. In the first place, you're bound to be turning it out on some live customers who are standing on your porch with their pillowcases open and their brass knuckles in their pockets. In the second place, these kids are surly when you don't deliver. Some of them are dressed like teen hoodlums. Some of these are not wearing costumes.

But I anticipate. The Halloween season at the Catatonia Arms begins in late September, when one hears the first tentative stirrings of anxiety: do you know yet what you're going as this year? For the next three weeks, ideas will be tried out on you, confidences shared, confidences violated, decisions made, abandoned, and remade, feelings injured, egoes unraveled. An air of secrecy masks an outbreak of whispered volubility. In the fourth week the excitement and tension escalate as people start to assemble the costumes they have finally settled on. I have seen a strong man—who shall remain nameless—break down in tears because his friend Roxie had already promised her chef's hat to Miguel, and a strong woman contemplate suicide because the fabric stories were sold out of fake rabbit fur.

If kids and grown-ups have to dress up on the same night, the result is disaster. The grown-ups can't get their hair moussed and their eyeshadow on because they have to answer the door every twenty seconds. After two hours of continuous interruption, they look menacing enough, even in drag, to terrorize the toughest of the teen hoodlums.

The good news was that this year, Halloween fell on Thursday, and the city fathers and mothers in their infinite wisdom had left it there, so the trick-or-treaters would show up on Thursday, while most of the grown-up festivities would be held on Friday. The bad news was that this stretched the whole business out, so that even though, as Moses had correctly noted, Halloween would be over soon, it wouldn't be soon enough.

On Friday night I actually had two—count them, two—events to attend. The Northside Cultural Arts Center was hosting a beaux arts ball at the Castle to raise money for new computer equipment. It would give me a good chance to meet some of the other board members and generally chat people up. Then there was the Stonewall Cincinnati affair in the Hall of Mirrors at the Netherland Hotel downtown. Kevin and Al were both involved in the planning of the Stonewall fete, so I had to put in an appearance there, too. And to think I used to stay home with Fred and watch *Night of the Living Dead.*

Having decided early on to give my nerves and my hormones a rest, I'd gone over to Mr. Tuxedo and ordered tails and a top hat.

"I'm going as Marlene Dietrich," I'd told Kevin.

"That's good, Mrs. C.," he'd said, and he looked a little envious, I thought, that I'd settled something. "Which movie?"

"I don't know. Whichever one she wears tails in."

"Well, are your tails white or black?"

"Black." I'd gone for the contrast with my white hair.

He'd nodded. "That'll be *Morocco*. She wears white in *Blonde Venus*." Kevin was all for authenticity. My standards weren't that high.

So here it was Thursday, October the thirty-first, and I had to stop in at Mr. Tuxedo to pick up my tux. That meant trying it on. I'm sure it will come as no surprise to you that tuxedos are not made for sixty-year-old women. The damn cummerbund felt like a corset.

"The sleeves are right," said the salesman, eyeing them critically, "and the pants length looks good. How does it feel?"

"It's a little snug in the waist."

He sighed. The Lord deliver him from old ladies who wanted to dress like twenty-year-old men, it said.

I studied myself in the mirror. I did look smashing, if I do say so myself. The top hat hurt my injured head, but I hoped the swelling would be down by the next night.

"Okay," I said. "Do what you can."

From there I drove downtown to Cappel's to pick up a derby for Kevin, who would spray paint it green for his leprechaun costume. If you want to know the truth, I think last year's Bette Davis imitation had drained him, and he was looking for something a little more straightforward.

When the word had gotten out that I was going to Cappel's for Kevin, everybody else wanted in on the act, and now I had a list that stretched from my fingertips to my elbow. Al wanted a small British flag for her Margaret Thatcher costume, confessing that she was afraid people would confuse her with Mamie Eisenhower. My daughter Franny, who was dressing up as Star Wars, wanted a bunch of little round mirrors and a large world map. Mel, who couldn't persuade Al to join her in a Reagan-Gorbachev duet, had found a Diana who was looking for a Charles. Mel owned her own custom-made tux, but she wanted anything that could be made into a polo stick. I didn't know what a polo stick looked like, but she'd drawn me a picture. My friend Mabel wanted green sequins for her Madonna costume. Moses wanted paper money. He wouldn't tell me what it was for.

If anybody in Cincinnati had stocked plastic polo sticks, it would have been Cappel's—a store modestly listed under "party supplies" in the Yellow Pages. Today the place was mobbed by frenzied shoppers, that glint of lunacy in their eyes. If you liked Halloween, Cappel's was to you what Harrah's was to a gambler. The thoughtless and indolent went to Stagecraft in Northside, where the costumes were already put together for you, but the hard core went to Cappel's.

I found everything on my list, and a few things that

weren't. I hoped the cats would like the little battery-operated skeletons I bought to clip on their collars. For Winnie, I bought a beagle-sized witch's hat.

I decided to drive home via Eden Park, and check out the Art Museum's Rookwood collection. Unfortunately I have this unerring instinct for the worst possible route from here to anyplace, the result of thirty-eight years of training by Fred Caliban, who never met a map he liked. If I ever do get sent to heaven—a very big *if*, I'll be the first to admit—they'd better have gas stations in hell. So I drove down to Fifth Street, because it's familiar, and wound up in the clogged traffic around Fountain Square, where some political event was going on. Somebody had set up a stage and sound trucks, somebody who'd no doubt hoped for a day about twenty degrees warmer than it was. Knots of people, probably campaign workers, huddled together for warmth. Their applause sounded loud and enthusiastic, even with the car windows closed, but I guess the clapping helped warm them up. I couldn't make out the figures up on the platform, but I could read the navy and yellow RE-ELECT HYDE banner even from that distance. There were banners and signs for several other Democrats as well, so it must have been a party campaign rally. As far as I could tell, they were preaching to the converted because the downtown workers were passing through at a pretty good clip.

Eden Park, when I finally got there, was showing off its fall colors. I paid my admission to the Art Museum and found my way to a long hallway lined in glass cases filled with Rookwood. There, vases glimmered like jewels, some in stunning bright colors, most in more subtle pastels. I passed over the brown ones with the Indian heads; much as I admired the technique, they didn't do anything for me. But the rest fascinated me, from the graceful irises and daffodils and poppies to the birds of various descriptions to the oriental fish swimming in a murky green or brown ocean to the fanciful crabs scuttling up the side of one vase. The shapes were fluid and graceful—not a murder weapon among them.

I returned to the information desk to ask if Dan Pratt was around. Kevin had touted him as Cincinnati's leading expert on Rookwood. I was given a map that lead me back through a maze of corridors and up the stairs. His office opened directly onto the hall. The door stood open and it was empty. There didn't seem to be anyone around to ask, so I stood and studied a display of blown glass until two men emerged from a nearby office. After a brief discussion, one turned and went the other way, and the other advanced toward me.

"Were you waiting to see me?" he asked.

"Are you Dan Pratt?"

I introduced myself, and he ushered me into the small neat office of a Type A personality. He was tall and lanky with black hair and wire rims; his dark complexion had been darkened still further by the sun.

"Nice tan," I observed.

He grinned. "I just got back from a conference in Mexico City. What can I do for you?" He started fiddling with a pair of paper clips on his desk, hooking them together and unhooking them.

I explained my connection to the Arts Castle murder, which he'd heard about.

"Have the police shown you the Rookwood vase that was found on the scene?"

"No. I hadn't even heard." He looked interested.

"It's a piece about this high." I held up my hands. "It's dark, with flecks of gold. I've heard it identified as Goldstone. It's decorated with a circle of red goldfish, and signed 'A.V.B.' "

He nodded. "Artus Van Briggle."

"Does it sound like something you've seen before?"

He considered before speaking. "It's hard to say without seeing it. It sounds very typical of his work—except, of course, that Goldstone could never be described as 'typical.' That would make it very special." He found another paper clip and attached it to the original pair.

"Special enough to make it valuable?"

"Oh, yes. Goldstone and Tiger Eye always command a good price. There aren't that many out there, you know. The average success rate on a firing for those effects was only about four percent."

"It has a label from the Paris Exposition of 1900."

"Even better." He looked impressed. "That means the pottery considered it one of their best pieces."

"Would you be surprised if a piece of that quality turned up out of the blue?"

"No, not really. You'd be surprised what people turn up in Grandma's attic or garage sales or out-of-the-way junk shops."

"You mean, somebody could have something like that and not know how valuable it was?"

"Oh, sure. Happens all the time. Think of what you've got at home. Suppose you'd inherited a box of miscellaneous vases from Great Aunt Kitty. Some of them strike you as more beautiful than others, but unless you know something about pottery, why would you think of them as valuable?"

"How much would it sell for?"

"It's hard to say. Perhaps a thousand dollars, perhaps more."

"Oh," I said. A thousand dollars was a lot of money for a vase, but it didn't seem enough to kill for.

"If a vase like that came onto the market, would people want to know its provenance?" I asked.

"Not necessarily. Again, because things are always turning up in an attic or basement, its appearance wouldn't be questioned. It's not like a T'ang dynasty bowl that's been around for a thousand years." He scrounged around on the desk and found another paper clip to add to his chain.

"Speaking of Chinese bowls," I said, "do you know Alex Parker?"

"Sure."

"Does he have any association with Rookwood?"

"He sells it from time to time, if that's what you mean."

"So he's an expert?"

"Well, I'm not sure what you mean. It's not his specialty."

"I've heard he has a tarnished reputation as a dealer."

"I've heard that, yes," he said cautiously, frowning at his paper-clip chain.

"Would you call him dishonest?" I put on my most ingenuous expression to take the edge off my attack Cat strategy.

He shifted uncomfortably. "I don't think it's appropriate for me to comment, Mrs. Caliban."

"Oh, go ahead!" I urged with a smile. "Nobody else is holding back."

He grinned at that and looked up. "Let me put it this way: I'd never buy a piece from him without seeing it first, and I'd never let him handle an absentee bid for me."

"What do you mean, about the absentee bid?"

"Well, say an out-of-town buyer hears that a piece he wants is going up for auction. If he didn't want to come to town for the auction, he—or she—would get somebody local to bid for him. Someone like Parker then goes to an auction with a list of buyers and bidding ranges—what each buyer is prepared to pay for a piece."

"So tell me what can go wrong?"

"Okay. Let's say that Parker has an assistant. The assistant is the one who holds the absentee bids and does the actual bidding. But then you notice that Parker is bidding, too."

"On his own behalf?"

"One might presume so. Or one might presume that he represents another absentee client. Except that he never makes the highest bid."

"So he just wanted to—what's it called—up the bidding? What's the advantage to him if his client has to pay more, unless—" I realized what he was getting at. "Unless he gets paid a percentage of the purchase price as a commission."

"Bingo."

"Isn't that illegal?"

"Not illegal, certainly unethical. And you have to see him in action to know what's going on. An out-of-town buyer won't know that Parker bid against him."

"But other people know."

"Those of us who know the people working for him, and who care enough to keep an eye on him, sure. That's how somebody like you can find out so quickly what his reputation is."

"You also said you wouldn't buy a piece from him that you hadn't seen first. Can you explain that?"

"I should have said a piece I hadn't handled first. On the day of an auction, the pieces for sale might well be on display in closed glass cases. So even if I was on the spot, I couldn't pick a piece up and examine it for damage or repairs. A reputable dealer will scrupulously report those things in the catalog. Alex is not scrupulous."

"So would you say that he lies, or only that he misleads?"

He grinned. "Since you've pressed me so hard, I'd have to say he lies. He might list a nick or a chip as a 'flaw,' suggesting that it happened during production, when any trained eye can see that it's post-production damage. Or he might simply fail to report a repair—there's a lot of that going around, but Parker's one of the worst."

That gave me something to think about, although it was a long step from lying to murder, or even arson.

"Do you know most of the local Rookwood collectors?" I asked him, watching in fascination as he began making patterns on the desk with his paper-clip chain.

"The major ones, I do," he said. "A lot of Cincinnatians collect Rookwood."

"If I mention some names, can you tell me if they're collectors, as far as you know?"

"I'll try."

Nobody on my list turned out to be a major collector. Gil Forrester, the obnoxious ex-pottery instructor, netted me a laugh, along with an "In his dreams." Some of the names were people he knew, some weren't, but if he thought any of them was capable of murder, he didn't volunteer that information.

I thanked him for his time and was out the door when I remembered a question I forgot to ask. I stuck my head back in the door and caught him dialing the phone.

"Yes?" He looked up, holding the receiver suspended.

"I'm sorry. I forgot. There was another mark on the bottom of the vase—a triangular purple mark that appeared to have been stamped in ink."

He put the phone down.

"What kind of triangular purple mark?"

"It was sort of—well, here, I'll draw it."

I picked up a pen off his desk, helped myself to a pad, and drew: a triangle, open at the bottom, with two semicircular lines for feet. I turned it around for him to see.

He stared at it. Then he stared at me.

"Are you putting me on?"

I felt my face flush with embarrassment. Had I just asked a really stupid question?

"Parker said it might indicate a piece that was for display only—not for sale. But I thought I'd better ask."

"He said *what*?" Pratt leaned back in his chair and studied me. He had gone pale under his tan.

"Don't you know what that is?" he asked hoarsely. "That's the owner's mark for the Justice Collection—a mark nobody has seen for nearly seventy years."

Sixteen

I sat down again. He abandoned his paper clips.

"We don't even know if it exists anymore—the Justice Collection. I don't even know if there's anybody still alive who has seen it. We've all heard about it, of course, and read about it. But nobody knows what happened to it."

And then he told me a story that made me wonder if he was pulling my leg. If he hadn't shown me several books that seemed to corroborate it, I would have sworn he was having me on. The story went like this.

Nellie Justice had run one of the most exclusive brothels in Cincinnati during the teens. Nellie herself was reputed to be beautiful and charming, if a bit aloof. She was generous with her girls, businesslike with her customers, and universally praised for her fairness as well as her business acumen—a rare combination in madams. She was, however, a very private person. But she had one passion: Rookwood pottery.

For some years admirers in the know eschewed the usual bribes for her attention—flowers, money, jewels, and clothes—and instead brought her gifts closer to her heart. Other pieces she bought for herself. She was even supposed to have had a young relative working as a decorator at the pottery. The result was a dazzling collection that some say might have been the finest ever assembled by a private collector outside of the pottery itself. It had been on display in the Rookwood Room, a separate room in her elegant George Street house, where it drew the admiration of all who saw it. These included respectable women, whose husbands and fiancés brought them there as if to an art gallery.

In 1917, the city had abruptly closed down its "restricted district," where prostitution was legal. All of the houses had been closed. Nellie Justice had disappeared, and neither she nor her collection had been seen since.

"You're making this up," I said.

"I'm not!" He held up both hands in protest. "Listen. It gets even better. The showpiece of the collection was a Kataro Shirayamadani. Do you know who he was?"

"The Japanese decorator?" Kevin had said something about a famous Japanese decorator at Rookwood. Most Cincinnati names are German, and it didn't sound German.

"Yes, and considered to be Rookwood's best. This vase was about fifteen inches tall, according to the reports. It was a Black Iris—that's one of the glaze lines—again, one of the most impressive glazes Rookwood produced. It was decorated with brilliant red poppies, which made for a stunning contrast with the black background. Actually, a very dark blue from the cobalt."

If this wasn't going to be on the test, he could skip the chemistry for all it meant to me.

"Rookwood pieces were rarely titled, but Nellie had given this piece a title and everybody knew it by that title: *The Red Emma.*"

He paused to let that sink in, but I was too slow on the uptake.

"You know who Emma Goldman was?" he prompted.

"Oh, that Emma. Wasn't she an anarchist?"

"An anarchist and a campaigner for legalized prostitution, apparently. So Nellie honored her by naming this vase after her. Everyone who ever saw it says it was so exquisite, it could take your breath away."

"So you're saying that Nellie Justice marked her pieces with a stamp, and that's how you know that none of them has ever shown up at a sale?"

"That's right. If anything had ever turned up, believe me, I'd know."

"But couldn't somebody sand it off—the stamp, I mean?"

"I suppose so, but it would probably show, and they'd risk damaging the other marks impressed and incised into the clay. And why, after all, would anyone remove such a mark? The Justice Collection might well be priceless—the story alone would increase the value of the pieces, even if they weren't the quality we've been led to expect. And your description of the vase you saw, by the way, certainly suggests an unusually high quality." He tipped his chair back. "Anyway, like I said, why remove a mark that increased the value of the piece? It would be like removing a Paris Exposition label—only more difficult, I should think."

"Could somebody fake the stamp?" I asked, remembering what Jan had told me about reproductions.

"Oh, sure, that wouldn't be hard, I don't guess. If we had an example, that would be one thing, but we don't—just a sketch, and several descriptions that agree that the mark was made using purple ink and a stamp. But a pot of that quality—here, let me show you."

He brought his chair back down with a creak and reached for a book on the corner of his desk.

"Here—there's a good example of Goldstone. Does that look like what you saw at the Arts Castle?"

"Yes, it does—the vase had those little gold sparkles in it."

"I'd have to see it to be sure, of course, but that glaze would be extremely difficult to replicate. As you already know, even Rookwood couldn't do it."

"So what you're saying is that it wouldn't do any good to fake a stamp unless you could produce a pretty high quality reproduction, which seems unlikely," I observed.

He nodded. "There are other glazes that would be easier to copy—that's why I say the piece you saw probably *wasn't* a reproduction."

"Okay. So why would somebody—anybody—take a valuable piece of Rookwood like that to the Arts Castle and leave it inconspicuously on a shelf of ordinary student pieces?"

"Hmm." Then he grinned at me. "This is pretty exciting, isn't it? I've never done this kind of detective work before. Let's see. Maybe we should start with why somebody would take a piece like that to the Arts Castle. Two obvious answers: they knew it was a fine example of Rookwood, and they brought it to show around; or they didn't know what it was, and they brought it to be appraised."

"Except, not only has nobody shown it around, they haven't even claimed ownership," I pointed out.

"Which means either it belonged to the victim, or it belonged to the murderer."

"Or to somebody who doesn't want to be implicated in the murder."

"Oh, yes, I see that. Hey, you're really good at this!"

"It's my job," I told him with a straight face. "Let's consider the other alternative. If somebody took it to the Castle to be appraised, whom would they have asked to look at it?"

"Well, they might have started with Frieda Katz," he said, taking up the paper-clip chain again, and unhooking its links one by one. "You know, here's this vase I found in my grandmother's cupboard when I cleaned out the house, and does it look like anything valuable to you, or can you tell me who to ask—something like that."

"Does Frieda know a lot about pottery?" I asked, surprised.

"No, I don't think so. But the general public doesn't necessarily know that. All they know is that she runs an art center, so she must know a lot about art. And if you don't know what you've got, you might be embarrassed to go right to an expert, in case it turns out to be a dimestore vase. You might well prefer to ask the director of the center where your kid takes African dance or your husband takes stained glass."

I thought about the gap in Frieda's attendance at the Thursday night lecture. I didn't like where this was headed.

"But why was the vase still there? And why was it on a shelf where it wouldn't be noticed right away?"

He shrugged. "You've got me there. It does tend to suggest, though—doesn't it?—that the vase belonged to the murder victim, or at least, that the victim brought it with him."

"Her," I corrected him automatically.

"Her?"

"The victim was a woman who worked as a part-time cleaning person at the Castle. Lottie Gambrel was her name. Mean anything to you?"

He shook his head.

"Okay, let me ask this. Alex Parker was lecturing on African pottery at the Castle that night. Might somebody ask *him* to appraise a vase like that?"

"Sure. Rookwood isn't his specialty, but he handles it all the time. Say!" he said as something apparently struck him. "Didn't you tell me that it was Alex who told you that stamp was probably a pottery mark of some kind?"

"Yes."

He leaned forward and narrowed his eyes.

"He knows better than that, that old rogue! He has to have known better than that!"

"I wondered about that," I said. "So why would he have misled me?"

"He's probably hoping to get his mitts on that collection!"

Yes, I thought. It made sense. Unless he already had his mitts on it.

"Say, this Lottie Gambrel—"

"Yes?

"Do we have any reason to believe that she actually owned the entire Justice Collection? I mean, could we find the rest of it?"

The bump on my head started throbbing when he said that. I saw no point in adding to my diminished condition by kicking myself, though I felt like it.

"Unlikely," I said. "Her house burned to the ground last night."

Seventeen

"I can't believe Arpad hadn't shown that vase to Dan Pratt, the city's leading Rookwood expert!" I complained to Moses after I told him the whole story.

"Come on, Cat! You know better than that. Rap's probably working three, four cases when he's not sitting on his ass down at the courthouse, waiting to testify." He gave me a look of reproof. "You should know better than to believe what you see on television."

We were preparing for the onslaught of trick-or-treaters. I'd panicked on the way home and bought three more bags of candy, only to find out that Al had done the same thing. We were dumping everything into a garbage can and mixing it all up with a broom handle. Sophie and Sadie had already retired to the basement. Winnie had chewed her witch's hat down to a spitball, and Sidney had shorted out his light-up skeleton by biting its legs off. Kevin had gone off to work wearing a cape and a Zorro mask. The hallway reeked of sugar.

We had already dragged four folding chairs out to the front lawn. The air was nippy, but the sky was clear. It wasn't the kind of weather that kids dread on Halloween—so cold or so wet that you have to spoil the effect of your costume with a parka or slicker, or risk pneumonia. But with my circulation, my hands and feet would probably be numb in another hour.

Meanwhile, Mel and Al were working on me to attend a wiccan celebration with them later on. They had friends who took Halloween even more seriously than we did. It was Sowhein, the wiccan sabbat—the day that marked the first day of winter on the pagan calendar.

"You know Moonspirit MacDavitt," Al said, handing out

Bubble Yum to Snow White and Darth Vader. "It's at her house."

"My suit's at the tailor's," I protested, exchanging a look with Moses. I dropped a few suckers into hard plastic jack-o'-lanterns and heard a muffled "thanks" issue from behind a Wolfman mask.

"You don't have to dress up," Al insisted.

"You really ought to go, Cat," Mel agreed. "It's your night—the night of the crone."

A couple of teenage boys wearing jeans and Grateful Dead T-shirts eyed our offerings critically as they held their pillowcases out. Maybe they were dressed like their parents.

"If it's the night of the crone," I said, "I want to spend it in a hot bubble bath with gin and Mary Roberts Rinehart."

"See, it's a celebration of the Mother Goddess as a wise old woman who knows lots of secrets," Al was explaining to Moses, who always liked to hear about other religions. "So on Halloween, she's the Dark Mother."

"If I had my druthers, I'd be the Invisible Mother," I muttered, thinking about my offspring and the ways in which they continued to impose themselves and their opinions on my life.

Our conversation was interrupted by the arrival of a rag doll, a ballerina, and a bunny rabbit-in-arms—Moses' grandkids with his daughter, Chrystal. Winnie circled them, barking enthusiastically.

Then things got kind of chaotic there for a while. Moses and Chrystal went into the house to get something about the time a group of *bandidos,* approaching from the west, collided with an angel, a spider, and four ghosts, approaching from the east. I was untangling a six-shooter from the hair of a sobbing seven-year-old angel, and Al was straightening out some of the spider's legs. Mel picked up a ghost off the ground and helped it to find its eyeholes again. The customers were piling up. A fairy dropped her wand in the shuffle, and a bride slugged a vampire she accused of leaking blood on her dress.

An Indian chief arrived, and while Mel was quizzing him about Native American history, I glimpsed a little black streak out of the corner of my eye. In no time, Sidney had wrestled a feather headdress to the ground. I was extricating my little feline hunter when the Indian chief, whose mood had soured considerably, made the mistake of insulting a pirate, whose sword, if blunt, constituted a weapon of some effectiveness when wielded with conviction.

Our stock dwindled rapidly. The cold seeped into our bones.

Leon showed up, shepherding a bevy of giggling little princesses and ballerinas. Since he was wearing a Ronald Reagan mask, I didn't recognize him until he tripped over a crack in the sidewalk, fell, and wiped out his whole chorus line.

Al was all for calling it a night when two kids showed up in jeans and T-shirts. The first stuck out his hand. I planted a sucker in it.

"Is that all you got?" he asked contemptuously.

"That's it," I lied, annoyed.

"Well, you can keep it," he said, and tried to hand it back.

Part of me watched with amazement as my fist shot out, grabbed hold of his T-shirt, and dragged him toward me.

"Listen, you little shit," I said threateningly. "I don't give a damn what you do at home, but at *my* house you take what you're given and say 'thank you,' goddam it!"

I had twisted the front of his T-shirt into a knot. Our eyes locked. Don't ask me why I called him "little"; I was standing on tiptoe. But my hormones chose that moment to think big, and I was flooded with fury. He might be wiry, but I outweighed him, no question about it. His friend had fallen back in a gesture of disavowal.

His eyes dropped. "Thank you," he mumbled.

I released him with a little push that sent him stumbling down the sidewalk. Behind me, everybody started breathing again.

Crone power, I love it!

Eighteen

I still wanted to know what Lottie was doing with a valuable Rookwood vase, if we were right in our assumption that it had been the victim, and not the murderer, who had carried the vase into the pottery studio and stashed it there. Now that I'd seen the inside of the Olmstead house, with its lavender-scented sofas and fringed lamps, the Rookwood vase seemed plausible, Leon's testimony regarding pickle jars notwithstanding. But how were the Olmstead house and its various occupants connected with the Justice Collection? That connection, between the respectable Olmstead drawing room and a defunct cathouse, seemed highly implausible.

What I needed was someone with a knowledge of local history, and when I recalled the scene at the fire, I realized that I had another reason to speak to the two retired schoolteachers, Malvina Deeds and Constance Petty, apart from their presence at the fateful Parker lecture.

I called on Friday morning and caught them headed out the door.

"It's Malvina you want if you're looking for neighborhood history," Constance Petty told me. "Of course, we'd both be glad to talk to you. We love to talk about history. But Fridays we work at the Historical Society."

I heard a voice in the background.

"It's Catherine Caliban." Constance's voice changed directions as she turned away from the phone. "She's a detective." Then to me she said, "Malvina says why don't you meet us for lunch at the restaurant in the Cincinnati Art Museum? We'll leave our brown bags at home and treat ourselves to something more interesting. That way, if it's specific information you want, we can go back to the Historical Society after lunch and look it up."

Detective work was wreaking havoc on my plans to evade the ten pounds you were supposed to rack up at menopause. Every time I turned around, I was power lunching. I reminded myself that I had a tux to squeeze into that night, then gave in and agreed to lunch.

I wasted another ten minutes on the phone with Yvonne. She didn't have anything to add to what I'd already heard. Yes, Jan had left her a note asking her to turn on the kiln. Yes, the kiln had been on when she went to turn it on. The controls were in the "on" position, the kiln was warm, and the cone had melted. Yes, she'd been surprised, but not surprised enough to call out the National Guard. She'd just turned the thing off. There are times when doing laundry is more gratifying than doing detective work.

The Cincinnati Historical Society was in the Art Museum complex in Eden Park. Just beyond it as you came up the drive was the Art Academy, which had apparently survived the years better than Rookwood Pottery, whose designers it once trained. Around back, facing the parking lot, was the Art Museum, where I'd met Dan Pratt the day before. At this rate I should probably take out a membership, I thought, as I paid my admission fee again. Two schoolbuses outside made me wary, but I thought it highly unlikely that the little monsters were scarfing down finger sandwiches in the tearoom.

Malvina Deeds and Constance Petty were already seated at a table facing the courtyard, which was filled with the flashy gold and wine-colored chrysanthemums of autumn. They didn't see me at first because they were arguing. I soon discovered that this was a pretty typical sample of their ongoing relations.

"Have a seat, Mrs. Caliban," Constance said, looking up at me out of the top of her bifocals. "Don't mind us. We fight all the time."

"Especially when one of us forgets to write something down," Malvina put in, giving me a firm handshake. She wore a wedding ring, I noticed. Both women wore skirts and sweaters—the kind of sweaters with stretched and pilled sleeves. Malvina's glasses hung on a chain around her neck.

"I keep telling you, I didn't forget to write it down. I just forgot where I wrote it down."

I felt right at home.

"I'll bet it's in your red notebook," Malvina said. "You look and see if it's not there when we get home."

Constance, rubbing hands that looked slightly contorted from arthritis, cracked her knuckles and winked at me.

"You're as bad as the kids," Malvina said, with a show of exasperation. "Mrs. Caliban's going to think you weren't raised right."

"Cat, please," I corrected her, "short for Catherine."

"Is this real cheese in this sandwich?" Malvina asked the waitress as we ordered. "It's not that light, low-fat plastic cheese they're coming out with, is it?" The waitress assured her that the cheese was real. "Good," Malvina commented, and I warmed to these women even more.

"Dr. Dexter won't like it," Constance warned.

"Dr. Dexter can go stuff himself," Malvina retorted. "You don't think he eats that trash he's always trying to push off on us, do you? Besides, if you tell him about that, I'll tell him about your popcorn binges, Miss High-and-Mighty, so don't you Dr. Dexter me."

"Don't you just hate the way these young doctors try to run your life, Cat?" Constance sighed. "I'm seventy-eight, and he's always after me about my blood pressure and so on. I said, 'What are you saving me for? Alzheimer's and cancer?' "

"They probably get a kickback from the nursing homes," I observed.

"Constance, Cat doesn't want to talk about our health,"

Malvina put in, slathering a cracker with butter. "It's boring."

"I heard you were teachers," I began. "Is that right?"

Constance nodded. "For more years than either one of us cares to remember. Junior high."

Junior high? I looked at them with a new respect. In that case, they would probably be able to run rings around Dr. Dexter on their hundredth birthdays.

"We both taught history," Malvina said.

"Then Malvina became the principal," Constance said. "That wasn't too long after Harold died."

Malvina nodded. "It took my mind off my troubles."

Constance snorted. "You mean, it gave you new troubles to think about. Anyway, now that we've retired from teaching, we're full-time historians." She rummaged around in the cracker basket. "You see any garlic sticks, Malvina? This is nothing but melba toast."

"There's some of those captain's wafers at the back," Malvina told her, "but they're all in pieces, look like somebody stepped on 'em."

"You said you worked at the Historical Society?" I asked.

"Oh, we don't have a job there," Malvina explained. "We go there to do research. We're working on a book about Cincinnati's black history from the Civil War to the civil rights movement."

"Really? That's interesting."

"We think so," Constance rejoined. "Our friends, who spend their time on fall foliage tours and gambling junkets to Atlantic City, think we're crazy."

Our food arrived. "Oh, good, french fries," was Malvina's comment. She had some kind of melt sandwich the color of a no-parking stripe.

"As I told Constance on the phone, I'm looking into the Arts Castle incident," I said. "I assume you know by now that the victim was Lottie Gambrel."

They nodded soberly.

"Yvonne told us. Poor Lottie!"

"Did you know her?" I inquired. I bit into a french fry with intense satisfaction. I'd been hanging out with the wrong crowd.

"Not well," Constance said, "but she went to our church. She struck me as quiet and hardworking."

"I think she had a job over at University Hospital," Malvina reported. "At least, that's what she told us. We didn't know her before she moved into the neighborhood, maybe—what? Six or seven months ago?"

Constance nodded and picked up the thread of the story. "Her aunt had died and left her the house, and some money, too, I guess. At first she was working the two jobs—the one at the hospital and the one at the Castle. But then I believe she had some health problems, and I guess she found out that Inez had left her pretty well off, so she stopped working at the hospital."

"When was this?" I asked, wondering if she hadn't discovered an alternative source of income instead—like, say, a priceless collection of art pottery on the premises.

"I don't know exactly," Malvina said. "End of the summer?"

"Did she ever suggest to you that she had found anything valuable in the house?"

The looked at each other speculatively.

"She mentioned some family Bibles once," Constance offered, "because she knew we'd be interested. And she said there were other papers in the attic that she'd show us some day, in case the Historical Society might want them."

Hell, I might as well be blunt. "Nothing about pottery, or vases—anything like that?" I ventured.

"You mean, because of that Rookwood vase they found?" Malvina's sources of information were excellent, and there wasn't anything wrong with her mind, either. "No, we talked about that. But the Olmsteads were wealthy people, and that was the family home. I'm sure Inez had nice things. It's hardly surprising that she owned a Rookwood vase."

I studied them a minute, then took the plunge.

"Would it surprise you to know that that particular vase came from a long-lost collection of Rookwood—a collection that everybody has heard about but nobody has seen?"

Constance dropped her fork with a clatter. "No!"

"Is that right?" Malvina asked.

They exchanged glances, eyes glittering. They had the looks of a pair of cats who'd been dining on Meow Mix when a school of tuna swam by.

"But you don't think the whole collection was hidden away in the Olmstead house, do you, Cat?" Malvina pursued.

"Of course she does!" Constance exclaimed. "And she thinks it has something to do with the house burning down."

"But that would mean—that would mean that the fire destroyed more than the Olmstead papers!" Malvina looked at me in alarm.

"If the collection was still in the house when it burned," I replied.

"How do they know this vase was part of the collection?" Constance asked.

"The owner used a special stamp to mark her pieces."

"Her pieces?" Malvina leaned forward eagerly. They had both stopped eating. "The collection belonged to a woman?"

"A prostitute named Nellie Justice, originally. Have you ever heard of her?"

"Nellie Justice. That sounds vaguely familiar," Constance said.

"You've probably got her in your red notebook," Malvina sniffed. "Along with all the other things you forgot to write down. When's the last time anybody saw this collection?"

"In the teens," I said, "right before all the houses were closed down."

Malvina nodded. "That would be 1917."

"Does it make sense that the Olmsteads would have acquired a collection like that?" I asked.

Constance narrowed her eyes and stared into the courtyard. "It's hard to say. They probably would have had the funds to do it. On the other hand, they were a very respectable family."

"Abstainers," Malvina put it. "Alcohol on the premises used only for medicinal purposes. Active in temperance."

"So you can imagine how they felt about brothels. I can't see them buying a collection previously housed in a bawdy house, can you, Malvina?"

Malvina shook her head. "The whole transaction would be out of character. For once, I agree with you."

"Do you know about the Olmsteads, Cat?" Constance asked me. "Who they were, I mean."

"No," I confessed. "Should I?"

"People don't remember them anymore," Malvina reassured me. "Phineas Olmstead founded the first colored newspaper in Cincinnati, the *Colored Messenger*, in 1868, and it was passed from father to son until the Depression, when it died."

"Lucius Olmstead, Phineas' grandson, wrote the first history of black Cincinnatians, published in 1925," Constance added. "It was called *A History of the Queen City's Colored Citizens*."

"Miss Inez was his daughter," Malvina continued. "She inherited the family home. I don't quite know how she and Lottie were related—cousins, I believe."

"Frankly, we were surprised that she left the house to Lottie," Constance said.

"Lottie told us they were kin," Malvina agreed, "but we'd never heard Miss Inez mention her. We thought she might have left it to someone in her brother's family. They didn't have children themselves, but there were Dorothy's sister's children."

"Even though Inez and Richard never did see eye to eye on

anything." Constance dropped her voice to a confidential murmur.

"Not that it was any of our business," Malvina insisted. "Miss Inez was more of an acquaintance than a friend."

"And we liked Lottie, and wished her well. I don't believe she'd had an easy time of it, and the inheritance seemed to have changed her life for the better," Constance mused.

"Unless she got killed for it, Constance," Malvina corrected her. "That will be a shame, if it turns out that she was better off without it."

"But getting back to this famous Rookwood collection," Constance said, "and whether or not the Olmstead family somehow acquired it from this prostitute. It seems much more likely, if less dramatic for our current purposes, that they acquired one vase out of the collection at some subsequent sale, without really knowing much about its pedigree."

"That doesn't explain the fire, though, Constance," Malvina pointed out. "Or the appearance of the vase in the room where Lottie was murdered. And are you going to eat those olives or just push them around the plate?"

"No," Constance responded, apparently to both questions, because she pushed her plate across to Malvina, then turned to me. "I don't suppose there's any possibility that the fire was an accident?"

"Doubtful," I said. "I was in the house minutes before it broke out, and I smelled kerosene just before somebody knocked me unconscious."

"Goodness!" Malvina exclaimed. She forked the olives onto her own plate, pilfered some carrot sticks to replace them, and returned the plate to Constance.

"It sounds like Cat's detective work is a little more dangerous than ours, Malvina," Constance said, rather wistfully.

"But yours might be helpful," I said, "if you can link the Olmsteads or Lottie Gambrel to the Justice Collection."

"We'll all go back to the Historical Society after lunch," Malvina declared, "and see what we can find."

"Dessert?" The waitress broke into our conversation as she cleared the table. Constance snagged a fistful of crackers just as the basket was disappearing, dropped them into her purse, and winked at me.

"I'm ready," Malvina agreed complacently. "How about you, Cat?"

Nineteen

Over raspberry torte and white chocolate mousse, I asked Constance and Malvina about the night of the African pottery lecture. I told them I was particularly interested in anyone who might have left the room during the lecture.

"I don't think we can help you there, Cat," Constance said. "Malvina's a little hard of hearing, so we sit near the front."

"We sit near the front," Malvina said acidly, "so that Constance can see the slides."

"Did either of you see Lottie at the Castle that night?"

They shook their heads.

"Do you remember anything at all unusual about that night? Anyone behaving strangely?" I asked without high expectations of success. I was beginning to suspect that most of the people involved with the Northside Cultural Arts Center behaved strangely most of the time, and I was no exception.

They frowned and thought.

"The Nagels were there," Constance recalled slowly. "They're such a lovely couple."

"And so good for the center," Malvina added.

"And that obnoxious young man—what's his name?" Constance said.

"I don't know his name." Malvina spoke with annoyance. "All I can say is that if he'd come through my school, he would have learned some manners."

"I think he's an artist," Constance told me.

"Gil Forrester?" I prompted.

"That's him," Malvina snapped.

"Of course, Frieda was there, and Brenda, Brenda Coats.

Now, there was something—I'd say a definite tension between the two of them."

While Malvina's attention was momentarily distracted by a flurry of squirrel activity outside, Constance purloined a raspberry from her plate. It was done so quickly and deftly that I'd almost persuaded myself that I'd imagined it, when Constance winked at me again.

"Things are always tense between them, Constance," Malvina objected, turning back to the table. "Don't go confusing Cat. The way you tell it, she'll think one of them pulled a knife on the other one and stabbed poor Lottie by mistake."

I didn't correct her choice of murder weapons. Instead, I asked, "Do you know why they don't get along?"

"It's Brenda's black arts center project," Constance said. "She's talked to us about it. She wants a black arts center in Walnut Hills—something similar to the Arts Castle, but more Afrocentric, as she would say."

"And heavily subsidized by grants and contributions, of course, so that classes could be low-cost or free," Malvina said, brazenly helping herself to a spoonful of Constance's whipped cream. "That's for the raspberry," she added.

"It's a good idea," Constance put in. "The arts center, I mean."

"But it would compete with the Northside Center for funding," Malvina continued, "so you can imagine how Frieda feels about it."

"Meanwhile, Frieda resents Brenda's presence on the board, because she feels that Brenda is exploiting the Northside Center for her own purposes—"

"—learning the ropes there, so to speak, so that she can go out and compete successfully against the center for funding."

"Okay," I said. "So who else do you remember from that night?"

"Well, Jan Truitt was there, of course." Malvina picked up the thread.

"She does lovely work," Constance enthused. "And she's a very popular teacher. Not everybody can do both."

"She seemed—well, frazzled," Malvina said. "But then, she's often muttering about deadlines and so forth. I guess she gets lots of orders for dinnerware."

"Jim Hyde was there," Constance said. "And that Dr. Salazar—the pediatrician—and his wife, who works at the library. I remember them because of the beepers. We don't like to sit near anybody wearing a beeper."

"But then it never fails—we end up next to somebody with one of those ridiculous alarms on their wristwatch!" Malvina lamented, then sneaked a peek at my wrist.

"And that night was a particular challenge," Constance continued, "because one young woman was wearing strong perfume, and we can't bear that, either."

"Makes us sneeze," Malvina confessed.

Mimi Finkelstein-Fernandez obviously cut a wide swathe wherever she went.

"But as to their behavior, they were all acting pretty much like they always do, as far as I could see," Constance summarized, confirming my suspicions.

It wasn't until we were passing the Egyptian pottery on our way out of the museum that I thought to ask them their opinion of Parker's lecture.

"It wasn't one of his best," Constance said thoughtfully.

"No," Malvina agreed. "We've heard him several times, and he's usually much more organized. He seemed kind of—distracted."

Distracted, was he? Maybe he'd had something else on his mind. Maybe he'd been thinking about some more recent pieces of pottery, made half a world away.

At the Historical Society we signed in at the front desk and received clip-on badges. I noticed that Constance's and

Malvina's were waiting for them and had a more permanent look than mine. By the time I had read all the rules, I was thoroughly intimidated and congratulated myself that my first trip was in the company of a pair of seasoned researchers. Would they search my purse and confiscate all my pens? My Swiss Army knife? My M&M's?

"You and I will take the Olmsteads, Cat," Malvina instructed me. "Constance will try to find out about Nellie Justice. That will be harder, and her instincts are better."

I didn't ask what that meant. I hadn't thought instinct had much to do with historical research; I thought you just used the card catalog and the reference books, but apparently not.

"This Nellie Justice, Cat. Was she white or black?" Constance asked.

"White, I think," I answered. But why did I say that? "I'm not really sure," I confessed. "Maybe I assumed she was white because she was represented to me as running one of the most exclusive houses and because the person who told me about her didn't say otherwise."

"It's probably a valid assumption, then," Constance said. "Though it makes the Olmsteads' acquisition of her collection more suspect."

Two hours persuaded me that I would never become a researcher. I was willing to admit that what researchers did had a lot in common with detective work. Hell, it *was* detective work. But it was all done in one place—and a dusty one at that. It involved a lot of reading of small type, when it didn't involve the deciphering of a faded handwriting that bore little resemblance to contemporary English script—it was all elongated loops and spikes and lines slanting up like a fleet of masts on a rough ocean. Letters were the worst to read. What they did, to save paper, was write a page, then turn the paper ninety degrees, and continue the letter, writing over the first part. Reading it was kind of like looking at an Escher print: you had to focus on one set of lines and ignore the others. How they read it by candlelight, even before it had faded to a faint antique brown, is anybody's guess!

Meanwhile, my hands and clothes were streaked with grime, my eyes were tired, my butt was sore, and I was all for skipping over anything that was too hard to read.

Constance and Malvina, on the other hand, worked with all the enthusiasm of foxhounds at the hunt. In fact, every now and then Constance would pass us with a strange look on her face, and an animal glint in her eye. A rakish brown smear across one cheek did nothing to lessen the effect.

"She's on to something," Malvina would observe succinctly. "Now, Cat, have you found anything in those letters?"

In two hours I knew more about the Olmstead family than I ever cared to know. To tell you the truth, I found it more than a little creepy to know them as intimately as I did, and reminded myself to go home and destroy any personal papers that might provide grist for a future researcher's mill. God knows what I'd find: old shopping lists, notes to the kids' teachers, recipes scrawled on the backs of bank deposit slips, reminders to Fred to take out the garbage.

After two hours what I did not know about the Olmstead family was whether they had ever acquired the Justice Collection, or anything that might have been the Justice Collection, unbeknownst to them.

"I don't think they ever owned it," I confessed to Malvina in despair. "Nothing I've read suggests that they were even remotely interested in art pottery. But I can describe the damask curtains Mrs. Olmstead ordered for the drawing room in great detail. I can even tell you how much the fabric cost her."

"Fascinating, isn't it?" Malvina said. She had one stubby little pencil stuck behind each ear, which made her look something like a shorthorn cow. "You're probably right about the Justice Collection, although you have to remember that we have only a small portion of the family papers. Just think what a limited perspective somebody might have on your life if they read only a hundred letters out of the thousand you'll write over the course of your lifetime. If only the house hadn't burned down! It just kills me to think what we might have lost!"

Old notes to Mr. Olmstead to take out the garbage? I thought involuntarily.

"There is one other thing, Cat, that makes me wonder," she continued, breaking in on my thoughts. "I found several references to prostitution dating from the early twentieth century."

Constance had arrived in time for this last remark. "The *Colored Messenger* was very active in the campaign to close the district."

"So maybe when it did close, the *Messenger*'s editor acquired the Justice Collection—why?" I mused. "To give a fallen sister enough money to start a new life? As a cheap investment?"

"Or to remove the spoils of sin from the marketplace?" Malvina speculated. "Who knows?"

"Tell me more about the campaign to close the district," I said. "I assume that there were colored houses—is that what they would have been called?—as well as white houses. Is that why the *Messenger* was involved?"

"There were colored houses, white houses, and even some mixed-race houses," Constance reported. "Many of them were on George Street in the West End, which was only three blocks long. Most of the colored houses were on Longworth Street—"

"Named for the Longworths of Rookwood Pottery?" I interrupted excitedly, remembering Maria Longworth Nichols.

"Same family." Constance nodded. "Anyway, during the Progressive Era, reformers attacked the houses as breeding grounds for syphilis and other diseases."

"The eugenics people were involved as well," Malvina contributed.

"Yes, but the black citizens had special concerns, apart from diseases," Constance said. "Most of the colored houses served an exclusively white clientele."

"Really?" I said, taken aback.

"Yes," Constance continued. "So you can begin to understand where black leaders were coming from. There was a lot of talk in the white community about white slavery—you know, the Mann Act dates from this period—but black leaders were concerned about prostitution as a new form of black slavery for the girls who got drawn into it.

"Then, too, most of the brothels were in a black neighborhood—the West End—not a white neighborhood. Black leaders saw them as promulgating other forms of vice as well as disease within the black community."

"So what was the 'restricted district'?" I asked.

"Somewhere along the way the city reached a compromise with the reformers: we'll allow prostitution, but only within a restricted geographic area so we can monitor and regulate it," Constance said. "Many cities reached similar compromises. After all, the brothels served local business interests. The reformers, of course, weren't happy with the compromise. They pointed out that syphilis was no respecter of artificial boundaries. And you can imagine what the black reformers thought of the arrangement."

"But within the district the brothels operated freely?" I asked. "The police never bothered the prostitutes?"

Constance and Malvina exchanged a look.

"I didn't say that," Constance replied. "The police did harass prostitutes, especially in mixed-race couples. An anti-miscegenation law was defeated in the Ohio Legislature in 1913, but the law nevertheless reflected a considerable amount of popular sentiment. The police were especially hard on white women, or any woman who looked white, accompanied by a black man. They even banned black musicians from playing in white houses."

"They could do that?"

"Remember, Cat, the South was right across the river," Malvina reminded me. "And Cincinnati practiced segregation in all kinds of public as well as private arenas—as you must remember if you were living here before the sixties. Of course they could do it!"

I thought a minute. "So eventually the reformers won?"

"It was the outbreak of the European war that finally closed the houses," Constance reported. "It took a federal law to do it. The U.S. government banned houses of prostitution within so many miles of army bases. At that time there were troops stationed just across the river in Fort Thomas, Kentucky. So the houses had to go."

"The sad part is that the prostitutes were just turned out on the streets," Malvina noted. "So while the reformers were congratulating themselves on all the 'lost sisters' they'd liberated from a life of sin, the girls were taking up street-walking a few blocks away from their former homes. Only now they were much more vulnerable, and much less financially secure. Before, they'd owed their livings to the madams, who had a lot of control over them, but not nearly as much control as the male pimps and gangsters who controlled them now."

"If we ever find anything on your Nellie Justice—and that's a big *if*," Constance said, "chances are good that the trail will disappear in 1917." She began collecting books and boxes from the table and stacking them on a nearby library cart.

"That's when the collection seems to have disappeared," I said.

"There you are," she said, spreading her hands in a gesture of despair. "She probably sold it off, a piece at a time, just to get money to live."

"But wouldn't a piece have surfaced before now?" I pointed out.

"I think we should check out William DeVou, Constance," Malvina said, reaching for a crusty old volume Constance had left alone and dragging it toward her across the polished wood of the library table.

"DeVou owned a sizable amount of West End property, Cat, including many of the George Street brothels," Constance told me. "He was married to a black woman and lived frugally in one of his own tenements—and he had a kind of passion for junk collecting. It's possible, I suppose, that he ended up with the collection, perhaps in payment of back rent. Or maybe he found it on the property after Nellie Justice left. Darn! I wish we had a Blue Book!"

I raised my eyebrows at her.

Constance grinned. "That's what they called the little directories of a city's red light establishments. The Blue Book was rather like the restaurant guides we have today, or the AAA guides to motels, except that there was no independent rating service passing judgment. Individual houses wrote their own entries, indicating their price ranges, atmospheres, and any specializations—*spécialités de la maison,* as it were. For example, you might have a house with—oh, say a nautical decor. Mutinies arranged for a price, that sort of thing."

"Constance!" Malvina chided her, not without a naughty little smile of her own.

"I'd be willing to bet that this Rookwood Room was featured prominently in the listing for Nellie Justice's house," Constance said.

"Not as some kind of—uh, atmospheric erotic prop, surely!" I protested. There flashed before my eyes a scene of debauched mutiny, peopled by men in their long underwear and women wearing the skimpiest of sailor suits and carrying Rookwood vases for some unimaginable sexual purpose.

"Oh, I doubt that," Constance reassured me. "She probably made it clear in her listing that she catered to a very refined clientele. Very cultured."

The sailor suits of my imagination metamorphosed into long, turn-of-the-century dresses. But what about their trains? I worried. Didn't ladies—and ladies of the evening—wear trains in those days? Surely, they weren't negotiating a room full of priceless Rookwood while trailing all their excess yardage behind them.

"Of course, Nellie Justice might have married," Malvina mused. "The madam of an exclusive house might well have had numerous suitors. And if the pieces in the collection were gifts from her admirers—well, that's a lot of admiration. She mightn't have married while her business was thriving, but afterward?"

"We can check the county courthouse." This seemed a grudging concession from Constance. "But it's highly unlikely that Nellie Justice was her real name."

"No?" I asked.

"No," Constance said. "Most prostitutes changed their names when they entered 'the life.' And even if it were her real name, what assurance do we have that she married in Hamilton County, if she married at all? No, I really think it's a shot in the dark. We're not that desperate yet."

"We're not?" I asked.

Funny, I thought. I was feeling pretty goddam desperate, in case anybody should ask.

Twenty

I left them muttering over their manuscripts, and headed home by way of downtown. Fingering a dim photocopy of a map, I turned down Central. Constance and Malvina had assured me that George Street didn't exist anymore, but I had to see for myself.

What I found was a short, unnamed street, larger than an alley, boxed in by a city parking lot and another building. It dead-ended into the expressway. I parked and gazed out over the concrete expanse.

Where, I thought, would my ladies have gone, trains or no trains, if they had died in the streets shortly after the district closed and been haunting their former homes ever since? What had they made of the bulldozers and earth-moving equipment when these had begun to excavate the very ground under their houses? Many had no doubt lived miserable lives in these brothels, but happiness was a relative thing, especially if you were poor and outcast, not to mention poor and outcast and black, at a time before welfare, Social Security, and food stamps. For some, the district may have provided the best home they had ever known, along with some semblance of a family. The closing of the houses may have fallen as a considerable blow, leaving them to wander the streets and seek shelter in doorways and flophouses, where the linens never approached George Street's standards of cleanliness. Without the practiced eye of a madam to scrutinize the johns, they had repeatedly fallen victim to violence from that quarter, until they found dubious rescue in the form of a male pimp, who turned out to be equally violent. The pimp came with a proliferating band of shadowy but dangerous associates always on the lookout for any woman who thought she could beat the system by running away.

So when they died, I thought to myself, surely some of them had drifted back to George Street, clucking their ghostly tongues over the decline of these often elegant houses into tenements. Then the houses themselves had disappeared, leaving behind a gaping wound to be cemented over. What was a ghost to do when she'd been told to "move on" once too often? The whole business was sad.

I was sniveling into my hankie when I started the car. With less than four hours to go until my first Halloween fete, I was hardly in a party mood. On the other hand, I was in the perfect frame of mind to identify with all of those fallen women that Marlene Dietrich had portrayed. Only I didn't think I could manufacture that air of careless indifference Marlene always presented to the world, swaggering around in her top hat and tails, hand in pocket, until the final reel when Gary Cooper or somebody left her in the dust.

I hummed throatily to myself and went home to pay my bills. I always try to take advantage of a bad mood to pay bills; that way I don't have to spoil a good one.

Four hours later my date was hammering on my door.

"Go away!" I shouted. "I vant to be alone."

Moses looked skeptical. "Ain't you got the wrong chick? Wasn't that the other one—the Swedish one?"

"I thought all white women looked alike to you," I said, downing the remains of a little gin mood-setter.

"They used to," he agreed, "till I got my cop training. Now I notice things like hair color. And I hate to tell you, Cat, but ain't none of these ladies under discussion got white hair."

"What are you talking about?" I said huffily. "Their movies were in black and white; they never had anything else."

"Suit yourself." He bent down to scratch Sidney's belly.

"But Kevin has that blond wig if you want it. I don't reckon he needed it to be a leprechaun."

I shook my head. "Mabel has it," I said. "Madonna."

As Moses straightened up, something fluttered behind him and caught Sidney's attention. Sidney was after it in a flash, and I had to pluck him off Moses' corduroy jacket and make him spit out the play money he was chewing on.

"Aw, damn! Did he get all my money?" Moses screwed his head around in an attempt to survey his back. This proved impossible, since two years of retirement from the force had added to his circumference, and the clothes he was wearing added still more.

"Just a C-note," I reassured him, holding up the soggy scrap of paper. "Mirror's in there."

I stood in the doorway of my bedroom while Moses admired his rear view in my full-length mirror. He was dressed in a ratty corduroy coat with some kind of logo pinned to the back. From holes in his pockets trailed streamers of paper money, Scotch-taped end to end.

"You're something to do with Home State," I observed.

"Wait. Lemme give you the full effect."

He turned his back and ducked his head. When he straightened up and faced me again, he was wearing heavy gloves and earmuffs—or, as my grandson Ben called them, "ear muffins."

"You're freezing," I said. "You're a frozen bank account. Very clever."

Moses looked pleased. To tell you the truth, I liked to encourage any sign that he was getting back his sense of humor where Home State Savings was concerned. He'd lost it when the Feds had closed the place down and frozen a good part of his life savings. Who wouldn't?

Sophie was sniffing at his coat with that look of concentration kitties get when they're trying to sort smells, checking every nuance against their memory banks.

"Where'd you get the coat?" I asked.

He shrugged. "I've had it. If my wife was still alive, she would have given it away years ago."

This was undoubtedly true. It was that kind of a coat. Anybody who's ever been married would have recognized it.

Sadie appeared in the doorway wearing her tragic expression, as if we were abandoning her for a season in Monte Carlo.

"Maybe I should take her along," Moses said thoughtfully. "She's got the right expression."

Al, Mel, and Kevin had already left, and I'd only caught fleeting glimpses of their various costumes. They were putting in only the briefest of appearances at the Arts Castle before moving on to the Stonewall Cincinnati dance. Kevin wouldn't be tending bar tonight, but he and Mel had responsibilities as members of the organizing committee.

"We have to show up early to worry," he'd told me.

Moses, meanwhile, had a new girlfriend, name of Charisse, but he hadn't invited her to come tonight because he hadn't thought she'd "feel comfortable." He spoke of her as a "very classy lady." We spoke of her as a pain in the ass, but not in front of Moses. It wasn't clear to us whether her alleged discomfort applied to us as white people, or to the Arts Castle crowd, or to the Stonewall contingent. In any case, it didn't make her a very good match for Moses, in my opinion. But there would be time enough to plot something if he ever announced his engagement. Kevin claimed to have several plans up his sleeve already, and he and Sidney, who had once been scolded for running Charisse's stocking, would discuss them for hours, then walk around looking smug.

Our housemates were just leaving the Castle as we were arriving. Kevin dragged me off into a corner of the foyer, eyes sparkling.

"Aren't you a little tall for a leprechaun?" I asked as he loomed over me.

"Listen, Cat, I have two words to say to you."

I searched my mind. "Lousy music? Punch stinks?"

"Marsha Francis," he stage-whispered in his most dramatic style.

"Who the hell is Marsha Francis?"

He shushed me, glancing over his shoulder.

"Marsha Francis. You remember. One of the people who left the room that night during the lecture. The one with the baby."

"Oh. That Marsha Francis."

"Ask her who left the room that night." He twinkled at me, and disappeared, like the overgrown leprechaun he was.

By the time I reached the ballroom, Moses was already dancing the tango with Mimi Finkelstein-Fernandez, who was dressed like a flamenco dancer. Gloves and earmuffs were nowhere in sight. I also spotted Leon on the dance floor in a skeleton costume; whatever he was doing, it wasn't the tango, but he was giving it his all and nobody seemed to object.

Me, I spent the first twenty minutes in the bathroom, watching Marsha Francis change and nurse her baby. Detective work is a thrill a minute, take it from me.

"We believe in getting out and doing things," Marsha told me. Both she and the baby were dressed in clown costumes, and it was a little hard to take seriously someone with a broad red painted-on smile and a ball on her nose. "Just because we're having a baby, that doesn't mean we're going to sit at home and vegetate. That's what we said."

I looked around the rest room. This was getting out and doing things? She must know every women's room in the city.

"I don't know what went wrong, really." She frowned at the baby as if he were holding out on her. He laughed delightedly and punched her in the eye. "He'd been an angel all evening, and when the lecture started, he was sound asleep. Then he woke up and started to fuss, so I took him outside. I never did get to go back in." She sighed. Her right eye was tearing.

"So you probably saw everybody who left the room during the lecture." I extracted a small notebook and pen from my breast pocket, where I was probably supposed to be keeping my monogrammed silver cigarette case.

"Well, maybe not everybody. We lasted ten minutes into the lecture before we had to leave. But I guess I saw most everybody. I told the police what I saw."

"Would you mind repeating it for me? I'm kind of conducting my own investigation." This sounded silly, even to me; if you were only "kind of" investigating, why bother? But Marsha wasn't that critical. Her intellectual faculties had probably been weakened by loss of sleep, judging from the lines of exhaustion in her face.

She unbuttoned her blouse, unfastened her nursing bra, and settled the baby.

"I don't see why not. But, like I told the police, I might not be remembering everything that happened."

I nodded, and she continued. The baby made little slurping noises.

"Well, we sat on that bench across from the door to the library, right next to the gift shop. Two little girls came out. They spotted the baby and came over to see him. I don't think they'd ever seen anybody nursing, either, though God knows they must have dolls these days that can nurse. I mean, if they can poop, they can nurse, don't you think?"

I didn't render an opinion. At a guess, I'd say the dolls that pooped probably came with a bottle, but what did I know? I was all for teaching little girls just how disgusting dirty diapers could be, though. Maybe they could invent a baby doll that nursed—preferably one that was teething as well. It could be the answer to teen pregnancy. Think about it.

"Maybe somebody else came out while I was talking to the

girls—I can't be sure. Then Frieda came out, and she asked if there was anything she could do for me. Then she went on down the hall. I think she's great, don't you? She's done so much for the center."

"Absolutely." I just hoped she hadn't murdered for it.

"Then there was another woman I've seen around—a black woman. Maybe she works in the gift shop, or else she's a board member—I don't know. I got the impression she was following Frieda."

Hmmm. Brenda Coats. Interesting that she hadn't made Frieda's list of people who'd left the room during the lecture.

"Right after her came this artist guy. At least, somebody told me he was an artist. I've seen him at lectures before, and he's always rude. I swear, for a while there, it was like a parade, because Jim Hyde came rushing out next. Well, you know who he is."

"And they all went down the hall?"

"Yeah. I began to think maybe there was some kind of an emergency committee meeting or something, though it seemed like a strange time to hold one."

"So what happened next?"

She shifted the baby to the other breast.

"Well, one of the girls' mothers came looking for them, and they all went back in. Then I went and stood in the door for a while, because he was asleep and that way I could look at the slides. Frieda and the other woman and the artist all came back."

"Were they together, would you say?"

"I didn't see, because I was watching the slides. Frieda and the other woman looked—I don't know—irritated, but I couldn't tell whether they were irritated at the artist or not. He looked—well, I don't know. He was just smiling."

"How long had they been gone? Frieda and Brenda?"

"Gosh, I don't know. I wasn't paying attention. Ten minutes? Twenty minutes?"

I sighed. The difference between ten minutes and twenty minutes could be the difference between guilt and innocence. "Did anybody else leave?"

I sincerely hoped not. As usual, I was being trampled by my crowd of suspects, which threatened to swell to the size of the *QEII* passenger list. I was beginning to think that Arthur Alexander Parker had been the only one not to leave the room during his lecture.

"The pottery instructor—do you know her? She left for a minute near the end. I ought to remember her name, since I once took that beginning pottery class from her, but I swear, having a baby has played hell with my memory."

Wait'll your hormones go altogether, cookie, I told her silently.

"Did you see where she went?" I asked aloud.

She shook her head. "She wasn't gone long, that's all I can tell you. You know, now that I think of it, there was somebody else who brushed past me, but I didn't see who it was."

"Did this person come back?"

"Not while the lecture was still going on. It was almost over by then. Oh—here's something. I remember he sneezed, and I heard him blowing his nose behind me." She slung the baby over her shoulder and gave him a series of practiced pats on the back.

"What about Hyde? Did he come back?"

"Oh, yes—sorry. Didn't I say? He was back before the others."

"So he left after them and returned before them?"

"That's right."

"Well, thanks, Marsha. You've been really helpful. It just complicates things that there was so much movement. Makes the place sound like Grand Central Station."

"You'd be surprised," Marsha said. "You think it's unusual because you probably don't notice all the movement normally. But if you sat outside rooms with a baby like I do, you'd realize just how much coming and going goes on."

She was probably right, I thought. I mean, here I'd left before I'd even fully arrived. So I went back upstairs to stay awhile.

Twenty-one

My date was dancing with a pleasant-looking black woman in a kind of gypsy outfit. Repressed he ain't.

"What the hell is that?" I muttered to myself, or so I thought.

"The bossa nova." A voice spoke politely over my left shoulder. I turned to see a white-haired black man dressed as an Arabian prince. "He's good." He nodded toward Moses. "Anybody who can keep up with my wife is good." He laughed.

I examined my companion more closely. He looked familiar, but I couldn't quite place him.

"Ralph Nagel," he said, anticipating my inquiry. "You've probably seen me in advertisements for the Nagel Funeral Home."

I shook his hand. "Cat Caliban. I came with Fred Astaire."

"Well, then, Ginger, maybe you'd like to dance." He offered his arm so gracefully that I took it before I remembered that not only did I not know the bossa nova, but even my cha-cha was rusty. My fox trot was completely submerged in my memory banks, along with the rules for bridge and a few old recipes for Tuna Surprise and Jell-O Salad. As we reached the dance floor, I also remembered hearing that Ralph and Ava Nagel were taking the ballroom dance class.

He bowed to me. "Shall I lead?"

I remembered that I was wearing a tuxedo. "You'd better. I left my instructions in my other coat."

A skillful dance partner who really knows how to lead can do wonders for the figure you cut on the dance floor. He or she can make the right moves so inevitable that you produce them without thought or effort. Dancing becomes instinct.

Your self-confidence swells, and you begin to imagine people on the sidelines turning to each other and saying, "And to think she's never set foot inside Arthur Murray!" Ralph Nagel was that kind of partner. Damn, he made me look good!

During a slower number we swapped chitchat about the Castle. He and Ava had taken Jan's beginning pottery class, but, he said, "We never felt that we had advanced far enough to sign up for the advanced class." He commiserated with me as I described my skirmishes with the pottery wheel. He'd also taken watercolor painting, oil painting, stained glass, paper making, flower arranging, Chinese cooking, ballroom dancing, line dancing, and yoga.

"We're going to try photography next," he told me.

That was about the time that Leon, who apparently had only one dance in his repertoire and executed it with equal alacrity on slow and fast numbers, got himself entangled with a teenage couple, and brought them all down in a heap. Luckily, the two victims responded with laughter as Leon's partner picked them up and they brushed themselves off. Leon was a disaster going someplace to happen, but most people didn't hold it against him because he was so good-natured and apologetic about it.

After a few dances we joined Moses and Ava, and I got my opportunity to ask about the night of the Parker lecture. Happily, Moses was in an indulgent mood, so he didn't spoil anything by questioning my right to question anybody.

"Ask Ava." Ralph nudged me. "She's the one with the memory. Of course, we already talked to the police."

"It's hard to know what to ask," I confessed. "But the police think the murder of Lottie Gambrel took place in the pottery studio some time that night, and it might even have happened during the lecture. I wonder, did you enter the building from the back, where the parking lot is, or from the front?"

"The front," Ralph said. "Easier to park the Seville on the street."

"So you didn't pass the pottery studio on the way in, and can't tell me whether the lights were on?"

"No," Ava said. "But they were on later, after the lecture. I remember that. I went to the rest room just after the lecture, and they were on then."

"Did you go in?"

Ava shuddered and shook her head. "No, and when I think how close I might have come to finding poor Lottie!"

"So you knew Lottie?"

Moses interrupted. "I don't mind your detecting, Cat, long's it doesn't stand in the way of more important business, like eating." He took me by the elbow and propelled me in the direction of the food table. "Me an' Ava been workin' up an appetite."

We stood over a plate of hors d'oeuvres that appeared to have been produced by the Little Chefs class for children—not that Moses seemed to care.

"You asked about Lottie," Ralph said. "We were acquainted with her, though not well. We spend enough time at the Castle to know all the staff and board members to some extent."

"Do you know about her connection with the Olmsteads?" I asked.

"Ralph asked her, just because he's interested in local history," Ava said.

"Miss Inez was a cousin of hers," Ralph confirmed.

"A cousin by marriage, or a blood relative?"

"Now, I don't know if I asked that, did I, Ava?" He frowned at his wife.

"You started to, I remember," she said, "but then the conversation took another turn."

Moses shoved an hors d'oeuvre in my hand, and I picked at it unenthusiastically. It looked like overworked and undercooked Play-Doh.

"Did you know the Olmsteads?"

"Not well," Ralph said reflectively. "Inez and Richard were the last of the line, as far as I knew, and Richard died a few years back. We handled his funeral—Inez's, too. I remember their mother and father."

"They were such a striking couple!" Ava put in. "She was such a beauty, and slender as a reed, but he was a big man—imposing, even."

"And Richard and Inez both died childless?"

"As far as I know," Ralph said, and looked to Ava for confirmation. "Inez never married, but Richard married a Dayton girl. We weren't close, though, because, of course, they were a good deal older than I was."

"Did you ever hear that they were collecting art pottery? Or ever hear that they had acquired a collection of Rookwood?"

Ralph laughed. "I would have been surprised. Richard had the aesthetic sense of a brick wall."

"But there's Inez, dear," Ava added gently. "She might have been interested. But we certainly never heard of it, if she was."

"And you never heard anything of the kind from Lottie—that she collected Rookwood, for example?"

"No," he said.

"I understand you own some Rookwood," I pursued. "Has anyone ever brought you a piece to authenticate or appraise?"

Ralph laughed again and shook his head. "I would have sent them away empty-handed if they had. I own a few pieces, but I'm no expert."

I could tell that my time was running out. The music was starting up again, and Moses was getting antsy. He'd removed his coat some time during the last dance and was down to slacks, sport shirt, and a very loose tie. I managed to ditch my hors d'oeuvre on a nearby tray.

I asked the Nagels if they had noticed anything unusual during the evening of the lecture, and if they could remember having seen anyone leaving the room. I asked this last with trepidation, as you can probably guess, since I didn't really want to add to my list of absentees.

"We really wouldn't have noticed," Ralph said. "We were sitting in the middle of a row."

"Except that somebody's beeper went off, Ralph," Ava reminded him. "We heard that. So did Alex. He looked annoyed."

"Absolutely right, dear," Ralph said. "That guy probably left."

"You don't know who it was?"

"As I say, we were sitting on the inside," Ralph said. "It could have been one of the doctors—there were several there, as I remember."

"Or Jim Hyde?" I prompted him.

"That's right," he agreed. "He was there, too, and he wears a beeper. So it could have been him."

"There was something else, too," Ava said slowly, studying her husband's face as if she could read it there. "What was it? Oh, I know! The gentleman with the cold! We decided he must have left at some point."

"The gentleman with the cold?" I echoed.

"Poor guy was sniffling and sneezing through most of the lecture," Ralph said sympathetically. "You know how you do when you're trying to be quiet and you can't because your nose is running?"

I nodded.

"And if you're listening it gets to be like background noise—it's annoying at first, and then you forget that you hear it. And then suddenly you realize that you don't hear it anymore. So unless his medication suddenly kicked in, I'm guessing he left the room."

That tallied with the sneeze Marsha had heard behind her.

"You're sure it was a man?"

They exchanged a puzzled look. "It sounded like a man," Ava said uncertainly.

"Come on, Cat!" Moses complained, shifting from foot to foot. "This is a ball, not a courtroom drama! We supposed to be dancin'!"

On cue a little devil popped up on the other side of the food table. She pointed accusingly at my abandoned hors d'oeuvre.

"You didn't finish your snack!"

I started guiltily. Maybe this was the Little Chef who had produced the snack in question.

"It was delicious," I said soberly, "but you're always supposed to leave something behind for the Great Pumpkin."

I danced the next two numbers with Moses, which proved to be a bruising experience, then bowed out. I moved to the doorway and began fanning myself with my top hat. Why didn't anybody think to put vents in these suits? How come Fred Astaire never looked overheated?

I was enveloped by a cloud of perfume just before I heard the familiar voice.

"Hey, Cat! You look great! *Muy distinguida, chica!* Are you somebody in particular I should recognize?"

Remembering Mimi's report on late-night television in New York, I doubted it. So I told her.

"I knew you looked familiar," she said, wagging a finger at me. "Listen, I'm green with envy you can get into one of those. I'd never get the pants past my hips!" She slapped her hips for emphasis.

That was how Mimi grew on you. She had so much enthusiasm, including more for your ideas than you had yourself. I complimented her on her flamenco dress.

"Say, didja see our guy Gerstley?" She turned away and craned her head. "Yo! Cuz!" she shouted. "Over here!" To me in a whisper, she said, "You wouldn't believe how hard it was to get him into a costume! *Hija!* We were over at Stagecraft for hours!"

Cuz?

"There, now don't he look nice?"

"Cuz" turned bright red and shifted from one foot to another. He was wearing a Dracula costume, complete with fangs.

"Very nice," I agreed.

"It's not easy to eat with these things in," he complained.

"Oh, go on!" Mimi said, and she actually punched him in the arm. "You know you love it! He wouldn't go for the blood, though," she told me. "Just one teeny little drop, I said. Don't be a shlump! Just one! But no."

He sniffed, and I glanced at him in alarm. His eyes were moist. But he was smiling.

"I think your costume is a model of restraint," I told him.

Speaking of restraint, or lack thereof, at that point we were swept up in a conga line led by none other than my erstwhile escort. It played hell with my train of thought, though I found myself recalling something Kevin had said about Mimi and Gerstley. I watched Mimi bouncing up ahead, turning to flash Gerstley a delighted smile. Could Mimi really be interested in him? It's true that he looked pretty debonair in his Dracula outfit, and holding on to his waist in a conga line tended to alter my perspective on him. But Mimi? Was it a case of opposites attracting? If she wasn't interested, she was wasting a hell of a lot of charm, like a thousand-watt bulb in a broom closet.

Well, after that little number, I wondered if Moses was plotting to prevent me from asking questions. I didn't have much breath left. I could also feel little bruises popping out on my heels: Leon had followed me in the conga line. Mimi took me into the hall to recover, while Gerstley went to get me some punch. I took a protesting Moses to the penalty box with me for five minutes' rest.

"I hope you took your heart medicine tonight," I wheezed.

He was as bad off as I was; he just didn't want to admit it.

When Gerstley returned, I worked the conversation around to the night of the Parker lecture.

"Gerstley had mentioned it, and I thought, what the hell? It could be really interesting. So at the last minute, I decided to go," Mimi reported "So me and Cuz, we end up sitting together."

"Cuz?" This time I did ask.

"Cuz" studied his feet sheepishly.

"Well, everybody's gotta have a nickname, right? I mean, you're Cat, and I'm Mimi, and Moses—what's your nickname, Moses?"

"Foggy," I answered for him, and Moses glared at me.

"No kiddin'? Hey, that's cute!" She reached up to pinch his cheek, and he flinched, as anybody would who saw those fingernails coming at them. She managed it, however, without causing any major blood loss.

I tried to redirect her attention to the night of the lecture. No, she hadn't noticed anything strange, and neither had Gerstley, when she let him get a word in edgewise.

"Did you notice anybody leaving the room?"

"We were sitting pretty far up in the front, weren't we, Cuz? We wouldn't have seen anybody leave."

"Did either of you leave?"

"Not us," she said. "We were enthralled. At least, once he got past the megillah with the maps of the ancient world and the migration of peoples and—ay, *caramba!* Enough already! I said to myself. Show us some pots. And he did. So I guess I got my money's worth." She winked at me.

"Cuz" shifted uncomfortably, so I directed the next question at him.

"And you didn't see anybody leave, Gerstley?"

"No," he said hesitantly.

"Are you kiddin'?" Mimi stepped on his line. "You could drop a bomb in the seat next to him and he wouldn't hear a thing. I never seen anybody so transfixed. And the amazing thing is, he don't even take notes, but he remembers everything! Go on—ask him! I bet he can describe every pot he saw at that lecture!"

"Well," Gerstley said with a modest little smile, "I am an art history professor, Mimi. It's just a trick of the trade."

"Thing is, he don't remember what he ate for breakfast! Go figure!"

With that profound conundrum on the table, Moses sprang up and announced that his time out was over, and he was going back in to dance. Mimi dragged Gerstley off in his wake.

Twenty-two

Frieda issued from the costume fray trailing a thin man whose air of placidity contrasted sharply with her own freneticism.

"I'm dying for a cigarette," she told me. Then she introduced him as her husband. I hadn't thought of Frieda with a husband; I'd kind of thought she was married to the Castle.

"I haven't seen Brenda yet tonight," I commented. "Have you? I thought she'd be here."

"No, I haven't seen her," she answered, and escaped down the stairs.

I let her go. If there was one thing I'd learned tonight, it was that there was a lot of lying going on. We experienced detectives know, however, that not all of the lies imply guilt. Some of them could be clumsy attempts to cover for someone else, who might or might not be the guilty party, the way my kids used to operate—like when Jason used to alibi Franny, not realizing that it had been the cat who'd broken Great-aunt Leda's cut crystal vase, or even that I'd always hated that vase and been glad to see it go. Some were attempts to repel suspicion like Teflon, to use a metaphor that was politically current; Sharon, Jason, and Franny had once insisted, unlikely as it seemed, that they'd all gone bowling together on the morning that the upstairs bathroom had flooded. Among those lies of the suspicion-repelling variety are the ones intended to divert attention from other unrelated criminal activity, like Franny's insistence that she and Heather had been studying at the library the afternoon our front window got broken, when in fact she and Heather had been attending an antiwar rally at U.C. Frieda's lies about the night of the murder might have fallen in any of these categories. I wasn't yet prepared to confront any of the liars until I'd had more time to sort out the lies.

Speaking of fraud, I had a few more potential liars to confront, and Gil Forrester, artist and thief, headed the list. When I didn't spot him inside the ballroom, I hunted up Jan, and she told me he'd gone already.

"Say, Jan, Marsha told me he left the room during the Parker lecture, and then came back."

"Gosh, Cat, she could be right. I just didn't notice."

"What about Mimi and Gerstley?" I asked. "Did either of them leave the room?"

She shook her head. "If they did, I didn't see them, or don't remember it. Sorry, Cat. I wish I could be more help."

"You can." I nodded at a man in Elizabethan dress who was dancing with a teenager in medieval costume. "You can introduce me to Jim Hyde."

Hyde was a handsome man with a chiseled face, wide-set intense gray-blue eyes, and curly black hair going artistically gray at the temples. I had watched as he courteously bowed to his partner at the end of the dance, offered her his arm, and escorted her to the punch bowl. Once Jan introduced us, he turned on me his warmest smile and introduced me to his daughter, Sissy.

In response to a look from her, he corrected himself.

"I beg your pardon, it's Cecilia. 'Sissy' is a name for little girls, not for fifteen-year-old young ladies." His eyes twinkled, but there was no disguising the pride in his voice.

He had reason to be proud. Cecilia had dark curly hair, delicate features, and his gray eyes with their blue-violet highlights. She was poised to be a real heartbreaker.

After passing out the appropriate compliments, I explained my interest in the death of Lottie Gambrel and asked him about the night of the Parker lecture.

"I'm only too glad to help in any way I can, though I've already told the police everything I know, Cat," he said. "I can't say I noticed anything at all unusual that night, anything that might shed light on this tragedy."

It was a little heavy-handed, but I made allowances for him because he was a politician, and politicians often forget how to talk like ordinary people.

Hyde excused his daughter to dance with a young man dressed like the scarecrow in *The Wizard of Oz*.

"Speaking of shedding light, I understand that you were called away during the lecture," I said.

"Yes, that's right." He frowned. "One of my staff members needed authorization for a statement to the press. Sometimes these things can't wait."

"That's why you carry a beeper."

"That's right. To tell you the truth, it makes me feel foolish, but my secretary insisted on it." He grinned at me sheepishly. "Embarrassing as hell when it goes off, too. Had to apologize to Alex later."

"So when you left the room, you went where?"

"Down the hall to the pay phone near the drink machines," he said.

"In the small alcove next to the entry to the pottery studio?"

"The pottery and jewelry studios, that's right."

"And you didn't see anything unusual, or hear any noises coming from the studio?"

"If I did, I certainly wasn't conscious of them," he said. "I think I can say with some confidence that I didn't hear anybody killing anybody. I may have been distracted, but I would have heard that."

Maybe, I thought. Maybe not. People don't make much noise when they're hit over the head. Take it from me.

"Can you tell me if the lights in the studio were on or off?"

"Let's see." He considered for a moment. "I suppose they must have been off, or I would remember them on. That is, the studios didn't register on me at all that night, so the lights must have been off, if you see what I mean."

I nodded. Those goddam lights must have been blinking on and off all night like a neon sign.

"And did you see anyone else in the hall, or hear anyone in the office?" I decided not to tell him that I knew several people had left the library just before he did.

He thought that over. "I didn't see anyone," he said slowly. "I did hear some voices coming from the office."

"Do you know whose voices you heard?"

"No, I really couldn't say."

"Did it sound like a regular conversation, or were the voices raised in anger?"

"I really couldn't say that, either," he said, somewhat uncomfortably, I thought. "To be honest, I wasn't really paying attention. I don't want to misrepresent anything."

This last comment sounded like a code: yes, the voices were arguing, but I don't want to be put in the position of getting anyone into trouble.

"Mr. Hyde, can you tell me what time you left the lecture and placed your phone call?"

"Jim, please," he corrected me genially. "Yes, it was just about eight-fifteen, Cat."

"And you never saw Lottie Gambrel at any time during that evening?"

He smiled. "To be honest, I don't even know that I'd recognize her if I saw her. I don't think I saw her. I didn't think I recognized her from the photographs the police showed me. Poor soul."

Was this reasonable? I had to admit that it was. The other board members who knew Lottie either knew her in a community context or spent time at the Castle taking or teaching classes, or both, like the Nagels. I doubted Councilman Hyde spent his evenings studying oil painting—unless he had a Winston Churchill complex.

He broke into my speculations about how he spent his evenings. "Here's Alex."

Alex Parker was dressed in some kind of Chinese getup, seemingly very expensive and definitely prerevolutionary. Maybe he was some kind of courtier, though from what dynasty I couldn't say. He appeared to be a walking advertisement for his own services.

"Jim." He nodded a greeting at Hyde. "I just came over to see how your investigation was faring, Mrs. Caliban. I hope you've been grilling Councilman Hyde. I'm sorry I missed it."

Leon chose this moment to trip over a shoelace and fall backward into the punch bowl, wiping out half the food table in the tidal wave that followed.

By the time we got Leon sorted out and the table reset, Parker had disappeared again.

When I turned back to Jim Hyde, he was gazing at something, transfixed. I couldn't read the expression on his face—repressed anger? Or just profound concern? I followed his gaze. He was watching his daughter, who was dancing with a good-looking black teenager in a Hollywood-influenced Arabian shiek getup. So, I thought, political alliances with the African-American community were one thing; personal alliances were something else again.

He felt me looking at him, and his expression changed. "I'm sorry, Cat. What were we talking about?"

"I was wondering how you felt about Brenda Coats' plan for an Afrocentric community arts center in Walnut Hills," I said.

"It's an interesting idea," he rejoined with a politician's tact. "We need more youth activities in depressed neighborhoods generally, and as you know, I'm a great supporter of the arts."

"But wouldn't it compete with this one for funding?" I asked.

"That's Frieda's position, of course," he said. "And perhaps it would, at first. But I'm convinced that a city like this one, with Cincinnati's commitment to the arts, could surely support two community arts centers. It's a matter of expanding the corporate funding base. That's what I would tell Mrs. Coats, if she sought my opinion: go after corporate sponsorship."

"And has she?"

"Has she what?"

"Sought your opinion."

He smiled. "Not very often, Cat. Not very often."

I opened my mouth to say something when a voice behind me said, "Councilman, you must introduce me to this charming creature." The accent was heavy Transylvanian, with a hint of Kentucky. I looked up to see another Dracula over me. This one wasn't Gerstley.

Jim Hyde laughed. "This is Cat Caliban, Count."

"My dear, I luff your neck," the count replied, bending rather too close to the body part in question. "Won't you come with me? I vant your blood."

He grasped me rather firmly by the elbow. I glanced at him in alarm, calculating how much bad publicity I would generate if I kneed him in the groin.

Hyde was still laughing. "It's a promotional campaign for Hoxworth," he said, naming our local blood bank. "They've got the bloodmobile outside. We thought it would be a good opportunity to help them out with their blood drive."

"But—" I sputtered, trying to dig my heels into the polished wood floor.

"It won't take but a minute, my darlink," Dracula purred, dragging me along.

"What about *him*?" I protested. "He should go first. He's on the board!"

"Doctor's excuse," the count murmured.

Why hadn't I thought of that?

"But my doctor would give me an excuse if she were here!" I wailed. "Listen, I'm a sick woman! My hormones are all shot to hell. Nobody wants my blood, trust me! Besides, I had a drink before I came!"

"Now, now, we just want your plassma, my dear," he said soothingly. "The nice nurse vill take care off you, and when you're done, she'll giff you a nice cookie."

Just inside the bloodmobile a nurse was bent over Alex Parker, waving an ammonia capsule under his nose. His body sprawled limply in a chair, face pale, eyes closed. This did nothing to boost my confidence.

Before I knew it, I was strapped down next to Moses, my eyes shut tight against the needle.

I have my share of courage. I do. I'm not afraid of large dogs or small boys. I can shout down an auto mechanic with both hands tied behind my back. I've even faced down desperadoes with combat artillery. But there's one thing I'm afraid of: needles.

Moses was looking none too chipper himself.

"I thought you cops were used to seeing blood," I said.

"Not our own," he responded weakly.

Well, I thought ruefully, this ought to put a crimp in his cha-cha.

Twenty-three

I don't know what I was thinking: Moses hardly missed a beat. One glass of orange juice, a cookie, and a Band-Aid, and he was ready for the Stonewall dance. The dancing, like the food, drink, and costumes, was wilder at the Stonewall affair, and the whole effect was quadrupled by the mirrors lining the Hall of Mirrors at the Netherland Hotel.

And speaking of costumes, I felt decidedly dull and unimaginative. The Grand Prize went to a phosphorescent salamander with a five-foot tail and an armful of gold tablets. In case you're not up on your religious allusions, this was a reference to the infamous "Salamander Letter," a recently unearthed nineteenth-century letter in which somebody claimed that Joseph Smith had received the Book of Mormon from a supernatural salamander rather than from the Angel Moroni. Two people had died in Salt Lake City this month in bombings apparently related to the sale of this politically hot item to a Mormon bishop. You felt bad for them, of course, but it was hard to keep a straight face when you read the whole story.

In the same category of borderline tastelessness was a perambulating Twinkie wearing a black armband. The armband marked the suicide of Dan White, who'd been convicted of killing gay San Francisco city council member Harvey Milk despite the first recorded use of the so-called Twinkie defense, citing junk food as a direct cause of homicidal impulses. Needless to say, there were no tears shed for Danny boy at the Stonewall bash.

By midnight, even Moses didn't care whether his partner was male or female. Judging from appearances, everybody on the goddam dance floor was leading anyway, or at least doing their own thing. By one, I had learned several new dances which I couldn't repeat now if my life depended on it. The last thing I remember, I was slam-dancing with a crowd of tall guys dressed like the Rockettes.

When Kevin tried to rouse me next morning, I rolled over and opened one eye.

"Rise and shine, Mrs. C! It's pottery day!"

I didn't even dignify this with an answer.

Al was next.

"Come on, Cat! This could be your lucky day at the wheel!"

"If I have to watch anything go around in circles, I'll throw up," I mumbled. "'Sides, I have to stay in bed and rebuild my plasma."

Moses, coward that he was, sent Winnie in next. She barked at me until I threw a pillow at her.

"Come on, Cat!" he said. "You ain't never gonna make detective if you let a little hangover keep you down. Some of your favorite suspects will be there."

"The only thing that comforts me," I told him, opening my eyes, "is the assurance that I look better than you do this morning."

"Don't count on it," he muttered.

Christ! I thought as I sat upright. Alcohol kills brain cells, and at my time of life, I didn't have any to spare. I couldn't even remember where I'd left my hands. Plus my feet, thanks to Leon, looked like the Blue Ridge at sunset. I stumbled off to find some aspirin.

We were a surly crowd at pottery class that morning. Even Mimi was subdued—a miracle for which I bless the patron saint of hangovers. Meanwhile, my head felt so heavy I was afraid I'd be caught opening my clay with my chin.

"Would you like to tell us how the case is going, Mrs. C?" Kevin proposed brightly.

"No, Kevin, I would not like to tell you how the case is going," I responded acidly. "There are too goddam many people telling too goddam many lies, starting with their goddam whereabouts at the time of the murder."

"Gee!" Ram said. "Maybe it was like that movie where they were all in it together, and everybody took a turn stabbing the guy!"

"I doubt it, Ram," Al said. "Cat's pot may have been heavy, but I don't think it took that many people to lift it." Which only shows the state she was in; tactlessness is Mel's forte, not Al's.

"You know, Cat, after we talked, I remembered something," Jan said. "I realized that I did leave the library at the end of the question-and-answer period, to look out the front window and check on the weather. They'd forecast a storm for later that night, and I wanted to get home before it broke. Sorry! I just forgot."

"Okay," I said, and made a point of wiping my hands and extracting a small notebook from my pocket. "Anybody else want to amend their statements?"

Nobody did. Gerstley averted my glare with a sneeze, and Mimi started talking to her clay.

"If I wasn't a board member, I would've left before I arrived," Brenda sniffed. "Alex Parker is so full of himself, he doesn't need my applause."

"But you didn't?" I pursued. "Leave the room during the lecture, I mean."

"I don't recall that I did," she said evenly. "Why do you ask? Does somebody say I did?"

Directly challenged, I admitted that somebody had.

"I may have gone to the rest room," she admitted smoothly.

"And do you recall having a discussion with Frieda when you went to the rest room?" I asked.

The room went quiet with held breaths.

"Who told you that?" she asked. Her clay wobbled on the wheel, then folded up like an arthritic fist. "I know, it was probably that son of a bitch Forrester." She laughed harshly.

"Listen, Frieda and I don't have 'discussions,' we have arguments. And if you want to know what that particular argument was about, you'll have to ask Frieda, unless your spy can tell you that." She narrowed her eyes. "And if you really want to know what happened that night, you'd best go and ask that weasel Forrester. He was the one hiding in the shadows. Ask him what he saw."

I tortured several lumps of clay that morning and produced—several lumps of clay. My efforts made no noticeable difference in them, except that they were wetter when I finished with them, and so was I. My only success lay in getting myself excused from mixing the glazes on account of being chemically handicapped. Jan believed that everyone should gain some experience in mixing glazes to further their development as potters. Me, I was plotting to ditch pottery for Barbie crochet as soon as this term ended. Or maybe I'd take shingle painting, which was Mabel's next project.

When we were heading to the car after another day of failure, Ram detoured me.

"Psst! Cat! Over here, in the bushes!"

Still stupefied from alcohol poisoning, I leaned over a bush and gaped at him.

"What the hell are you doing in a hedge? Isn't your mother coming to pick you up?"

"Shhsh!" He looked over his shoulder as if he thought the KGB were hiding in the next hedge over. "I got some information. Come through here."

"Through here" was an opening in the hedge that was more the size of a slender teenager than an arthritic menopausal woman with a hangover. I emerged on the other side with a new crick in my back, squatted painfully and wondered how I would explain this to the ambulance driver when she arrived.

"It might not mean anything," he said, doubt creeping into his voice as I rubbed my back. I remembered that his mother was a massage therapist, and wondered what lengths she was willing to go to just to bring in a live one. Barely live. "It was something I saw last night."

"Go on."

"I was going to the bathroom, see? And I spotted old Mimi sneaking down the hall."

"'Sneaking'?"

"Well, she was walking real quiet and kind of looking around."

He was right: that sounded like sneaking to me. Mimi didn't do anything quietly.

"When I came out of the men's room, and saw her on the phone, I decided to investigate. So I kind of walk past, like I'm not paying much attention, you know? And she smiles at me, but then she turns her back. So I stop outside the alcove and listen. I couldn't hear much, 'cause she was talking real soft."

"Mimi?"

"Yeah." He gave me a significant look. "Anyway, I heard her start to hang up, so I zipped down the hall and out the door, only I leave the door open, see? So I can watch her. And I see her putting something in a coat pocket where that coatrack is, on the other side of the hall?" He checked to see that I was following this intricate narrative. "Then she goes off around the corner, and I figure she's going back to the dance. I had to go through a bunch of pockets, 'cause I didn't see which coat she put it in."

"You did what?" I asked, amazed at his brazenness.

"And at last—" He paused dramatically. "I found it. A little yellow slip of paper like the one I saw in her hand."

"You didn't steal it!"

He rolled his eyes. "What do you take me for—a doofus? Of course I didn't steal it! That would have given everything away! I found a pen in another coat pocket and copied down on my hand what was written down on the yellow paper.

Then I put it back. So then—I go back in the men's room, see, and copy it down on a paper towel, then wash it off my hand."

I hoped to God he had not swallowed the damn paper towel, or I could be in for a long drawn-out saga.

But no, he produced it with a flourish.

"And here it is!"

On the scrap of paper, scrawled in an adolescent hand, was an address: 127 S. Mound, #5.

"I think it's in the West End," he said. "I looked it up on the map. Of course, it might not mean anything," he added dejectedly, experiencing the deflation that frequently follows adventures of this kind. He studied my face for signs of approval.

"On the other hand," I said, "it might just crack this case wide open."

He grinned appreciatively.

Twenty-four

One twenty-seven South Mound was not, as I'd fleetingly hoped, the address of Gil Forrester's studio, where I'd entertained hopes of finding a stash of hot Rookwood. It was the right neighborhood for an artist's studio; lots of artists rented space in the gallery district around Third and Fourth Streets, and on the western fringes of downtown. In fact, the South Mound address was easily within walking distance of Forrester's studio, which, according to Jan, was at 562 West Third Street. I'd decided to pay him a little surprise visit on that Saturday afternoon. But I detoured past the Mound address first to see what there was to see.

The building did not, in fact, appear to house artists' studios at all. It was a large warehouse that had been subdivided into smaller storage units about the size of an auto mechanic's bay, and Number Five was one of these. In earlier days Cincinnati had thrived on river commerce. Goods would have been unloaded a few blocks south of here and stored in one of the area warehouses, or, by the mid-nineteenth century, loaded onto trains, whose weathered tracks still crisscrossed the streets.

Whatever there was to see in this building, however, was hidden behind layers of grime that had probably originated with the first locomotive in the vicinity. There was only one set of windows, and although the place was pretty deserted on a Saturday afternoon, I felt too conspicuous to start scrubbing at the dirt to look inside. Besides, I didn't clean my own damn windows; you can bet your Electrolux I wasn't going to volunteer to clean other people's—especially when they were such slobs.

The door, naturally enough, was locked. I confess I felt that prickle of feline curiosity. I didn't think that whatever was standing behind Door Number Five was a new washer-dryer or a trip to Bermuda. Was I loitering within breaking distance of the Justice Collection? It was enough to tempt a woman to burgle in broad daylight. But I decided to return at night, under that traditional cover of darkness we detectives like to work in—at least, till middle age, when our night vision goes all to hell.

The West Third Street building was a storefront, with offices and studios on the second and third floors. Just my luck: Gil Forrester was on the third floor, 3-B.

I paused on the second floor landing to catch my breath.

"Do you know if Gil Forrester is in?" I asked of a young woman in paint-smeared coveralls who passed me, going down.

Her eyes crumpled with mirth. "Ask me if I care."

Such a popular guy.

Three-B was at the end of a long hall—naturally. I arrived panting and took a moment to stick my head between my knees so that I wouldn't collapse on Forrester's doorstep. The reversal of blood flow did succeed in keeping me conscious by waking up my hangover and reminding me how long it had been since I'd taken any aspirin. Well, I thought, let's play the glad game: the bastard couldn't possibly sour my mood.

But he could, because he had the nerve not to be at home for my surprise visit. Either that, or his hangover was worse than mine.

I glanced down the hall. Nobody cares about Gil Forrester, said my bad angel. If anybody catches you breaking and entering, they'll probably stop to give you advice. On the other hand, I was fresh out of credit cards. Christ! It was high time I invested in some professional equipment, like a set of picklocks. Then I wouldn't be caught standing around in hallways like this, choosing between my library card, my

Blue Cross-Blue Shield card, and my Golden Buckeye card.

Just to tempt fate, I tried the door. It wasn't locked.

This had to be an oversight on his part. Nobody had ever mentioned "cooperation" in the same breath with "Gil Forrester."

I stepped inside.

Gil's studio took up a good third of the top floor of the building. Shelves of finished pots lined the wall on my right. In front of me, shelves filled with unfinished pieces served as room dividers, cutting off parts of the room from view. I could see beyond them a counter and sink, and an open window above them. The windows to my left, overlooking Third Street, were also open, and the room was chilly. A stiff November breeze rustled the curtains over the drying shelves.

That made me uneasy. At the Castle we never wanted our pots to dry too fast because then you couldn't trim them without a power sander. Maybe it was different for professional potters who worked around the clock seven days a week, but somehow I doubted any of them would encourage this much air circulation throughout the studio.

I cleared my throat. "Mr. Forrester?" I called.

I didn't expect an answer; in fact, he probably would've scared the shit out of me if he had answered. Head and heart beating a syncopated rhythm, I began to examine the pots on the shelves.

Forrester's work was competent but undistinguished. Even I could tell that much. His signature pieces seemed to be bowls the size of watermelons, but they could have been mass produced. His glazes tended toward the blues and browns, with relatively little surface decoration. On the top shelves were row upon row of toothbrush holders and soap dishes, and my lip curled with the sneer of the newly initiated. Pure commercialism, I scoffed—forgetting for the moment that I myself had produced that very week something that was well on its way to becoming a toothbrush holder. I had not set out to make a toothbrush holder, but that was another story.

The drying shelves told a story of their own. I frowned at the curtains flapping wildly against pieces swathed in plastic. Other pieces, uncovered, had turned the light brown of bone-dry clay—and yet, they hadn't been trimmed. Some were still sitting on the bats on which they'd been thrown. Looking around nervously to make sure I was still alone, I did the unthinkable and tried to lift one and inspect it. It stuck to the bat, confirming that it had dried in place without a trimming.

In for a penny, in for a pound. I gently uncovered a bowl and saw that something—presumably the heavy curtain—had damaged its rim. And it was now bone dry as well, which meant that it couldn't be repaired.

Gil Forrester had not opened the windows; someone else had. Was I about to become the fall guy for a really nasty practical joke? I resolved to complete my inspection quickly, and split.

The wind shifted, and I caught a faint unpleasant smell, like a neglected refrigerator. When I rounded the shelves, would I discover the remains of meals past? I held my breath just in case.

I scanned the area beyond the shelves for signs of spoiled food, and saw only a McDonald's bag on the floor. On the right an old cot had been shoved up against the wall. The counter that ran across the back wall ended in utility sinks on both sides, and under the right one was a small refrigerator, which I eyed with suspicion. In the middle of the floor on that side was a potting wheel, and on it, turning slowly, was a bone dry, half-thrown bowl.

It gave me the creeps, I can tell you! I went over and stomped on the foot pedal to stop the damn thing, then glanced nervously over my shoulder again. This was no time for a panic attack, I informed my hormones sternly.

Something caught my eye on the counter behind the wheel. It was the colors I noticed first: jewel-like purples and reds, delicate pastel blues and grays. These were not colors in the Forrester palate. Moreover, the shapes of these four pieces did not show Forrester's heavy-handedness; they were buoyant, carrying the eye up along graceful lines. Forrester's pieces were like stolid camp guards, while these were ballerinas—columbine to Forrester's zinnias. I turned one over. There on the base, stamped into the clay, was the double-looped "RP," surrounded by tiny flames. But the purple scales of justice, telltale monogram of the Justice Collection, were missing.

I checked all four pieces. To my consternation, none of them carried the mark of the Justice Collection.

I turned and surveyed the other pieces atop the counter. None of them looked remotely like Rookwood. One of my pet theories—that Gil Forrester wanted the Justice Collection in order to attempt copies—bit the dust. Judging by his work, Forrester was no more capable of imitating Rookwood than I was.

Okay, maybe that was an exaggeration. He was slightly more capable than I was. We could both make toothbrush holders, but his were intentional. Still, I doubted Rookwood had ever turned out a toothbrush holder.

There remained the other possibility: that he wanted the Justice Collection because it was valuable. It wasn't easy making your living as a potter. The Justice Collection could buy a lot of clay and cobalt.

I continued my tour. Projecting into the room on the left hand side in the corner was a large electric kiln—about twice the size of the one at the Castle. I gazed at it thoughtfully, wondering if the building owner knew it was here, wondering why anybody would allow such a large electric oven in a building as old as this one. And on the top floor. Still, I thought, there has to be another one somewhere. Big as it was, this one wouldn't accommodate enough bowls the size of Forrester's to make it worth the cost of the electricity, especially given the apparent pace of his production. This was clearly the toothbrush holder kiln.

But it was plenty big enough for some things, I thought, as my stomach sank to my shoelaces. I'd just noticed that the gizmo on the side of the kiln was down, but the controls were still turned to "high."

"Oh, hell!" I said out loud to whoever was listening. "It's not fair! It's not my turn!"

I considered retreating on my little cat feet, my footsteps muffled by my Adidas. Of course, there was that woman I'd passed on the stairs; she'd remember me. She'd only have to describe me to someone in Homicide circles, and the jig would be up. After all, this would make—how many? I cast back to the beginning of my career, less than a year and a half ago and counted on my fingers: four. Four dead ones to one live one, presumed dead, and that was a kitten. It was enough to give a girl a complex.

This kiln opened on the side. I unlatched the door, and peeked in. There was a lot of something on the top shelf, which was mounted a good third of the way down. I discovered that the whole shelf slid out.

The shelf was covered with a pile of dust the color of bone.

I deduced that Gil Forrester had posed his last obnoxious question.

Twenty-five

"We've got some drug-sniffing dogs that don't have a record as good as yours." Lieutenant Arpad towered over me where I sat in the hall, my legs crossed and my back—physically and metaphorically—against the wall. He was wearing a pair of Dockers, a sport shirt, an orange-and-black windbreaker, and a Bengals cap. He shook his head slowly. "I had tickets on the forty-five yard line, you know what I'm sayin'? The Bengals were down by six, and Brooks was fading back for a long pass to Boomer when my beeper went off."

"I'm sorry," I said humbly.

"You ought to go on and get yourself licensed," he continued, lowering himself awkwardly to the floor. "You're wasting your talent without it. Though exactly what you should be licensed as is another question. 'Mortician' comes to mind."

Originally I'd sat down there to try to remember what it was I wanted to ask him. Instead, I'd dozed off while officers and technicians filed past. I didn't even know at this point if the remains had been removed from the studio. I didn't suppose they'd needed a full body bag; a Ziploc bag would've done.

"You want a statement?" I asked him.

"Just hit the high points," he said, "including the part about what you were doing prowling around the guy's studio when he wasn't available to let you in. You can give them the unabridged version down at the station."

I explained about finding the door open, glossed over the etiquette of entering uninvited, mentioned the various indicators that something was amiss.

"Uh-huh," he said, eyes closed. I couldn't be sure he wasn't replaying the game in his imagination, and I sneaked a peek at his ears to make sure he wasn't plugged into a radio.

"At least it wasn't my pot that killed him," I volunteered cautiously. I'd spotted a lump of melted metal among the ashes, but as soon as the words were out, I realized that the metal could be anything—a button or rivet, something he'd been carrying in his pocket, a ring. Notice, too, that having leaped to the conclusion that the ashes belonged to Gil Forrester, I was unwilling to entertain alternatives.

"No, apparently not," Arpad agreed. "Killer must've decided there were easier ways to do it—lighter, more portable. *If* it was the same guy."

God, he must be crabby, I thought. He'd learned enough about pottery to join the ranks of the jokesters who thought my work a fair target for abuse.

"So why did you want to see Forrester?" he asked.

I considered him thoughtfully. Even crabby, he was an improvement on my usual interrogator, Sergeant Fricke. So I told him what Brenda had said about Forrester—that he'd been lurking in the shadows the night of the first murder.

"He probably wasn't away from the lecture for more than ten or fifteen minutes," I said. "And I don't have any way of knowing whether they were the crucial ten or fifteen minutes. But it was worth a follow-up."

He nodded. "I guess you saw the Rookwood."

The Rookwood! Damn, it was something about Rookwood I wanted to ask him. Have I told you that I was having these memory problems even before I got hit over the head?

"Yeah," I admitted. "But it wasn't the right Rookwood." That was it! Where was the Justice Collection? "Say, Lieutenant," I pursued. "Have you guys figured out whether the Justice Collection was in the Olmstead House when it burned?"

"Not yet," he said, standing up with some effort. "There's

some evidence that at least one piece from the collection was there, but it could have been a plant. There's a fellow from the Art Museum supposed to come take a look when Arson has it all together in one place."

"Dan Pratt."

"That's the one," he said. He rubbed the small of his back. "I'm getting too old for this."

Somebody called him from the other end of the hall.

"There was a smell," I observed as he turned away. "Refrigerator?"

He grimaced. "Worse than my college days."

"Say," I continued, trying to build on the improvement in his mood, "you wouldn't by chance have learned who inherits Lottie's estate, would you?"

"Yes, indeedy!" he said too gleefully for comfort. "That would be Mrs. Brenda Coats."

He waved as he strode down the hall. "Keep your nose clean," he called, leaving me with my mouth open.

Brenda Coats! What the hell business did *she* have inheriting the Olmstead estate? If she had been tight with Lottie, I'd never heard of it.

Moses had much the same reaction when I talked to him later in the afternoon—shortly after a nap had restored my normally genial demeanor.

He was giving Winnie a bath, bending over the bathtub in his shirtsleeves, and he was as wet as she was. So was Sidney, who was watching from the edge of the tub. He stopped when he heard my news, holding soapy hands suspended in midair.

"Brenda?" he echoed. "Brenda inherits from Lottie? Is she kin? She never mentioned it, if she was."

"I don't know, Moses," I admitted. "But we should find out."

His curiosity wasn't sufficient, however, to make him

change his tune about my interference in a police investigation.

"Look, Cat," he said, "you think Forrester was offed because of something he knew, and you're probably right." The enthusiastic tail wag I received when I appeared in the doorway had emptied half the tub, so now my tennies squeaked and sloshed on the tile floor.

"Hard to figure any connection between Lottie Gambrel and Gil Forrester, unless she caught him stealing from the center again," he went on. "That would explain her death, maybe, but not his. So it stands to reason he died because he knew who killed Gambrel. You figure it out, you be next in line. Hey!"

Winnie had spotted an errant bubble and jumped for it. I stepped back, but I wasn't fast enough.

"Maybe I'd better give Sidney swimming lessons," I observed.

"Wouldn't hurt," Moses admitted, giving Sidney a pat on his wet head. Sidney lifted one black paw, shook it, and started to wash it. "Long's he got this bath fixation, he gonna be in the path of the flood."

I had awakened from my nap with a disturbing thought, and I voiced it now.

"Do you think Forrester was killed because I asked the wrong person the right question?"

"Hard to say, Cat." Moses lifted an armful of wet beagle out of the knuckle-deep puddle of water remaining in the tub and wrapped her in a towel before she could shake herself dry. "That's a possibility. But the cops been asking questions, too. And you don't know what role, if any, the Olmstead fire plays in all this."

"No, though I'd be willing to bet it has something to do with the Justice Collection."

"Yeah, but here's the thing, Cat," he said, wiping wet glasses on a wet towel. "The Justice Collection is not exactly a marketable commodity, you see what I'm sayin'? It's the same with any famous artwork: you can sell it for a bundle at an open auction, or you can sell it to an unscrupulous private collector. If it's stolen, you got no choice. But you got to have the contacts. In this case, we talkin' 'bout a whole collection somebody's got to unload. And your expert doesn't think it's too likely that anybody would try to remove that owner's mark on the bottom of the pieces."

"So we're back to a killer with contacts in the world of unscrupulous art collectors," I said. "In other words, an unscrupulous art dealer. In other words, Parker."

"He's the obvious choice," Moses agreed, drying Winnie's ears. "Maybe too obvious. Jan must know some collectors. So should Frieda. So, for that matter, should Forrester. And Gerstley's an art history professor, with a specialty in pre-Columbian pottery," he reminded me.

"Hell, we might as well throw in Mimi Finkelstein-Fernandez," I groused.

"On the principle that she knows everybody," Moses agreed.

"And Brenda, because she's on the Arts Center board." I sighed. "Only now it turns out she'd own the collection anyway. So she wouldn't need to steal it, and she sure wouldn't burn down her own house."

"Assuming she knew that it *was* her collection and her house," Moses remarked.

"Say, Foggy," I proposed, "why don't you call up your old buddy Rap and ask him how come Brenda inherits?"

"'Cause I ain't that interested, that's why not. I 'magine he'll tell me when he's ready. You so curious, why don't you call up your classmate Brenda and ask her how come she inherits?"

Winnie slipped away, planted her feet on the soggy bath mat, and shimmied from head to toe, spattering the few remaining dry spots in the bathroom.

"Well, I just hope that officer who took my statement took my advice while he was at it and searched the building," I said.

"That's standard operating procedure, Cat," Moses said.

"I wish I'd looked myself," I grumbled. "There's bound to be another kiln somewhere—like in the basement, maybe—and an elevator. He couldn't have done all his firing in that kiln in his studio. He could have the whole Justice Collection stashed somewhere else in the building. I should've looked!"

"Cat, read my lips," he admonished me, opening the door to allow dog and steam to escape. "The next body you find in a kiln could be your own."

Twenty-six

That's why I didn't invite Moses along that night. But I hadn't killed off enough brain cells to be utterly incapacitated: I did invite Mel.

"Just me?" she asked. "I could probably round up some of the Lesbian Avengers."

I shook my head. "This storage unit isn't that big. And I'll have my Diane."

So that's what we were doing, dressed in dark clothes, prowling around outside the warehouse at 127 South Mound Street about nine o'clock that Saturday night.

"Oh, hell!" I said under my breath. "Somebody's there."

A light shone dimly through the dingy glass. The door, however, was closed. A car was pulled up outside the warehouse. I couldn't see its color in the dark, but it didn't look especially familiar.

"Let's wait awhile," I proposed, "and see what develops."

We had parked my car a block away to avoid calling attention to our little nocturnal visit, and now I congratulated myself on my caution. We crouched behind a pile of crates across the street from the warehouse. The air was nippy, and the sky was black. Thunder rumbled in the distance.

Fifteen minutes later, by my watch, a second car pulled up outside and parked next to the first. A tall figure emerged. When he reached the door, I saw his face in the faint light: Gerstley. He opened the door and went in.

"Things are getting too damned interesting," I told Mel. "Cover me. I'm going in."

"Cover you?" she whispered back. "Cover you?! With what? I'm a practitioner of aikido, not a SWAT officer!"

"You know what I mean! If I don't come out, or if you hear shooting, do something useful!"

"Well, in that case, we should have brought a cellular telephone," she was grumbling as I crossed the street.

The door now stood slightly ajar. Inside, I heard voices—Gerstley's, and another one with a Spanish accent. I crouched down, pushed the door gently, and slipped in.

The place was piled high with packing crates. There was a relatively clear path from the door to the back of the warehouse, and a side path. I crawled along this side path, which ran parallel to the front of the warehouse, and settled in to listen.

"It's a mistake, okay?" the Hispanic said. "It has to be a mistake. I can call on Monday and let them know."

"I think I'll do the calling," Gerstley said quietly. "I'll speak directly to Ferrón."

"Why would you want to do that? He won't know anything about it," the other man said.

Gerstley answered him in Spanish. Great, I thought, if only I'd brought my Spanish pocket dictionary.

I poked my head around the corner, where the path continued to the back of the warehouse again, to see if I could see them. I couldn't quite. I edged around the corner on all fours, gun in hand, pausing to read a packing label. The crate was addressed to Dr. Gerstley Custer, 127 South Mound, #5. So this was Gerstley's storage space.

Gerstley sneezed. And then—damned if I didn't feel a corresponding tickle in my own nose!

I clapped both hands to my nose, nearly braining myself with the Diane. The explosion, when it came, made a tiny sound.

"Who's that?" the Spanish accent called.

I heard a gasp of surprise from Gerstley. "What the hell is *that* for?" he exclaimed. "Are you out of your mind? What's going on here?"

Between my thighs I felt a spreading warmth.

"Get up!" the Spanish accent commanded. "Come out where I can see you!"

I was damned if I was going to stand up in my condition! To make matters worse, I felt another wave of heat engulfing my body.

"Don't move!" I heard him say, possibly to Gerstley. Now I saw him standing in the path, between the piles of crates, pointing a gun at me. "Get up!" he ordered. "Get up or I'll shoot! What's the matter with you?"

It's a long story, I thought. "I can't get up," I told him.

"Don't fire that thing in here!" Gerstley put in, both anxiety and authority in his voice. "These pieces are irreplaceable! What's the matter with you?"

"What's the matter with *you*?" the Spanish accent echoed, waving his gun at me.

I pitched forward and closed my eyes. Do the unexpected—that's my advice. It always throws them.

Turns out I wasn't the only one with a surprise, though.

"Drop that gun! Now!"

I opened one eye. Behind me, feet planted, knees bent, arms straight, gun steady, eyes blazing, stood Mimi Finkelstein-Fernandez. She was dressed all in black, with a lightweight black jacket that was uncharacteristically unfashionable. Swell, I thought. Now I'm having hallucinations along with my hot flashes.

Poor Mr. Spanish Accent didn't know what to do. None of this had been part of his game plan.

But before he could decide, Gerstley decided for him. In a rush Gerstley tackled him from behind, forcing his gun arm up, then bringing it down hard on the edge of a crate. The gun clattered to the floor, and I picked it up.

The two men stood panting and stared at me. I sat up with my back against a crate and my wet butt against the cold cement floor, and started at Mimi. By now, I was shivering.

"Give it here, Cat," Mimi ordered me.

"No," I said. What the hell was going on here? And where in hell was my backup? Changing into her gi?

"Cat!"

"I said no, Mimi," I told her firmly. "You've got one already."

"*Madre de Dios!* This is a fucking bust, Cat!" she exclaimed in exasperation. "Don't screw this up for me!"

She looked so sincere that I gave it to her, however reluctantly.

"Yours, too," she added.

"No," I said firmly. "But I'll put it away. How's that?" I stuck it back in my pocket.

She glared at me and spoke softly into a metal disk attached to her jacket.

Three armed men appeared at the door, wearing jackets that matched Mimi's. They began moving up the aisle.

She slapped at her shirt pocket. "Oh, hell! Where'd I put it now?" She felt her other pockets, cursing softly in Spanish. "Here it is." She pulled a slender black case out of her back pocket and flipped it open. I saw a glint of metal.

"Finkelstein-Fernandez. U.S. Customs. Miguel Suarez de Zamosa, you're under arrest for smuggling and receiving stolen property. You schmuck!"

Twenty-seven

One of the men handcuffed Miguel and led him away. Mimi, meanwhile, was trying to talk me into getting up off the floor and following her outside. By now we were quarreling in low voices, conscious of the stares of other agents.

"I like those jackets," I said, gesturing at hers. "The ones with 'Customs' on the back. I want one."

"*Caramba, loca!* We're from Customs, not the Salvation Army."

"I want one," I repeated. "A nice, long one."

She didn't get it, and who could blame her? I was willing to bet that the one health condition *bubbes* and *abuelitas* gave short shrift to was menopause.

She heaved an exaggerated sigh, turned on her heel, and stomped off. Gerstley stood there looking at me, face frozen in an expression of blank amazement.

"Did you know about her?" he whispered at last.

"No, of course not," I said. "In fact, if I were guessing what her profession was, law enforcement would be pretty far down the list. But what the hell are *you* doing here? What is this place?"

"It's a space I rent to store artifacts."

"Nice neighborhood," I observed.

"I'm an art professor," he pointed out. "I can't afford Hyde Park."

Mimi returned with an oversize jacket, which I struggled into. Then she helped me up.

My backup was outside, shooting the breeze with a couple of Cincinnati cops who'd shown up to watch their cohorts in action. Must've been a slow crime night; all the criminals were as hung over as I was. I got most of my information from Mel, who learns a hell of a lot more by being quiet than I ever will from being nosy.

"The Customs people have had Gerstley under surveillance for a while," she told me. "See, he's such an expert that he does consulting work for museums and galleries all over Latin America and the U.S. He travels a lot, but people also ship things to him—either because they need them identified or because he's curating an exhibition. Funny, isn't it? Al says he's real reserved."

"*Reserved* is a euphemism for what Gerstley is," I said.

"Well, anyway, some valuable artifacts have been disappearing from different sites in Mexico—a Mayan dig in the Yucatan and an anthropological museum in Mexico City. I gather that the Mexican authorities contacted Customs because they suspected that some of these artifacts got shipped to him. I don't know whether he's involved or not."

"It was the other guy they slapped the cuffs on," I reported. "Miguel something."

"So does that mean Gerstley's clean?" she asked.

"I don't know," I confessed. "But he was arguing with Miguel. And Mimi walked away and left him standing there, so I guess she wasn't worried that he was going to bolt."

"That's unlikely, if he really loves the artwork and isn't just in it for the money," Mel speculated. "He'd want to stick around and make sure the Customs agents didn't break anything."

"You have a point."

"So I gather that the crates weren't full of Rookwood after all," she said.

"No, I guess not." I sighed.

"Look on the bright side, Cat," Mel said on the way home. "You've just eliminated two murder suspects."

"I suppose so," I said dejectedly.

The next afternoon Mimi and Gerstley were sitting in my

living room. To be more precise, they were sitting side by side on the couch, knees touching, holding hands. It was cute, but utterly bewildering. Just when I'd decided that Mimi was playing up to Gerstley for investigative purposes, she'd surprised me again.

"As soon as I got to know him, I knew he couldn't be involved," Mimi was saying. "It was his graduate assistant, Miguel Suarez. He was a plant—part of a ring that included an employee of the Museo Antropológico and a worker at the Yucatan site. What they'd do is, they'd hide relatively small pieces inside a legitimate shipment to Gerstley."

"I supervised all the unpacking, though," Gerstley put in. "That's what gets me. The bastard made a copy of my key, went down there and unpacked shipments to remove the stuff that wasn't legitimate, and repacked the crates and boxes! So when I was supervising what I thought was the unpacking, it turns out he'd handled all the stuff already! If I ever get my hands on him—"

I gaped at him. This was a whole new side of his personality: Gerstley the Avenger.

Mimi patted his knee. "He had to be pretty careful, *querido mío,* or he would have aroused your suspicion."

"But he did arouse my suspicion, damn it!" Gerstley exclaimed. "I'd had some minor breakage in the last six months, and I couldn't account for it. These days you ought to be able to ship anything anywhere, properly wrapped, and be pretty confident of its safe arrival. If we didn't have that kind of security, we wouldn't be shipping such irreplaceable artifacts to begin with. So I was seriously troubled by the damage. But I never suspected Miguel, because I thought, of course, I'd watched him open every crate and unwrap every piece. Besides, he was one of the best graduate assistants I'd ever had—smart, knowledgeable, experienced, and willing."

"You're too trusting, boychik," Mimi said, smiling at him

affectionately. "Miguel was a *gonif* who knew just how to play up to you."

"So tell me about last night," I said. I'm all for young love, but if I wanted it in my living room, I'd turn on *The Young and the Restless*.

"I received an anonymous call," Gerstley replied. "A muffled male voice told me that the light was on in my warehouse. Well, at first I thought it was a crank call. Then I thought, 'Gee, I must've left the light on.' But it bothered me. So eventually I did what they wanted me to do: I went down there."

"And fell right into my little trap." Mimi winked at me. "We had the place bugged. We could have moved in and arrested Miguel, but we needed evidence that Gerstley wasn't involved."

"I can't believe she set me up," he wailed. But he didn't look too unhappy.

"Anyway, even though we had Carlos Ibarro there from the Museo Antropológico, we wanted Gerstley's help if he wasn't involved," Mimi said. "We were there until three in the morning, cataloguing all the pieces.

"But we nearly lost the whole operation when you showed up, Cat. *Chica!* What were you doing there?"

"Looking for a lost collection of Rookwood," I confessed. And told her the whole story.

"But I would never have blown my cover if it hadn't been for you!" I said.

"What do you mean? I had to go in to protect you!"

"Yeah, well, next time you show up to protect me, bring your gun and leave your perfume at home!"

"I thought I did!" she said, crestfallen. "You could smell it?"

"Ask Gerstley," I retorted. "He sneezed first."

Gerstley looked utterly uncomfortable.

"Can you smell it now?" she asked anxiously.

I sniffed. I could, but it was faint—too faint to provoke a sneeze. And suddenly something else fell into place for me.

"That's why you left the lecture!" I said to Gerstley accusingly. "Someone thought you had a cold, but it was Mimi's perfume!"

His face turned the color of tomato sauce. He looked stricken.

Mimi laughed. "Oh, Cuz, it's okay! I already figured that out. That's why I covered for you. I knew you'd be embarrassed if you had to explain the real reason you walked out. Here the poor guy's recovering from some tropical bug he brought back from the Yucatan last month, and he's got allergies on top of that! So I really have gone cold turkey on the perfume." She sniffed at her wrist. "But I guess it takes a while to wear off. Anyway, I never wear that much normally—it's against department regulations."

Mimi was intrigued by the developments in the murder case.

"My boss calls up the day it was on the news about the body in the kiln," she said. "He wants to know who we rubbed out, and why we torched the body. 'Boss,' I said. 'I got nothing to do with it, *lo juro,* on my grandmother's grave, may she rest in peace.' But that murder investigation didn't make things any easier, I can tell you. You had to wonder whether Suarez was involved."

"So Brenda inherits this dead lady's money," she went on after a rare nanosecond of silence. "*Hija! Qué cosa*, no? You think she'll get enough out of it to start her own art center?"

"Don't know," I confessed. "She'll probably collect insurance on the house, but who knows if it will cover the cost of the repairs. I just wish I knew the connection between her and Lottie."

"Could be anything, really," Gerstley offered helpfully.

Mimi stood up, hauling Gerstley to his feet.

"Well, Cat will figure it out.

"Come on, *amado.* You promised me a tour of the pre-Columbian collection at the Art Museum. And you know how it turns me on to hear you talk art." She winked at me.

She dragged him to the door, where he turned back for one final word.

"Meshuggeneh," he said, and was gone.

Twenty-eight

"So Thanksgiving is what—three weeks away?" I said dejectedly. "I'd just like to have something to be thankful for when we pray over the turkey and vegetarian lasagne."

I'd wandered up to Moses' apartment, where a football game was on and the beer was cold. It was halftime, and Moses was pretending he wasn't interested in the halftime show.

"I've looked for that damn Rookwood collection in two perfectly good places—Gil Forrester's apartment and Gerstley Custer's warehouse. And it wasn't in either."

"No, but you found a dead body, or what was left of it, and a shipment of smuggled artifacts," Moses said. "Most detectives be happy with that."

"Well, excuse me for my ignorance and inexperience," I replied, a little snippily, "but I was under the impression that a detective's first obligation is to the guy that's paying the bill. I thought I was supposed to be getting results for my client, not for the Cincinnati P.D. or the U.S. Customs Service."

"Who's your client?" he asked in surprise. "The Cultural Arts Center? I don't recollect that they asked you to horn in on the police investigation. And I surely don't think they planning on paying any bills."

"I'm doing it for their own good," I said, falling back on the formulas of motherhood. "They'll thank me for it some day. And I'm not asking them to pay the bill. It's—what do you call it?—pro bueno work."

"Pro bono," he corrected automatically, sneaking a peek at the bouncing, buxom halftime entertainment. "You been hangin' with Mimi too much lately, girl."

"Anyway, I wish I knew why Lottie's house got torched," I said. "That's another mystery. Did somebody remove something from it? Something so obvious that the next of kin would notice it was missing? Or did they look for something and not find it, and then torch the house in case it was there for somebody else to find? Or did they search the house carelessly and then burn it down to cover up the fact that a search had been made?"

"You were there, Cat," Moses pointed out. "What did you see?"

"Not a thing," I admitted. "Not a goddam thing. Just a nice comfortable old house, lace cloth on the table, and family photos on the end tables—that kind of thing."

"Well, then," he said, scratching Winnie's ears, "didn't nobody make what you're calling a careless search, or you would've seen signs. Unless the searching was confined to the third floor."

"Where I didn't see anything but stars." I sighed. "And speaking of next of kin, was Brenda Coats really related to Lottie? If she was—"

Moses nodded. "You right, Cat. Most murders are committed by family members."

"Say, Moses, you been talking to Arpad? You know if they've had those pottery fragments analyzed yet? The ones from the Olmstead house?"

"I wouldn't know," he said. "Why don't you call and ask him?"

We watched a beer commercial in silence. Obviously the company had no interest in selling to white-haired menopausal grandmothers.

"You go out with Charisse last night?" I asked.

He nodded.

"Where did you go?"

He groaned. "Opera."

"I thought you didn't like opera!"

"I didn't," he agreed. "Still don't. Was about this Spanish chick, but they were singing in French. Don't ask me why."

Moses is more sophisticated than he pretends, so this was his way of registering disapproval.

"Better than ballet," I observed.

"That's where we going next weekend," he said morosely.

"Moses, are you sure this Charisse is your type?"

He bristled. "Didn't know I had a 'type.'"

I didn't say anything for a minute. Then I said, "You ask her over to watch the game with you today?"

He shot me a look.

Case closed.

Twenty-nine

On Monday I called Dan Pratt and asked him whether he'd completed his analysis of the pottery fragments found in the rubble at the Olmstead house. I figured, why bother the police when you don't have to?

"Yes, I have, in fact," he replied, lowering his voice as if our topic were international espionage. "It was really interesting, Cat."

"And—?" I prompted him.

"Well," he said. "There were some Rookwood pieces destroyed by the fire, no doubt about it. I even saw a few shards which showed parts of the Justice Collection monogram."

"Oh, hell!"

"But, Cat," he continued, "in my humble expert opinion, the Justice Collection in its entirety could not have been in that house when it burned."

"Oh?"

"Most of the fragments were from considerably less distinguished pieces than we've been led to expect from the Justice Collection. A lot of them were production ware. I'd say that at most we have fragments from two higher quality pieces, but that's simply not enough. And then—" He paused dramatically. "There was the ink."

"What do you mean?"

"It seemed to me that the purple ink from the monogrammed shards didn't match our sample—that there were two distinct shades. I didn't know enough about chemistry to say whether the fire could have done that, though I supposed it could. House fires don't burn evenly, you know, so I imagined it was possible that the uneven heat could account for the difference in coloration. It was also possible that Nellie Justice could have used two different inks—a new brand when the first one ran out. But I suggested that Lieutenant Arpad have the ink tested. He did. It wasn't the same ink—by a good seventy years!"

"You're kidding!"

"I'm not! The ink on one shard was considerably older than the ink on the others, though the monogram appeared identical. So of course the lab took a closer look at the owner's marks as well. They weren't the same, either."

"But that means—" I sputtered.

"Yeah," he said. "Somebody went to a lot of trouble to persuade everybody they should stop looking for the Justice Collection."

So the Justice Collection was presumably alive and well, and in the hands of some unscrupulous, possibly homicidal, person with the kinds of contacts necessary to dispose of a stolen collection of art pottery. The same person who'd knocked me over the head and burned down the Olmstead house. That meant there was one more logical place to look for it—unless it had been crated up and shipped to Latin America inside a legitimate shipment of antiquities. I didn't think it had.

I'd need some help on this one. I called around and made the necessary arrangements, then sat twiddling my thumbs till school let out. I turned on the television, but between soap operas and campaign commercials, I couldn't find anything I could bear to watch. So I picked up the Mary Roberts Rinehart I'd been reading—one of those mysteries in which the detective is a spunky older woman. I could really relate, as my daughter Franny would say.

At four forty-five I stood in front of Parker Gallery. In one hand I held a leash. Attached to the other end of the leash was one of the largest, clumsiest dogs I'd ever had the misfortune to meet—a dog named Junior acquired by my friend Louella during my last case. At the moment he was standing on my foot. Stuck to the other hand was a pint-sized garbage dump, my grandson Ben. He was wearing a ripped T-shirt liberally splashed with Kool-Aid, and brown corduroy pants with an unidentifiable yellow substance ground into both knees. His hair was matted, his face sported a contrasting Kool-Aid stain and a Mickey Mouse Band-Aid, and his nose was running. He was chewing on a plastic dumptruck. To Ben's left was Leon, who maintained a firm grip on Ben's T-shirt, though whether to keep Ben out of trouble or to steady himself was not immediately apparent. His hightops weren't laced all the way up, and four shoelaces dragged the ground.

We all tried to squeeze through the door at the same time. Junior edged the rest of us out by a nose. Ben left a small, sticky red handprint on the glass door.

Todd, Parker's assistant, shot up from behind his desk like a salmon and hurled himself at us.

"You can't bring them in here!" he sputtered. "You'll have to leave!"

"Grammy, he didn't say please." Ben studied him disapprovingly, one finger up his nose.

"Excuse me?" I said, giving Junior just enough leash to sniff a brass coatrack within striking distance of the display window.

"I'm sorry," Todd said sternly. "No animals, no children." He contemplated Leon as he tried to come up with a rule that applied to teenagers as well.

"Oh, he's not a child," I replied genially. "My grandson's just short for his age. And Junior here is his seeing-eye dog."

Hearing his name, Junior wagged his tail, thwacking a tall porcelain umbrella stand and causing it to rock. Todd dived for it and caught it on the way down.

"Is Mr. Parker in?" I asked. I knew he was; I'd had Louella call and make an appointment to show him a set of vases she'd inherited from a missionary great-aunt.

But Parker was already bustling toward us from his private cubbyhole.

"Mrs. Caliban!" he cried. "What is all this?"

"Oh, Mr. Parker!" I said. "I'm so glad you're here. Leon's been studying China in school. You remember Leon, from the Arts Castle beaux arts ball?" I watched as it registered on him who Leon was and just how much destruction Leon had left in his wake. "Anyway, I was telling him about all the nice Chinese porcelain you had, so I brought him down to show him."

"Chow m-mein," Leon intoned, getting into his role.

"Mrs. Caliban," Parker scolded, "you can't expect to bring a dog and a small child into a shop like this with so many breakable items."

"Oh, but I do!" I insisted. "If we leave Junior in the car, he barks his head off, and if we leave Ben in the car, he honks the horn."

"Honk, honk!" Ben bellowed.

I gave the leash a little more play, and Junior responded to Ben's racket by leaping at him, barking loudly. Junior's tail continued to sweep a two-foot arc. I inched forward, dragging my entourage with me.

"Mrs. Caliban," Parker protested as Todd scurried to move a lacquered table of porcelain bowls out of Junior's vicinity. Parker smiled at me patronizingly. "I really doubt you have enough funds to cover the breakage even if we allowed your little friends to look around."

He didn't get it yet. Have you ever noticed how willing people are to believe that once your hair turns white, your brain cells are shot? Not that Parker didn't have his own share of gray, but he no doubt thought that on him it looked distinguished; on me, it was simply a mark of dottiness.

"I know you're right." I sighed. "You'll have to sue me and I'll have to declare bankruptcy. And in the meantime, all your lovely pieces will be gone. Oh, it makes my heart race, just to think about it! Better get the bag ready, Todd!"

I swayed a little for dramatic effect and stumbled toward a locked glass cabinet full of vases.

"Look out!" Leon shouted, flailing his arms wildly, and knocking his elbow into a tall chest. On top, two brass figurines toppled over. One fell to the floor, where Junior picked it up. He growled at Todd's attempts to retrieve his prize.

Parker got it. He went white as porcelain.

"You wouldn't!" he gasped.

"Try me," I said.

In the silence that followed, as Parker struggled to decide whether to call my bluff, Ben piped up.

"Grammy, I got to go the the bafroom!" he wailed, peeling his hand off mine and clapping it to his crotch. He was now anchored only by Leon's tenuous hold on his T-shirt.

Parker looked at Ben and recognized how little stood between him and total annihilation.

"What do you want?" he whispered.

"I think you know," I said.

"I have no idea," he said.

"Leon, take Ben back to the rear of the store," I said. "There's a bathroom through that door in the back."

"What do you want?" Parker repeated, moving to block Leon's passage.

"The Justice Collection."

"The Justice Collection?" He frowned. "Whatever would I be doing with the Justice Collection?"

"But you know what it is," I said, narrowing my eyes. "Last time I was here, you didn't seem to know—didn't even recognize the monogram."

"I'm gonna pee my pants," Ben announced.

"Well, I didn't remember it at the time," he said. "Remember, I didn't claim to be a Rookwood expert. But the police have mentioned it to me since then—Lieutenant whatshisname, Arpad."

We stared at each other.

"Grammy, can I pee in that pot?" Ben pointed to a large round vase, conveniently placed on the floor and about the right height.

"Sure, honey, go ahead," I told him. Then I bent down to Junior's collar and fingered the catch on the leash.

"All right, all right, damn it!" Parker caved in ungraciously. "Todd, for God's sake, take him back to the rest room." To me, he said, "Maybe I don't have the collection, but I know where it is."

"I know where it *was*," I said, "so I'm hoping that its current resting place is more fireproof. And don't try to give me any bullshit about the hired help! You're not the trusting type. Nobody as crooked as you are ever is. *You* went into the house, *you* removed the collection, and *you* burned the place down after planting some evidence that a crossing guard could see through. *And* you bashed me over the head! You bastard!"

"H-h-he the one busted your h-head, M-miz Cat?" Leon asked and turned on Parker. "You b-b-bastard! You b-better not m-mess with M-miz Cat no more!"

Junior barked ferociously, putting in his two cents on my behalf.

Parker closed his eyes as if he had a very bad headache.

"Could you please remove that beast from the premises now?" he said.

"Maybe you'd better take him outside, Leon," I agreed.

"Okay," he said and shook his fist at Parker, "b-but I b-b-better not catch you m-messin' with M-miz Cat!"

And with that he stumbled backward over his shoelaces. Junior broke his fall, and they departed without so much as a chipped cup to their credit.

Leon sketched a wave as they passed through the door. *"Chow,"* he said. *"Sayonara."*

Most people don't think of Leon as a dangerous kid. Most people think of him as friendly, helpful, and polite. *Dangerous* is a word they might more readily use to describe Leon's three older brothers, who were all bodybuilders. But Leon, in his own way, posed a threat to be taken seriously.

Todd had thoughtfully decided that we needed some privacy and was keeping Ben entertained out back. Maybe he'd found a few unredeemable casualties for Ben to finish breaking.

"I think I know where the collection is," Parker resumed, collapsing into the chair behind the desk. I pulled another chair closer and sat down. The chairs together probably cost more than all the furniture in my apartment.

"Yeah, right," I said. "You have this friend who has a problem."

"You can't prove I was ever in the house," he said evenly. "As a matter of fact, I wasn't."

"Got a good alibi, have you?"

He pursed his lips. "I don't see why it should come to that. I have an acquaintance—not an employee, you understand, but a business associate to whom I'd happened to mention something. You see, the dead woman, Mrs. Gambrel, had called me to ask whether I could appraise a collection of Rookwood."

"She knew it was Rookwood?" I interrupted.

"Apparently," he answered. "Difficult to imagine that one could live in this city for any length of time and not recognize the Rookwood logo."

I bet I could round up a few thousand, but I let it pass.

"She said it had been stored in an attic for years, along with other things belonging to her grandmother."

"Her grandmother!" I ejaculated. "Was her grandmother an Olmstead?"

"I have no idea." He frowned.

"Right," I said. "Provenance doesn't interest you."

"Not at that point it didn't," he said snippily. "Until I see what I'm dealing with, I don't care whether the grandmother is a Taft or an Olmstead or a Smith. I don't take on many of these grandmother's attic cases; ninety percent of it is junk, and very little of the remaining ten percent is Chinese. But she did mention an odd purple mark on the bottom of all the pieces. I admit that intrigued me."

So he was back to confessing he knew all about the Justice Collection.

"I'm not a Rookwood specialist, as you know," he continued. "But to find a collection like that, of such high quality, intact after all these years—well, who could resist? She proposed to meet me after the lecture and show me a piece or two from the collection."

"And?"

"She never showed up," he said. "I expected her to approach me at the reception. I even popped into the pottery studio at one point on my way to the rest room. The lights were on, as I've already told you, but there was no one there."

"Uh-huh," I said. "So you decided to pop over to her house a few nights later, steal the collection, and burn the place down. Seems kind of a drastic payback for a missed appointment."

"I keep telling you, that was not I," he insisted. "My—associate—remembered the story when he heard about the remains in the kiln on the news Saturday morning. He drew his own conclusions—conclusions which I must say I considered extremely far-fetched when he finally got around to sharing them with me. But by that time the burglary and—all the rest were a fait accompli."

"'All the rest' is called arson," I put in helpfully. "It's a felony offense."

"That's what I told him," he countered. "I also pointed out

that if he got caught, he would no doubt become a leading murder suspect, since by the time I learned what he had done, we knew the identity of the victim and knew that he had guessed right. I advised him to take his story to the police, but he refused. Needless to say, he became even more reluctant to go to the police after Forrester was killed. Instead, he offered me a generous commission to sell the collection."

"How nice for you. Congratulations."

"Yes, well, I suppose that's all water under the bridge now," he said glumly. "Unless you'd be amenable to a partnership?"

I shook my head. "No way. I don't take on partners I don't trust, much less phantom partners. You want to know what I think happened? Here's what I think. Maybe you killed Lottie, maybe you found her dead. I'm kind of sketchy on the details there. But I think you cremated her. And I think you, Arthur Alexander Parker, not some asshole associate, not elves or Elvis, but *you*, you went to her house, knowing that she wouldn't be around to disturb you because of the aforementioned cremation. You stole the Justice Collection and torched her house."

"You'll never prove it," he said.

"I don't have to," I said. "The crime lab will. You'd be amazed what they can do these days with microscopic evidence."

That got his attention. He plucked nervously at his beard.

"My acquaintance was extremely careful," he said.

"Maybe," I conceded, "but he doesn't know jackshit about burning down a building. He wanted to destroy all the evidence in the attic, so he started the fire there. He got a lot of bang for his buck, because the roof collapsed. But your professional arsonist knows that fire burns up, and that means no arsonist worth his reputation will start a fire in the attic alone. The Olmstead house may look pretty bad from the street, but there's more of it left than you'd think. That provides the lab technicians with a lot to work on."

"My acquaintance was extremely careful," he repeated. "However, I might be able to persuade him that it would be in his best interest to return the collection, anonymously, as it were." He sighed.

I shook my head. "Anonymously, as it were, is not good enough. Christ, Parker, you think I'm the only one who can figure this stuff out? Arpad is going to be right on my heels. You may be the leading expert at deceptive and fraudulent transactions in the art world, but you're strictly bush league when it comes to breaking and entering, burglary, and arson. And, as you so perceptively point out, there's now a second set of ashes to account for. If you've burned anything in the past two weeks, you'd better start worrying."

He sighed again. "Perhaps I should consult my attorney."

"Good idea," I agreed. "This is Monday. If I don't hear by Friday morning that you've returned the collection, I'll call Arpad and tell him what I know."

"Forgive me for pointing it out," he said evenly, "but you don't *know* anything."

I laughed. "Friday morning," I repeated.

He nodded and went to call Todd. Todd carried Ben through the gallery and received a sticky kiss for his trouble. He already sported red handprints on both cheeks.

At the door Parker said, "You wouldn't happen to know who the Justice Collection's new owner is, would you, Mrs. Caliban? I'd still hope to handle its sale."

"I do," I said. "Brenda Coats."

His face registered shock. "Brenda?" he echoed. "But why?"

"Does it matter?" I asked, studying his face.

"No," he admitted glumly. "Ah, well."

Leon had Junior's leash wrapped around his legs like a maypole streamer. He was perusing Parker's front window.

"My Aunt B-Bertha got a b-bowl look just like that one," he told me, pointing to a porcelain beauty perched on a small pedestal. "She k-keep her teeth in it at night."

Thirty

"So, do you think Parker is our killer?" Al asked.

She and Mel were raking leaves when I got home. Kevin, who had the night off, was watching and kibbitzing, but refused to help because it was against his principles. He insisted that the leaves should not be raked until the maple just the other side of my property line dropped all of its leaves, which would happen in the next two weeks. In Kevin's view leaf raking was not a project to be undertaken twice. Me, I couldn't see the point of doing it once. One stiff wind and all your leaves ended up in your neighbors' yards, and all their leaves ended up in your yard anyway.

"Not really," I admitted. "If he'd left me in the Olmstead house when it was burning, then I'd take him more seriously as a murder suspect."

"If he'd left you in the Olmstead house when it was burning, you wouldn't be around to take anybody seriously," Mel pointed out.

"The situations could have been entirely different, though, Cat," Al said. She was raking everything into neat little piles, going after every last leaf. A breeze was blowing, dropping leaves on her tidy strips of lawn. It teased her piles and picked up little eddies of leaves and pine needles. "I mean, he could have killed Lottie in the heat of the moment, so to speak."

Al said, "He probably did kill Lottie that way, since he used your pot. Obviously he didn't bring a murder weapon with him, and he couldn't count on finding one there."

After a brief silence I ended it. "Unless he knew my work." They'd all wanted to say it, but had held back. "Which he—or she—could have done if they were in our class."

"Any of them could have done it," Kevin volunteered.

"Brenda inherited, and she's sturdily built. Jan's slight, but she's strong."

"I can't see Frieda wielding a pot that size, though, can you?" Al asked. "She might be familiar with Cat's work, but I don't think she could lift that pot easily." As she paused to consider, Sidney streaked out from behind a bush and charged her pile, that maniacal look in his eyes that cats get sometimes. He landed in the middle of it, agitated it like a Mixmaster, and raced off, leaving leaves scattered everywhere.

"Are we eliminating Gerstley and Mimi from contention?" Kevin asked, at least in part to distract Al. "Because I bet both of them could have done it."

"If this were an Agatha Christie mystery, it couldn't be them because they're young and in love," I said. "But seeing as how it's real life, I don't think we should grant them immunity. I assume college professors and Customs agents commit their share of murders." I stopped.

"Have we found out yet whether Brenda was related to Lottie?" Kevin asked. "That's the part that intrigues me. I mean, we didn't know Lottie at all, and we don't know Brenda well, but they seem such an unlikely combination."

I thought of my own relatives. "They must have been related, then; that's the only explanation. Is that my phone?"

"Moses will get it," Mel said. "He's working on your sink."

In that case I didn't want to go in my house at all. He'd have everything that lived under the kitchen sink spread out on the kitchen floor. Who knew what was under there? Probably some rotten zucchini and desiccated eggplants left over from gardening season. Brillo pads from ages past. Screws and hooks and other unidentifiable doojiggers I'd found when I moved in and was saving until I figured out where they belonged. Socks that had vanished into a black hole in the washing machine and come out under the sink. I shuddered.

"Cat! Phone!" Moses called.

The voice on the other end was breathless. "Cat, we've had a brainstorm!"

It was Constance Petty. I heard Malvina's voice in the background, giving me that stereo effect you always got with them.

"I'll tell her!" she said. "It was Malvina's idea. You know how hard it is to track prostitutes. But Malvina thought of another group that might be easier to track."

Malvina's voice again.

"No, not that easy," Constance continued. "But marginally easier than prostitutes, and with a longer lifespan: musicians!"

I didn't want to dim her enthusiasm, but I wasn't trying to track a tuba player, I was trying to track a prostitute. And I didn't even know for sure whether I needed to track her anymore. I knew that the Justice Collection existed, and I knew where it was, more or less. Nellie Justice seemed moot.

But Constance was still talking. "You go see Alabama Toomey. He can tell you about Nellie."

"Who?" I said.

"Alabama Toomey. He played piano in the district in the teens. He wasn't allowed to play in a white house, but somebody told us they thought he knew her."

"And he's still alive?" I asked. I admit I felt a prickle of curiosity, if nothing else.

"Not just alive, he's still performing." A muffled voice, and then, "Yes, I'm telling her, Malvina. He performs Thursday nights at Cory's in Clifton."

"But that wouldn't be a good place to interview him," I objected. "Don't you have an address for him?"

"Not an address. We know he lives on Cutter Street, though, around West Ninth. You could probably ask around down there. People in the neighborhood would know him."

"He must be in his eighties," I said.

"Nearer ninety than eighty," she agreed. "And Cat: Malvina wants me to tell you that the deal is, you take notes and let us know what you find out."

"Sure you don't want to come with me?" I asked. I didn't want to be entrusted with a fact-finding mission on their behalf; I knew I wouldn't ask the right kinds of question.

"Hold on." There was a muffled consultation.

"Malvina will go with you," Constance told me. "Wait a minute, I'll put her on."

So Malvina and I negotiated. She wanted to make the trip today, since it was the only day on which the Historical Society was closed. She picked me up at four-thirty, and by five we were standing in a dimly lit, musty-smelling neighborhood bar, confronting an elderly black man who didn't look a day over seventy. He had bony shoulders and an expansive belly, as if everything had sunk to his middle. He had brown eyes the color of milk chocolate, a broad nose, and a bushy gray mustache bordered by deep clefts that ran between nostrils and chin when he smiled. He wore a dark suit that hung loose on his shoulders, a thin dark tie pulled loose.

We confirmed that he was Alabama Toomey.

"Alabama, Sweet Bama, Baby Bama, Bama, Jr., Albert Toomey, Jr—that's me, all right," he said in a slow drawl. "You ladies lookin' to get my autograph?"

"Naw, it ain't that, Bama," one of his cronies shouted from the bar. "They from the Census, come to find out if you dead yet."

"Naw, it ain't that, either," someone else put in. "They from the Internal Revenue Service, come to tell you you been overpayin' on your taxes, and how would you like 'em to pay back all that money they owe you?"

Toomey acknowledged all the hilarity with a smile. I was beginning to realize the wisdom of Constance and Malvina's decision to send Malvina only. Two white women, even if accompanied by a black one, would have aroused suspicion.

"Mr. Toomey, we want to ask you about somebody you used to know a long time ago," Malvina said.

"Well, now, my mem'ry gettin' kinda spotty," he answered, still smiling. " 'Long time ago' for a man of my years be kinda tricky to reconstruct."

"Why don't you buy him a drink, Miss Lady?" came one of the voices from the bar. "It might help him remember."

"Hell, why don't you buy us all a drink?" came the other one. "Help us remember, we help Bama."

"I thought you was drinkin' to forget," said his companion. "That's what you always tellin' me."

So we bought a round of drinks and sat down in a booth with Alabama Toomey. Malvina asked if she could tape record the interview.

"Don't do it, Bama!" advised one of the onlookers. "Next thing you know, why, you be hearin' that tape in court, and the judge be shakin' his head over you."

"Maybe they gonna put me on the radio," Toomey suggested. "I speak my mind, anyway—nothin' else to do at my age. Don't matter none to me who hears it."

Malvina turned on her small portable machine.

"I heard you started your musical career playing in houses of ill repute," Malvina began. I guess after a career of teaching young people, she couldn't bring herself to call them whorehouses.

"That's right," he agreed placidly. "Some of the best work I ever had. Educational, too."

"What year would that have been?" Malvina asked. "Do you remember?"

He nodded. "Yes, ma'am, that was in nineteen and fourteen, before the war—First World War, that was. I was seventeen years old, and I come home with a pocketful of money, every night of the week. Ten, fifteen dollars in change. That was a lot of money for a boy in those days. Man,

I was on top of the world! Bought one of those old crank washers for my mother—what you call them things? I bought it at Sears and Roebuck, Anthony Wayne was what it was called, because my mother, she used to say, come Monday, she say, 'I'm visitin' Anthony Wayne today. Y'all come on, and bring me your clothes.' "

"Did you always play at the same house, or did you move around?" I asked, intrigued.

"No, now, in them days, I played different places," he said. "I was young, didn't nobody know me yet, you know. I moved around."

"Did you know a madam named Nellie Justice?" Malvina asked.

He was drinking a shot of whiskey and a beer chaser. He drained the shot, then set the glass down carefully before responding.

"I didn't never play no white houses," he said. "Wasn't allowed. White citizens was all hot and bothered about white women consorting with colored men. Didn't seem to care none 'bout colored women with white men. But the other way 'round—they didn't like that at all." The lines in his face now looked like scars.

"But did you know her?" I persisted.

"Yes, I knew her," he said.

"Mr. Toomey, something that once belonged to her has just turned up again, and it's related to a murder case," Malvina said gently, sensing, as I did, the change in mood.

"Murder?" He frowned.

"I tol' you to keep clear of this, Bama." One of the bar buddies piped up. "You gonna land your ass in court for sure!"

Toomey ignored him. "What was it? This 'something' that belonged to Nellie?"

"Her collection of Rookwood," I said.

His eyes went soft and he looked down at his glass, then

moved it around a little on the table. "She always was crazy 'bout them vases," he said. "I always figured—" He broke off, as if suddenly conscious of his audience.

"A woman was murdered," I said. "There was a piece of Rookwood found at the scene, and we have reason to believe that the rest of the collection was in her house at the time. It had Nellie Justice's owner's mark stamped on the bottom of it."

He half-smiled. "Them purple scales of justice. I remember." Then, more seriously, "Who died?"

"Her name was Lottie Gambrel," Malvina told him. "She inherited the house from a cousin, Inez Olmstead, when Miss Olmstead died six months ago."

"So Inez died," he said slowly, as if trying to process all of the bad news we'd brought him. "And Lottie. She was a pretty thing when she was little. And spirited. She have Josie's looks, but her grandmother's temperament. Love beautiful things like her grandmama, too. And now she dead, too." He stopped a minute, and then looked up. "I'ma give you ladies a piece of advice: don't ever get too old. When everybody you knew is dead, and they children dead, and they grandchildren dead—" He paused for effect. "You too damn old."

I shivered. I made a mental note to ask my mother if she felt that way. Me, I could think of a whole bunch of people I wanted to outlive just to spite them.

"So you knew Lottie, too?" I prompted. "And Inez? What was their connection to George Street and Nellie Justice?"

He stared down at his beer. "It ain't my place to be tellin' what some folks might not want told. No, sir, it ain't my place."

"Mr. Toomey," I said, "we're trying to find out who killed Lottie Gambrel and another person, a young potter named Gil Forrester. We think it has something to do with the Justice Collection, but we're not sure. Lottie hadn't lived in the neighborhood very long, and nobody seems to know much about her. I can understand your wish to honor people's secrets. But if there's anything you can tell us that you think would be helpful, we'd appreciate it."

He shook his head sadly. "George Street was a long time ago. Don't even exist no more, 'cept in folkses' mem'ries. And ain't many of us left who remember that far back. Don't see how it could have anything to do with this here murder."

Malvina switched off her machine. We stood to go, and he stood to shake hands.

When Malvina took his hand, she said, "Mr. Toomey, I've spent nearly fifty years studying the history of the African-American community here in Cincinnati. After a while, you develop an instinct for what's important. I can't explain it, but other people who spend years doing research in libraries and archives understand what I mean. I have an instinct about this matter we've been discussing. I know that George Street was a long time ago, but the past has a way of living on. Slavery did. African language and speech patterns and ways of thinking did. My instinct tells me that these questions Cat is asking about Lottie and Inez and Nellie are important. I don't know why. I don't even know if they'll explain Lottie's death. But they are important."

He studied her earnest face for a minute.

"Well, Mrs. Deeds," he said finally, "I reckon there's things in the public record you could find, if you know how."

And having thrown down the gauntlet, he turned back to the bar for another shot.

Thirty-one

Okay, I admit I was curious. But I was also increasingly inclined toward the view that the distant past didn't have much bearing on Lottie's murder. She might have been killed for the Justice Collection, whether by somebody who wanted it or by somebody who wanted it to remain hidden I wasn't prepared to say, but I didn't think it mattered much how she came by it. I was much more interested in how Brenda Coats came by it, and whether she knew she was Lottie's heir, and when she knew it.

Something had been bugging me, though, and as I thought things over that night in the bathtub, Sidney looking on from the edge of the tub and a glass of wine resting on my chest, I figured out what it was. So much in this case led back, as it so frequently does in Cincinnati, to race. Inez and Lottie and Brenda were black; Nellie Justice, as well as the second murder victim and most of the suspects, were white. Nellie had been the original owner of the Justice Collection. My first question had been how a prostitute's art collection had come into the possession of a prominent family of moral reformers. But maybe there was a more important question, one Constance had raised earlier. How had that collection crossed that vast divide between black and white Cincinnati? There's a reason why the heart of the city is bisected by a street named Race.

If I was curious about Nellie, however, Malvina was obsessed. On Tuesday morning, before I'd even gotten my eyes open all the way, she called from the courthouse. She had something to show me, she said. I offered to buy her lunch.

We met at Rookwood Pottery in Mt. Adams, up the hill

from Eden Park and the Cincinnati Historical Society. The original pottery had been converted into a restaurant, where you sat inside the large cylindrical kilns to eat. Malvina had Constance in tow.

"Malvina's put everything else on hold," Constance told me. "We're giving Project Nellie top priority."

Malvina launched into her story. "Of course, there was little point in looking for Nellie's records—birth or marriage certificate, because 'Nellie Justice' probably wasn't her real name."

"And she could have been born before the courthouse burned down in 1884," Constance added, watching to see if I followed her.

I was hazy on the details of how, when, and why an angry mob attacked the courthouse in the 1880s, but I didn't want a digression, so I nodded.

"What we did find was this." With a flourish, Malvina produced two photocopies and laid them before me.

The first was a birth record for a Charlotte Miranda Justice, born 1930 to a Gabriel Abraham Justice and a Josephine Cecile Justice, née Washington, at General Hospital in Cincinnati. The second was a record of marriage, dated 1953, between Charlotte Miranda Justice and Thomas Edward Gambrel.

"Nellie was black?" I asked softly.

"Either she was, or her lover was, or both," Malvina said. "But I think she was passing. 'Miranda' was Inez's mother's name: Miranda Root Olmstead. So there was a family connection, and I'm guessing it was a blood connection. Nellie probably realized that she could make more money as a white prostitute than a black one, and—who knows?—command more respect."

"Remember, too, that the police arrested white prostitutes who were consorting with black men," Constance pointed out. "She could have avoided that by working in a colore house that catered exclusively to white men."

"Except that if she even walked down the street with colored gentleman friend, like Alabama Toomey, she woul have been picked up," Malvina said. "She looked white."

My eyes had filled with tears I tried to blink away. Goddam menopause, I thought; I never used to be this susceptible.

"What kind of a life must it have been for her?" speculated sadly. "A hard profession, and a dangerous one Pretending to be something she wasn't. Dan Pratt describe her as reserved. Hell, no wonder she was reserved! Sh couldn't afford many relationships with black men, coul she? I wonder how well she knew Alabama Toomey?"

"You saw his face when he talked about her, Cat," Malvin said. "What do you think?"

"I think he was in love with her," I said. "Do you believ that relationship was ever consummated?" I had a sudde thought and scanned the birth certificate again.

"Gabriel couldn't have been his, Cat." Malvina anticipate my concern and reassured me. "Toomey would have been to young. You know, Constance, I wondered at the time why h called her 'Nellie.' A man of his age and his backgroun should've called her 'Miss Nellie,' even if she was prostitute and even if she was black. He'd known her as quit a young man, and she would have claimed some prominenc as one of the leading George Street madams. It was obviou he respected her, so the 'Nellie' implied an intimacy that couldn't explain."

I set the two documents side by side. "This change everything."

"What do you mean, Cat?" Constance asked.

"Suppose the Olmsteads never bought the Justice Collec tion," I said slowly, working things out as I went along "Suppose there *was* a family connection between Inez Olm stead and Nellie Justice, and Inez was just keeping th collection for Nellie, because she had a house and a place to store it."

"It probably wasn't Inez," Malvina noted. "Inez was just a little girl when the district was closed down in 1917. It would have been her mother, Miranda."

"Anyway," I continued, "the point is, the collection still belonged to Nellie when she died, whenever that was, and to her heirs afterward. One heir was murdered. How many others are there?" I shook my head. "Shit, I've been making the same damn mistake everybody makes in this fucked-up society. I've been making assumptions based on appearances. I won't make it again. Now, when I go looking for possible heirs, I'll know—"

"It could be anybody," Malvina affirmed.

"Three cheeseburgers with fries?" The waitress's arrival lightened our mood.

I glanced around at the brick walls.

"Anybody else think it's hot inside this kiln?"

Thirty-two

"Well, I reckon it ain't no harm in tellin' you the story now, seein' as how you know about Nellie and the kids and all. Inez gone and left her house to Lottie, so don't seem like she was 'shamed to acknowledge the connection. And they all dead," Alabama Toomey said. "I been thinkin' on it, what's best to do. And I reckon if it be any help to Lottie, why, I owe her that—to tell the truth, I mean."

We were sitting in the same bar, same booth, twenty-four hours after our last visit. As far as I could tell, the bar didn't have a name, just a Hudepohl sign. Some of the same commentators were warming the same barstools as the day before. In fact, they looked as if they hadn't moved since the day before. But they didn't look any drunker, either.

Malvina and I exchanged glances.

"We only know about one child, Mr. Toomey," Malvina said. "We only found one birth record, and that was Lottie's."

"Well, you know, folks was kinda lax about those things in the district," he said. "It wasn't much better anyplace in the West End. What did the government need to know you was born for? It only brought trouble on down the line, that's what folks thought. You didn't go to the hospital in them days, why, you just called in the neighborhood midwife. And there in the district, the houses kept them midwives busy."

"So what's the connection between Inez Olmstead and Lottie Justice Gambrel?"

"Nellie Justice come from a place down in Georgia. My family, we come up from Alabama; that's how my daddy got his nickname, and I got mine from him. Anyway, Nellie had an older sister, name of Miranda. Miranda come up to Cincinnati lookin' for work, and after she was settled, Nellie come up, too. Only things didn't work out too good for her, not like they did for Miranda. Oh, Nellie was young and good-lookin', and I reckon she lost her heart to the first fancy man come sniffin' 'round. One thing followed another, like they do, and one day Nellie runnin' the most exclusive house in the district, with a sister married to Mr. Lucius P. Olmstead, colored newspaper editor and general mucketymuck and leader of the fight to close down the district."

He laughed and shook his head. "Life's funny that way, sometimes," he said.

"Now, Inez was one of Miranda's girls," he continued. "And Lottie was Gabriel's daughter, so Nellie was her grandmother. Gabriel and Inez was first cousins."

"Did Inez ever meet her infamous aunt?" I asked curiously.

"Oh, yes, they met. The sisters used to visit, but only when Mr. Olmstead was off editin' or crusadin' or some such thing. Miranda lost her first two children as babies, then Inez come along, so she just naturally got a lot of lovin', from her mama and her aunt, too. I reckon Inez figured when she died she could do somethin' for Nellie's granddaughter, kinda make it up to Nellie for the hard life she led. Her brother Richard had already died, and he didn't have no kids, and didn't never get on with her anyway. That's how I figure it."

"Had Inez met Lottie?" Malvina asked.

"Now, that I can't tell you," he said. "Last time I saw Lottie, she was a little bitty thing, just out of diapers. No, I lost touch with all them folks, long time ago."

"Did Gabriel grow up in the district?" I asked.

"No, you didn't keep children in the district if you could afford to send 'em away," he explained. "He lived with a family out in Loveland. Real nice family, had a little farm. Nellie paid his keep, went to visit when she could. He was happy there, and she wanted him to grow up happy."

"Who were the other children? Nellie's, I mean," I pursued.

He studied his empty glass before he spoke. "There was a

little girl born first, Rose was her name. That was before I knew Nellie. Nellie was only twenty, didn't have no money at the time. So she gave up Rosie for adoption. I believe it liked to killed her. It was different with Gabriel. He knew who his mama was, and she got to see him from time to time. She placed him with a nice colored family, like I said."

My ears tingled. "Was the family that adopted Rose black or white?"

He looked up at me, eyes tired. "I wouldn't know about that."

But he did know, I thought. And he won't tell me.

"Does the name 'Brenda Coats' mean anything to you?" I asked. "She's Lottie's beneficiary. Is she related to Lottie?"

"I wouldn't know that, either," he said.

Something else he was keeping to himself.

"That's two children." Malvina picked up the thread. "Were there others?"

He blinked hard. "There was one," he said. "But she died, a long time ago." The answer seemed wrung from him.

"Yours?" Malvina prodded gently.

He nodded. "Her name was Belle Charlotte Toomey. Charlotte—that was Nellie's real name, one she was christened with. I wanted it to be her first name, but Nellie said no, she didn't never like that name, so we picked 'Belle,' because it sounded like 'Nellie' and because it means 'beautiful' in French."

He reached slowly into his pocket and drew out a battered black leather wallet. He extracted a plastic case, and handed it to us. It was a formal family portrait: a proud young father, a heartbreakingly beautiful mother, and an infant.

"Was Nellie older than you?" I asked, knowing she must have been.

"Eleven years," he replied. "I was eighteen, she was twenty-nine, when the baby was born."

"What happened to Belle?" Malvina had put on her bifocals to study the photograph.

"Turn it over," he directed us.

Back-to-back with the family portrait was another photograph, this one of a pretty girl in her mid- or late-teens. She looked very like her mother, but more fragile, almost ethereal.

"That was taken two years before she died," he told us.

We just looked at him.

"Sickle cell," he said in a hollow voice.

Sickle cell. I didn't know much about it, but I thought it was one of those diseases that involved two parents who were carriers and a strong element of chance. What had Nellie ever done, I thought, to deserve such rotten luck? But the question answered itself: nothing. Luck was just that: luck. Nobody deserved to live the life she'd lived. Certainly not Nellie herself.

"What happened to Nellie?" I asked softly.

"She died in an influenza epidemic in January of 1919," he said, gazing at the family portrait we'd returned to him. "She died in a rented room in Loveland. Wouldn't even let the kids come near her. Didn't want them to get sick. But I was with her, at the end."

His voice dropped to a whisper. "Never expected to live long after that—a week, a month, a year. I couldn't imagine living without her. Sometimes, I still can't."

Thirty-three

"But why didn't Gabriel ever go back to the Olmstead house and collect his inheritance?" I asked Malvina in the car.

"Maybe he didn't know he had one," she replied. "He was nine when his mother died, and he lived in Loveland. Toomey lived in Cincinnati."

"But he saw Toomey later, or at least, Toomey once saw Lottie when she was little, so they must have kept in touch," I pointed out. "And Toomey knew about the collection, knew where it was."

"Maybe Gabriel was embarrassed to go knock on the door of an aunt he'd never seen and identify himself as the illegitimate son of a prostitute," she rejoined. "Or maybe his aunt was dead by the time he was old enough to do it, and he didn't want to confront his uncle. We can find out when Miranda died."

"I'm counting on you and Constance to find out a hell of a lot of things," I told her. "And fast. Got time for a strategy session?"

"Not now, Cat," she said. "I need to get to the polls and vote."

Election day! Shit! I pounded my fist on the steering wheel in frustration and hit the horn, to the obvious surprise and annoyance of a Buick in front of me. Nobody ever arranged things on my schedule! Not my kids, not my husband, not the rest of the world!

I dropped Malvina off, found my own polling place, and punched the ballot with a sinking heart.

I watched the returns that night with the same queasiness. Hyde had won easily, along with the rest of the city council incumbents. The best that could be said for the whole business was that it wasn't a presidential election year. I watched Hyde acknowledge his victory, flanked by his lovely wife, Laura, two daughters, and a son, James III. I turned off the set.

For the next several days Constance and Malvina bounced back and forth between the courthouse and the Historical Society, while I pursued my own inquiries. I interviewed so many people, by the end I was forgetting whose family I was asking about, and I'd get my cover stories mixed up. Newspaper reporter was my favorite one, but it didn't work with everybody, so sometimes I had to be an old schoolmate or just a genealogical busybody. You'd be surprised how much people are willing to reveal about their families. In fact, the crazier their families were, the more they wanted to talk. I got an earful of paranoid aunts, homicidal cousins, and sociopathic siblings. It's a wonder anybody's sane.

On Thursday Arpad called to tell me that Alex Parker had confessed to removing the Justice Collection from the Olmstead house for appraisal. He claimed to have been given a key by Mrs. Gambrel on the Monday before she died, and authorized to transport the collection to his home, where he could use his extensive private library for reference. He had not confessed to murder or arson, had in fact been reluctant to tell his story to the police for fear of becoming a suspect in those crimes. He claimed to have noticed some things which, in retrospect, convinced him that someone else had been searching the house.

Could that be true? I asked myself. Had more than one person gone traipsing through the house, plundering its treasures? Or was Parker cleverly acknowledging my own presence in the house, uncertain whether the police knew of my little escapade? I admitted that it was possible, even plausible, that someone else had been through the house, looking for something quite different from a set of hand-decorated nineteenth-century vases.

"Do you believe him?" I asked Arpad.

"Officially, I have to believe him until I can prove he's lying," Arpad said. "Between you and me, I hope the arson people can pin that on him, but it's going to be hard now that he's provided us with an explanation for any fingerprints we find. If we find 'em on a charred can of gasoline, though, that would do the trick."

Given Arpad's skepticism, I didn't see any point in reporting the story that Parker had told me, or in suggesting that he changed his story more often than he changed his underwear. I asked Arpad how the investigation was going in general, and he was fairly noncommittal. He asked me if I'd found out anything, and I was fairly noncommittal.

I called Constance and Malvina to give them a chance to complain about how hard this kind of work was, and to give them some encouragement. I put in some time in the library myself, down at the U.C. College of Medicine. Things went on that way until Sunday night, when we all agreed that we had just about all we were going to get.

What we didn't have was the proverbial smoking gun, and it seemed highly unlikely that we were going to get that.

So Monday morning found me planted in a plastic chair down at the Investigations Bureau, across a bruised Steelcase desk from Lieutenant "Rap" Arpad.

"I know who murdered Lottie Gambrel," I said. "And I know why. What I don't have is evidence."

He looked at me over a Styrofoam coffee cup, elbows on the desk. "I've got evidence," he said. "But I don't know who did it. Call."

So I laid my cards on the table.

"Suppose you were a successful white politician with a good chance of being the next mayor of Cincinnati. In fact, you were feeling so good about your career that you'd begun to talk, in private, of course, about a run for Congress. Suppose someone showed up one day and told you that you were the great-grandson of a black prostitute, and not only a black prostitute, but a woman who passed as white and ran one of the most exclusive whorehouses in the red light district of her day. And not only that, but according to this person, you were her second cousin, as well as first cousin to Brenda Coats, one of your most outspoken critics. Suppose this person said she could prove it. How would you feel?"

He regarded me impassively. "I'd say a successful black entrepreneur or two in my family tree would be a hell of a lot more respectable than a white slave-owner who beat his slaves and sold off his own illegitimate children. But I don't hold family against anybody, Mrs. Caliban. You can't choose your kin."

"You're not playing the game right," I objected. "I didn't ask how you, Lieutenant Arpad, would feel. I asked how a successful white politician with an eye on Congress and possibly—who knows?—the White House would feel."

"From what I hear, wouldn't be the first time we had African-American blood in the Oval Office, but I get your drift," he conceded. "If I were a white politician under those circumstances, I'd likely be upset. But if you're asking me if I'd kill somebody to suppress that kind of information—well, that seems a little far-fetched to me."

I gave him a minute of silence to think it over.

"Am I supposed to have known about this little wrinkle in my family history?" he asked.

"That's a good question," I said. "Let's say you knew, at least, that you had African-American blood."

"And how would I know that?"

"Oh, let's suppose you found out that you had sickle-cell trait," I said.

"Sickle cell?" He raised his eyebrows and shifted uneasily in his chair. "I don't like to hurt your feelings, Mrs. Caliban, but this story is getting wilder and wilder."

"Ten percent of the African-American population are sickle-cell carriers," I pointed out.

"But how would you even know if you were a carrier or not?" He looked uncomfortable. "Hell, I could be a carrier, couldn't I? It doesn't show up on routine blood tests."

"No," I admitted. The next part was tricky, and I didn't know if he'd buy it. "Nowadays, they screen newborns for sickle cell, but in the past, unless you requested a screen for it—like when you got married or thought about having children, you didn't find out you were a carrier unless you suffered some kind of rare condition that can affect people with sickle-cell trait."

"I've heard something about that," he said. "Keep going."

"As far as I can tell, the problems are most likely to show up in pilots and military recruits," I said, "and I think they all have to do with oxygen deprivation. There are some other possible signs, like blood in the urine, but since I'm writing this story, I'm choosing the oxygen deprivation plot. Let's say you join the Navy, and start training to be a Navy pilot. What would make you leave the training program after your first few high-altitude flights?"

"This is all speculation, right?" He cocked an eyebrow at me.

"I know he left the training program, and I know he always cites 'health reasons,'" I responded. "He's got this inspirational speech he gives, all about learning to deal with disappointment. The story ends with the heavily decorated hero coming home to his wife and kiddies after a tour of duty in Vietnam."

"So in this story you're concocting—" He leaned back in his chair, hands behind his head, elbows out. "Is Lottie Gambrel a blackmailer? Does she arrange to meet up with our future mayor at the Arts Castle and tell him to pay up or she'll give away his family secrets to the press?"

"That's one possibility," I agreed. "But on the other hand,

the worst thing anybody's had to say about Lottie is that her standards of cleanliness were too high and she did her job too well. Nobody seems to have known her very well, unless her friends and relatives have been contacting you?"

He shook his head.

"So maybe she had left town for a while, until she inherited the house in Northside, and only then found out," I suggested. "Anyway, it's also possible that she told him about his family because she genuinely thought he'd want to know. I mean, I'd just as soon forget most of my family, including my kids half the time, but family connections are really important to some people. Or maybe she offered him a share of the proceeds from the Justice Collection, except that she probably didn't know how valuable it was. Or maybe she offered him part of the collection or some other memento of his great-grandmother."

"If so, then she should have made the same offer to Mrs. Coats," he said.

"Maybe she did," I said. "We'll have to find out. Or maybe she told Brenda that Brenda would inherit the bulk of the estate, and then decided she ought to offer something to our future mayor, even if it was just a token. She might not even have planned the encounter at all. If he'd had any prior warning, you'd think he would have picked a more efficient weapon. He did the second time."

His eyes were closed. He was trying to picture this bizarre scenario. "So she says, 'Guess what? Your grandmother and mine was a black prostitute and we're cousins and I can prove it,' and his political career flashes before his eyes, and he picks up your pot and hits her with it. I don't know." He opened his eyes. "Seems like he'd be the ideal candidate—a black moderate who thinks like a white man."

"I agree," I said. "The Republicans would probably offer him a vice-presidential slot if he'd switch parties. If you want my opinion, I don't think he was thinking too clearly. In fact,

I don't think he was thinking at all. I believe he reacted on an emotional level to something he didn't want to hear. The thing he'd always feared most appeared before him: a black relative. And it was worse than he'd thought, because Nellie had been a prostitute, which made his grandmother illegitimate."

"You white folks sure do obsess about some strange things," Arpad cracked. "So, anyway, he kills her, stuffs the body in the kiln, and disposes of his black relative."

"Well—" I said slowly. "I kind of like Parker for the role of pyromaniac. I think he found her dead, removed her keys, and burned the body to buy time so he could search her house for the Justice Collection."

"But what about Forrester?"

"I think the mayor followed Parker's lead on that. He'd heard about how Lottie's body had been destroyed in the kiln, and he recognized the possibilities for delaying discovery and obscuring the time of death. I never said he was dumb."

"But why did he kill Forrester?" Arpad started doodling on a pad in front of him.

"I think Forrester tried to blackmail him. I think he heard something the night of the murder and drew his own conclusions." I shifted and resettled. Damn, these chairs were hard! "I think he heard the mayor's beeper coming from the pottery studio, and later on he remembered that and decided to capitalize on it."

"But, wait, where does Brenda Coats fit in?" he wanted to know. He started sketching Nellie's family tree as I had represented it, with Nellie and Miranda at the top.

I handed him a chart I'd already drawn.

"Rose was Nellie's first child, and as far as most people know, Rose only had one child, the mayor's daddy. But I found a certain garrulous lady in her late seventies who confided, after three sherries, that Rose had a second child, a daughter, who was given up for adoption because, in her words, 'there was something wrong with the baby.' She didn't know what it was, only that it was something so scandalous that none of the older people would talk about it in front of the children. I'm guessing the baby was dark-skinned."

"But how could anybody track this family through all these adoptions?" he protested.

"Somebody kept track," I said simply. "Maybe it was Miranda's daughter Inez, or maybe it was Lottie. Or maybe each of them had a piece of the history and put it together. Nellie seems to have inspired a lot of loyalty in the people she was close to, so I think they'd have wanted to keep track out of respect for her memory."

"So let me get this straight." He leaned over and peered at me. "You want me to take to my boss this genealogical chart"—here, he dangled it in front of me—"and a speech about dealing with disappointment and ask please can we arrest the next mayor of Cincinnati, Jim Hyde?"

Thirty-four

"I told you I didn't have much," I said grumpily. "*You* were the one who said you had evidence. Well, what have you got?"

"Hell, I got a shitload of physical evidence—I just don't know who it applies to!" he exclaimed, waving an arm in exasperation. "Say I've got physical evidence that appears at both crime scenes. I can't go out and search the houses of everybody associated with the two scenes, especially with the Arts Castle, hoping to connect them to the evidence I've got. That's assuming it doesn't just mean that the second victim visited the first crime scene at some point in the last few weeks."

"Well, at least you can search his place," I pointed out. "Gil won't object. Oh, but the problem is you don't know if this evidence, whatever it is, was taken to the Castle by Gil, or if the killer brought it in from outside. But now I've told you who the killer is, can't you establish probable cause for search warrant?"

"Well, if this were the neighborhood crack dealer, yes, I probably could, but my luck doesn't run that way," he said, eyebrows bouncing for emphasis. "Far be it from me to shake your confidence in the criminal justice system, but it takes a hell of a lot more to prove probable cause to suspect the mayor of murder than to prove it against Joe Citizen."

"And I don't suppose you've got any fingerprints," I said glumly.

"One measley set of partial fingerprints," he admitted. "Not good ones, but it's something."

"Where'd you get that?" Didn't this guy watch prime-time television in between campaign dinners and town meetings?

"We lifted them off one of the Kevlar gloves by the kiln," he said. "They don't belong to any of the pottery students or teachers. I figure he looked around and spotted the gloves afterward, put 'em on to search her, or handle the body and kiln, or wipe down everything he'd touched. He either forgot that he put the first glove on with a bare hand, or he didn't think we could lift a fingerprint off it." He demonstrated with his hands.

I stared at him. "So what's the problem here? Go ask the man for his fingerprints. He's a board member of the center. You can explain it that way if you don't want to arrest him on the spot."

He sighed. "It's just not that simple when you're dealing with the mayor," he said.

"Okay," I said reasonably. "Call the Navy. They must have his fingerprints on file. They can probably also tell you if he has sickle-cell trait." I paused. "They wouldn't tell me," I muttered.

"That's a thought," he mused. "But I don't want you to get your hopes up," he added. "A good defense attorney can shoot holes in circumstantial evidence like shooting fish in a barrel. And I think we can rest assured that Jim Hyde will have the best defense attorney money can buy. Prosecutor may not even be willing to take the case to trial without better evidence than what we got."

Well, I hadn't exactly started my career in detection as Rebecca of Sunnybrook Farm. You don't sustain your innocence through three teenagers. And even if I had, Watergate and the proliferating revelations about J. Edgar Hoover would have soured my perspective. But more than a year and a half of closer acquaintance with the criminal justice system helped me understand why they called it that: the whole goddam justice system was criminal.

So it wasn't a big surprise when the days dragged on with no visible results. The future mayor's smile was just as bright a week after my meeting with Arpad as it had been before. And this despite the Navy's confirmation that the fingerprints were Hyde's, and that he was a sickle cell carrier who'd been transferred out of the pilot training program after several episodes of hypoxemia. I learned all this from Moses, who ran into Arpad at a P.D. basketball game.

"I don't understand all this sickle cell stuff too well, Cat," he told me later. "I mean, I know it's bad news if two carriers marry, but how sick can you get from being a carrier?"

"I don't understand it that well, myself, Moses," I said. "But you're right. If you're a carrier, and you marry another carrier—or I should say, if you just have kids with another carrier—your kids have a one in four chance of developing full-blown sickle cell anemia, because they inherit it from both parents, so it's like a double whammy. But carriers don't necessarily know they're carriers, because they aren't usually sick, except in rare circumstances. If the oxygen level in their blood drops, though, the hemoglobin cells which are carrying the trait will sickle just like they do in full-blown sickle-cell anemia. Sometimes it happens to military recruits who've just been exercising too hard."

"That so?" He pushed his recliner back to his favorite semirecumbent position and propped a beer on his stomach. "In that case I better not exercise too hard. Hand me that book over there on the coffee table, Cat."

"This one?" I asked dubiously, picking up a battered black leather-bound book about the size of an old Webster's dictionary. It looked at if it had been thrown out of a moving vehicle into a brushfire, and then rained on. I turned it over. It was a Bible.

"Arpad gave me that to give to you," he said. "They found it in the Olmstead house, on a first-floor bookshelf. Belongs to Brenda Coats now. He thought maybe you'd like to take it to her."

I opened it carefully, and something fell out. But before I

could bend to retrieve it, my eyes fell on the page before me: *Charlotte Mary Root, b. Macon, Georgia, 5 January 1887*, it said, in an elegant, old-fashioned hand. Added in a different hand was: *d. Loveland, Ohio, 17 January 1919.* There followed the names of Charlotte/Nellie's three children, Rose, Gabriel, and Belle, each birth recorded in the careful script of their mother, the marriages and deaths recorded in a different hand. In the next generation the second hand took over, although the handwriting deteriorated over time. They were all there: Rose's children, James Robert Hyde and Pearl Letitia (Hyde) Cormer, and Gabriel's daughter, Charlotte—Lottie Justice Gambrel. There were no children for Belle, just the date of her death at eighteen. Then the next generation: James Robert's son, James Robert, Junior, and a daughter, Susan; Pearl's daughter, Brenda Helen; and Lottie's son, John, who had died in 1979. Marriages were meticulously chronicled as well. The last births recorded were those of our future mayor's children, Margaret, Cecilia, and James Robert III.

I stooped, ignoring the crick in my back, and picked up the folded piece of thin paper, and a yellowed envelope. Unfolding the delicate paper carefully, I read:

> *My dear sister,*
>
> *As you have always been kind to me and mine, I am moved to impose upon your generosity once more. I have entrusted all of my earthly treasures to you, except for the ones I value the most highly—my children. I do that now, in the form of this good Book, which has often been my friend and consolation in my darkest hours. I wish it to have a more secure home than I can provide. Should I never return to claim it, I implore you to record here those events of greatest consequence to tracing the*

history of my small family, cast to the winds as we are. I wish Gabriel to have it, with his mother's love, when he is of an age to appreciate it. To Belle I bequeath my best emerald ring, to be given her on her wedding day with her mother's most affectionate wishes for health and prosperity. The rest of my property you must divide between the two children as you see fit, for much as I would wish to leave Rose a token of her mother's love, I know it to be unwise. Ever in your debt, I remain, your affectionate sister—

Charlotte

Inside the envelope was a small, slender ring, a large square-cut emerald and diamonds sparkling against a dull background of tarnished gold: a present to a daughter who never lived to see her wedding day. And wrapped inside a piece of tissue paper so thin and brittle that I feared it would disintegrate at my lightest touch was another gift: a lock of wavy black hair.

Yes, I thought. I most certainly wanted to talk to Brenda Coats.

Thirty-five

When I tracked her down at Brenda's Fashions in downtown Walnut Hills, she claimed to be as bewildered by events as I was. And I believed her. I watched as her beautiful violet eyes, surely a part of her grandmother's legacy, expressed shock, distress, and outrage, by turns.

She took hold of both ends of the tape measure she had draped around the neck and pulled it tight when I got to the part about Jim Hyde.

"You're not serious!" she exclaimed. She leaped to her feet and retreated a few steps, creating a minor whirlwind that stirred the brightly colored fabric hanging from the racks. "Cousins! You can't be serious!"

The implications were even harder to take.

"I never liked the man," she said, "but I never thought—" She trailed off.

She wept over her great-grandmother's Bible.

"Do you think Lottie was ever going to tell me, Cat?" she whispered, fingering the emerald ring. "I never had much family, I would have liked—" She narrowed her eyes. "I never had much family, and now that I've found them, they're all dead, except for the bastard that killed them. I don't suppose I can make a donation to the prosecution?"

So that was when I had to tell her. She took it more quietly than I thought.

"I know, Cat," she said bitterly. "He's got money and political clout, and he's white—at least in the minds of the powers that be. He'll never get what he deserves, will he?"

"No. But there might be a way," I said carefully, "to give him some of what he deserves. And I know some people who might be willing to help."

It was time to give up on the Old Boys Network, which we didn't have access to, anyway, and trust in the Old Girls. So we went to the Woman's City Club.

The room was a large, low-ceilinged church basement that looked like any other church basement. It was filled with long metal folding tables covered with the remains of box lunches. At one end of the room you could see a speakers table and a microphone, but you had to crane your neck to see around the thin posts apparently intended to supplement the rock on which the Christian church was founded. The room was filled with women, some dressed in power suits, others in fashionable dresses, all of them in hose. I'd had to stop at the Circle K to buy a pair so that I'd fit in. Otherwise, I fit in just fine; half the women in the room were my age or older.

"Anybody else hot in here?" I asked. "Or is it just me?"

Around the table a gratifying number of heads nodded.

This was the Woman's City Club, where Cincinnati's most interesting, interested, and influential women came on Fridays to eat lunch and hear informative, educational programming on everything from women's health to women's art to women's history, not to mention that perennial favorite, Queen City politics. By so doing, they were following a tradition of power lunching that began in 1915, three years before the restricted district had been closed down—an event not unconnected to the club's activity in the area of city planning and municipal reform. Not that these women were narrow-minded. There was a rumor that Emma Goldman had once addressed the club.

Now, two weeks after the election, the "new" city council members—who turned out to coincide with the old city council members, this being Cincinnati—had been invited back to the club to analyze the election and discuss what we could expect in the near future. To tell you the truth, I was surprised by the turnout. As candidates, all of the speakers had appeared at the club a month ago. Monday-morning quarterbacking the Cincinnati election results seemed to me an enterprise about as stimulating as speculating on the identity of the next Republican presidential nominee. Somebody could get up and say, "People vote for the names they recognize," and we could all go home. Maybe the crowd had something to do with my own little band of rabble rousers, who were strategically placed around the room.

I napped through the announcements, acknowledgments, and opening remarks by the council members, but when the question period arrived, Brenda Coats dug her elbow into my side.

"This is it, Cat!" she stage-whispered.

We still had to sit through a lengthy discussion of infrastructure before I was called upon.

"I have a question for Jim Hyde," I began genially. He smiled at me, and I smiled back. "Is it true that your great-grandmother ran one of the most exclusive brothels in Cincinnati?"

The smile froze on his face, and his rosy color betrayed his shock, dismay, and embarrassment. He laughed, a little too loudly and long.

"If so, this is the first I've heard of it, Mrs. Caliban," he said, and exchanged amused glances with his fellow council members.

"So Lottie Gambrel never told you about your great-grandmother before she was murdered?" I pursued.

Under control now, he favored me with a look of astonishment. "I'm afraid I never had the pleasure of a conversation with Mrs. Gambrel, on that or any other subject. In any case, I think this is hardly the occasion for discussing personal matters."

He looked to the moderator for help, and she called on someone else. Out of the corner of my eye, I saw an *Enquirer* columnist slip a notepad out of her purse, bang her pen on the table, and start writing.

After a spirited exchange about riverfront development, Brenda took the floor.

"I'd like to go back to Mr. Hyde's grandmother," she said. "Is it true that your grandmother was African-American?"

"I don't know where you're coming up with these absurd allegations," Hyde began angrily.

"Are you ashamed of your African-American heritage, Councilman?" Moses asked from somewhere behind me. (Yes, members of the opposite sex were welcome at Woman's City Club luncheons, and they didn't even have to wear hose.)

"I am *not* black!" he retorted vehemently. Then he seemed to take hold of himself. A sizable minority of the audience was black, and many, if not most, had voted for him. "If I were, of course, I would take pride in that. Now I really don't think we're here to discuss my lineage."

The columnist's hand moved in rapid jerks across the notepad. The poor distraught moderator called on someone sitting on the opposite side of the room from Brenda and me: Al, our legal representative.

Al stood up. "I don't want to discuss your family background, Mr. Hyde," she said disarmingly. "I'm interested in your military career. I believe you've often spoken of your disappointment in being forced to leave the Navy's pilot training program." She looked down at the table and fingered some papers in front of her, the way trial lawyers do when they're setting a trap. "You've cited 'health reasons' for that abrupt change in your training, but isn't it true that you had suffered the effects of sickle-cell trait during high-altitude flights? Isn't it true that the Navy tested you at the time and informed you that you were a sickle cell carrier?"

"What is this?" he demanded. "I didn't come here to be put on trial. I came to discuss the problems and needs of this city, and I will not be intimidated by these bizarre allegations!"

The room was abuzz, but if he was hoping for sympathy, he was out of luck. The Women's City Club was an open forum, and no one understood that better than the women in the audience. Some of them had been coming for fifty years. If a city council member got publically skewered at a Friday luncheon—well, it wouldn't be the first time. The columnist was writing so fast, her pen was smoking.

Now Kevin rose, up in front. "Gee, I don't know about the rest of you," he said boyishly, "but I'd kind of like to hear more from these ladies"—he gestured at us—"about what they're saying and where they're getting their information."

Heads nodded, including, I noticed, the columnist's.

"Oh, by all means," Hyde sneered. "I'd be very interested in hearing where they're getting their information." Now he was going to try and bluff his way out.

Brenda stood up, holding a black leather-bound book. "Why, I found it right here in our family Bible, *Cousin* Jim," she said acidly. "It was there on the bookshelf all the time—in the Olmstead house in Northside. The police found it after the fire. Your great-grandmother's niece, Inez Olmstead, recorded your whole family history here, right down to your children—Margaret, Cecilia, and James the Third."

"Now, I wonder," I said, rising to stand next to Brenda, "If you'd be willing to swear on your great-grandmother's Bible that you never spoke to Lottie Justice Gambrel on the night she was murdered, and she never told you she could document your family history."

"Mrs. Caliban," he said slowly, "are you accusing me of murder?"

"Certainly not, Mr. Hyde," I said. "My legal counsel advises me not to accuse you of anything I can't prove."

Thirty-six

"And then," Brenda reported, "all hell broke loose."

The occasion was the end-of-class potluck, moved from Saturday morning to Saturday night to encourage greater consumption of food and alcohol. The rule was that you had to eat off of something you'd made, so I was using one of my rectangular slab-built casserole dishes. Two of the sides had separated from the base during the bisque firing, but if you propped that end up with a fork, nothing fell out the bottom. I was saving my sunken cat bowls for dessert.

Student pots from the latest firing lined the shelves under the windows. But in the place of honor, at the head of the table, stood a stunning vase, vibrant red poppies exploding against a black background: *The Red Emma.*

"Wow! Wish I could've been there!" Ram enthused. His dinnerware was a perfectly round dinner plate, trimmed to perfection and beautifully glazed. "So did the cops arrest him?"

"Can't," Moses said, helping himself to another of Mimi's enchiladas. "Don't have enough solid evidence against him to take it to trial—yet."

"Even with a fingerprint from the gloves?" Jan asked.

Moses shook his head. "Defense attorney would say that proved he handled the gloves. Doesn't prove he killed Lottie, or even that he put her body in the kiln."

"He'll never hold elective office in this city again, though," Kevin mumbled around a hunk of Brenda's cornbread. "Or anywhere else."

"What made you think of Hyde, Cat, when you heard about the sickle cell?" Jan asked. "It could have been anybody."

"Stupid, really," I admitted. "But he avoided giving blood

on Halloween. No reason for him to have done that; they wouldn't have screened it for sickle cell, anyway. But it made me think he might be sensitive, at least, or paranoid, at worst."

"I heard he told the cops he'd kept his racial background under wraps because he didn't want his children to know they were African-American," Jan said.

"That's what he *said*," Brenda confirmed. "But Cat and I don't buy it."

"His kids are growing up in a different world. My guess is that they're not nearly as upset about it as he is," I agreed. "I just don't think he wants to admit it."

"So, Brenda," Gerstley put in, "I'm still not clear on this. Did you know Hyde was your cousin?"

She shook her head. "Not until Cat told me. My mother knew she was adopted, but she didn't know who her birth parents were, and she sure didn't know why they'd given her away. I didn't even know that Lottie Gambrel was my cousin, so I was floored when I heard I'd inherited. But I thought, well, maybe she'd heard about the Walnut Hills African-American Art Center, and she thought it was a good idea." She sighed. "Funny to think that Inez Olmstead kept track of us all those years. I still don't know if Lottie found out about me from Inez or from her own father. I'll tell you something, though: the shock he had when he found out he was related to me couldn't have been as bad as the shock when I found out I was related to him!"

She broke off. "Say, Gerstley, this is good," she added. "What all's in here, besides chicken and chili peppers?"

"He's got an asbestos mouth, for a gringo, I'm telling you," Mimi observed. "Al, pass me some more of Cat's broccoli."

Okay, I admit it; I'd taken the whole freezer thing in hand and accelerated our arrival at the next layer of garden produce by bringing broccoli to the potluck. Isn't that what potlucks are for? Aren't they the culinary equivalent of garage sales?

"And meanwhile, Mimi was spying on Gerstley because of the stuff that was being smuggled out of Mexico, but that was just coincidence, right?" Ram was trying to piece things together. "It didn't have anything to do with the murders, did it?"

"That's right, *boychik,*" she said, "and you nearly blew my whole operation by putting Cat on his tail!"

"This rice dish is vegetarian, isn't it, Ram?" Al asked, peering into a bowl.

"Yep," he affirmed. "No dead chickens."

"But we still don't know for sure why Forrester died," Jan mused.

"We still don't know any of this for sure, Jan," Moses reminded her. "It's all speculation on Cat's part. Reasoned speculation, maybe, but speculation all the same."

"It makes sense to me that he figured out who the killer was," Al said. "I like Cat's explanation—that he heard Hyde's beeper go off when Hyde was in the pottery studio."

"It makes sense to me that Gil tried to blackmail somebody," Jan said. "I guess his criminal tendencies finally caught up with him."

"And speaking of criminal tendencies," Kevin pursued, "my favorite part of the story is the way Cat forced a confession from Alex Parker! Wish I could've been there for that!"

"You're way too tidy," I protested.

"*Caramba, chica!*" Mimi exclaimed. "Even if I was allowed to pull a stunt like that, which I'd get my ass fired if I ever so much as thought of putting the agency at so much risk, I wouldn't have the *chutzpa* to pull it off!"

"Well," I said modestly, "I remembered what Mel had said about Gerstley not wanting to see any of his beloved artifacts damaged, and I knew it would be true of Parker, too. There were things he valued more highly than the Justice Collection—all of them breakable."

"'Course, if it turned out he didn't know anything, the Catatonia Arms be up for sale right now," Moses muttered. "And if he was the killer—"

"Come on, Moses," I objected. "He wasn't going to shoot me, two kids, and a dog in the middle of all that antique porcelain, and on Fourth Street in broad daylight!"

"So you really think he's the one that burned the body?" Brenda asked me.

"Yeah," Jan said, "what *did* happen the night of the murder, anyway? I still don't know."

"I think—and this is purely speculation—that Lottie and Hyde bumped into each other that night. Maybe she saw him coming down the hall, or maybe she was hanging out here in the studio, waiting for Parker. I don't know why she hid the vase—maybe because she didn't entirely trust Parker and wanted to talk to him first, or maybe because she saw Hyde coming and she didn't trust him.

"We'll probably never know what she said to him," I conceded. "But she had family on her mind, and maybe she succumbed to an impulse to tell him about his background. Personally, I don't believe that she was a blackmailer. Maybe she felt guilty about leaving her estate to Brenda and wanted to offer him a keepsake. Whatever she said, it really unnerved him, and I think he acted on the emotions of the moment.

"I don't think Hyde was thinking too clearly that night, and I doubt he knew enough about the kiln to consider disposing of the body that way. Once he found out that she hadn't been identified, though, I think he may well have entered the Olmstead house the same way I did and searched it for anything related to his family background. Parker may not be lying when he says that somebody else had been searching the house, and he may not mean me."

"But if he was looking for the Bible, he didn't find it," Ram added. "I think it's awesome that it survived the fire!"

"It think it's pretty awesome myself," Brenda agreed.

"Well, I'd like to propose a toast," Mimi announced, standing up and raising a tulip-shaped ceramic cup of wine. Kevin abandoned the ceremonial cutting of the cheesecake and turned toward her.

"To Cat," she said, "who cracked the case of the cracked pot!"

"May her evidence grow stouter and her pots thinner!" Gerstley added, to everyone's surprised delight.

"Hear, hear!" they shouted.

The flush I was willing to attribute more to the wine than to my hormones. But when tears sprang to my eyes, I knew it was all over.

"I have a toast, too," I croaked, before I lost control of my voice altogether. I turned toward *The Red Emma*. "To Nellie, and to justice—any way you can get it."